LET NOTHING ASTONISH YOU

This book is a work of fiction. References to historical events, real people or real places are used fictitiously. Other names, characters, places, and events are products of the author's imagination. Any resemblance to actual events, places, or persons, living or dead, is entirely coincidental and not intended by the author.

Copyright © 2026 by Lauren Opper

All rights reserved.

No portion of this book may be reproduced in any form without written permission from the publisher or author, except as permitted by U.S. copyright law.

May 17, 1869
Auguste Maurier
Maurier & Lawrence Cabinet Makers
New Haven, Conn.

Dear Sir—With utmost admiration I offer you my compliments. I encountered your exquisitely crafted cabinet in Bishop Crawford's library on my last visit. His Excellency informed me of your name and permitted me to mention his own in this inquiry. I write to commission a nearly identical cabinet for my study here at Glenhurst Castle in Glamis, Connecticut. I will, however, require four unique specifications.

First, the material upon which I insist is beechwood, painted black in imitation of ebony. Second, the piece is to measure eight feet in height, ten feet in width, and three feet in depth. Third, I ask for a single window of leaded diamond quarries on the upper half of the left-hand door only. The right-hand door is to remain of solid wood. Your ornamentation of the Bishop's cabinet delighted me, especially the three hooded arches at the top with dropped points and five petal rosette motif. Please keep this decoration the same for mine.

You may find my final request unusual. It is nevertheless imperative for the piece. My cabinet must have a false back, which will allow discreet passage between my study and bed chamber. I will disclose to you the design I devised for this secret egress when you visit Glenhurst personally. I await your acceptance of this commission. Until then I remain

Respectfully yours,
Ernest G. Glenmore

CHAPTER ONE

Friday, March 31st - 6:00 p.m.

"Beast!" said Jade Glenmore, as the man in front of her raced out of the cold into Dolce Far Niente without bothering to hold the door. Since reaching her fifties, Jade's tolerance for poor manners had plummeted. She wasn't shy anymore about letting offenders know it. Inside the restaurant, walk-in hopefuls waited on wooden benches lining the foyer, where Justin Marotta, the owner's son, kept order, aided by Sinatra's civilizing croons. Through the doorway on the right, patrons filled the dining room decorated in blue and gold Art Deco wallpaper. Lewis Waterhouse, Glamis' fantasy novelist of renown, paid his bill at the zinc and brass bar. His eyebrows jumped with pleasure as he spotted Jade. He saluted her, a strand of his shoulder-length silvery white hair slipping free from behind one ear. Jade waved back to him.

As she reached the front of the line, Justin greeted her from his dais. "Your rigatoni is almost ready. It'll just be a minute."

"Thank you. I'm in a hurry to get home. Here comes your father." Jade half raised her hand to Sal Marotta, who had just extracted himself from a table of guests and was now strutting over to Jade with a fiery twinkle in his eyes. He had never directed this kind of look at her before in their close to forty years knowing each other. She prayed Lewis would hurry up with paying his bill and intervene with one of his signature quips.

"My favorite customer." Sal swooped in to kiss Jade's cheek. "Business is good, see?"

"I do. It's a madhouse."

"Your order, Jade." Justin held out a paper to-go bag.

"Thank you so much," said Jade. "Goodnight, Marottas. Must be going."

"Why are you in such a hurry?" asked Sal. "Why not stay and have your dinner here tonight? There's room at the bar. I will make you the best espresso martini."

"I never drink those," Jade said. "I'd be up until dawn."

"Would that be so bad?" Sal asked.

"Ghastly. I intend to be asleep by nine."

"How about next Friday you'll stay and eat with me? It's a date?" Sal asked.

Jade shook her head before she could allow herself to entertain the thought. Lewis' nineteen-year-old nephew Scott had taught her about 'the friend zone', a kind of psychological pen where one contained the men in one's life who were not good romantic prospects. That was exactly where she intended to keep Sal corralled. Moreover, she never ate dinner at the restaurant. Sal should know that. "Unlikely. I'm a creature of habit."

"Wait one moment," Sal said. "I'll bring you a special dessert. Chef Paul made a lemon custard tart. You can't miss it. I'll be back!" Sal dashed off to the kitchen.

"What's come over him?" Jade asked Justin.

"Not sure," he said. "Dad's been bouncing off the walls all day. My wife Sarah's parents are moving here tomorrow. Greta and Carl. Dad is determined to make Carl his best friend."

"That's so nice," said Jade.

"It would be, except Carl doesn't love Italian food. I didn't mention it to Dad before Sarah and I got married. I haven't seen a way to break the news to him since."

"In the grand scheme of things, that's pretty minor," Jade said.

"The other problem is you can't get anything past Carl, so if my dad takes offense, Carl will figure it out. He was a homicide detective for the Houston Police Department for years."

"Well, if it isn't you."

Jade turned at the sound of Lewis Waterhouse's voice. The author stood in the doorway to the dining room. Jade enjoyed his casual, but serious expression zeroed in on her. She usually preferred polite smiles and formal greetings. She had to admit with Lewis it was fun to dispense with them. "Picking up your Friday to-go order?" he asked.

"Trying to go," she said. "Sal is foisting a dessert on me. Then I will be on my way home."

Sal emerged from the kitchen and placed a cardboard box into the bag and presented it to Jade with care. "Prepare for an explosion of love in your mouth!"

Lewis' eyebrows threatened to touch his hairline.

"Call me later and tell me what you think about this dessert. Promise?" Sal asked.

"No promises," said Jade. "I am exhausted from this week. I need my rest before the big day. I'll see you tomorrow for my brother's party?"

"Of course. Tomorrow night at The Castle. Justin and I will personally deliver the catering for Merlin's celebration. Arielle and Chef Paul and I have been talking about all the details. Everything will be perfect."

"I'm sure it will be. Until tomorrow." Jade zipped her coat up to her chin. "Night, Lewis."

"I'll walk you home." Lewis held the door for her and followed outside. "Dark and slippery out here. Take my arm."

"As long as you're not escorting me out of pity," said Jade.

"You must be confusing me with someone else. I don't do pity escorts. Brr!" Snowflakes spangled Lewis' stubble beard.

"Fine, walk with me. I won't ask why you are insisting on it. Your motives will out soon enough."

Across Main Street, her brother's new blood-red sports car gleamed in front of Thane's cigar bar. "I shouldn't bring it up, but that's Merlin's birthday present to himself."

"So that's how your brother spends the family fortune. On a car," said Lewis. "What does the license plate say?"

"Hotspur. What he named it." Jade pressed her lips together to avoid saying more.

"One night his fancy new sleigh might get acquainted with my house key."

"Beast!"

"I'm not," Lewis protested. "You are the one breaking our only rule. No talking about the scumbag—"

"Stop," Jade interjected. "Our only rule remains a good one. Quick, let's talk about anything else."

"Fine, here is a subject more fascinating to me. Do I sense a spark between you and Sal Marotta? Would you date him?"

"Hardly! If I did would you be insane with jealousy?" Jade asked, frantic butterflies rising in her stomach as they always did when she freed herself to flirt with Lewis.

"You do toy with me wickedly," he whispered teasingly in her ear. "Does 'hardly' mean a little bit? How could you."

"Lewis Waterhouse," she grinned. "Do you presume to have the right of first refusal on me?"

"Just curious. He seemed extra attentive." Lewis gave her a sly look as he tucked his silver hair behind his ear. A nervous gesture, Jade thought.

"Is that why you're walking me home? To get what your nephew Scott calls 'the tea', I think?"

"Has he taught you what 'a snack' is yet?"

"No! Do you know how to use it in a sentence? Demonstrate if you dare!"

"I dare, give me a second." Lewis had never looked more mischievous. "I was at the bar at Dolce Far Niente. I spotted Jade Glenmore in the foyer. She looked like a real snack."

"That sounds very naughty!" Jade laughed.

"I suppose it is. You'll have to ask Scott for more information. One forgets exactly what it means."

"You have not, Lewis."

"Getting serious for a minute, my dear Jade, the real reason I wanted to take this stroll with you, besides basking in your stimulating company, is to thank you. Scott is getting a lot out of the internship with you. It's giving him purpose, structure, a good mental challenge and distraction for his mind. He needs all that right now."

Jade was pleased to hear it. Scott Waterhouse had been working part time as a Marketing and Collections Intern for Jade's family's museum (and ancestral home), The Glenmore Pace Castle, for the past three weeks. Lewis' late sister, Maeve Waterhouse, had been married to Merlin, so when Lewis told Jade that his other sister's son needed a place to land after going through a rough patch, Jade had been happy to help. After all, Scott was essentially family, even if Jade hadn't known him before he moved to Glamis. It turned out he and Merlin didn't get along. Merlin seemed to have forgotten he was Scott's uncle by his first marriage. Merlin all but ignored Scott whenever he was around him.

"We're enjoying having Scott," said Jade. "He is intelligent, curious, and resourceful. I'm encouraging him to make another go at college. Doesn't his mother want him to finish his education? He's what? Twenty?"

"Nearly. Pamela is in London performing in the West End and seems inclined to let her only son do what he wants. When she was his age, she ran off with a playwright who turned out to be a complete scoundrel. I guess to Pamela being involved in a scandal at the cusp of one's adulthood is a necessary rite of passage. As much as I love her, she's different and difficult. I'm working on Scott. You Glenmores are keeping him busy, between the work with you at the museum and his job at The Marina with Robin. Hopefully, we can all keep the trouble-prone lad on the righteous path, while I peck away at the keyboard."

"How *is* your latest book going?" asked Jade.

"An infernal rat's nest."

"I would have thought after all those bestselling, award winners you've written it would be a breeze for you."

"As it turns out, accolades can't cure my chronic imposter syndrome."

"What's new in the world of your hero Lord Talon de Fey?" asked Jade.

"de Fey is uncovering a villainous cabal which unleashed the kalbrenious pox on the kingdom."

"Dastardly. I can't wait to read it!"

Lewis moved on to his next subject. "Scott's fond of your sister-in-law, isn't he?"

"Yes. He certainly is."

Scott had been spending time with Merlin's new wife, Arielle, who worked as Head of Collections at the Castle. Jade had asked Arielle to help manage Scott and to come up with assignments that would be both helpful to the museum and learning opportunities for the bright young man. What started out as a manager and intern relationship in a matter of days had morphed into a playful friendship. It worried Jade, but she thought it was a one-sided crush on Scott's part. It was natural he should admire Arielle. She was an attractive woman. The two had similar interests in history and…poetry. Scott followed her around like a puppy. Jade had to admit to herself Arielle indulged his adoration too much for comfort.

Lewis and Jade reached the intersection at High Dunsinane Road, which led down to the river. With no cars coming uphill or downhill, they crossed the street. On the other side, Main became Paddock Calls Court, where Jade lived.

"And would you say Arielle is fond of Scott?" Lewis asked.

"I'm sure Arielle sees herself as a mentor to him."

"That's a relief," he said. "Keep an eye on them, would you? Married women have found young Scott's charms irresistible before."

Jade tilted her head at Lewis. "Oh?"

"I'm referring to his time in Paris. I didn't go into this before, but he and a certain high-profile socialite made the French papers. Her husband was killed. It got out that she had a young lover. The poor kid was in over his head. Pamela and I retrieved him back stateside before it got any uglier."

That cleared up one mystery: why her nineteen-year-old intern owned an impeccably tailored, designer wardrobe. Not that she concerned herself much with haute couture, but she had spotted the name "Tom Ford" on the label of Scott's favorite blue suede jacket lying on his office chair. It now made sense he had been taken in hand by someone with deep pockets and champagne taste. It upset Jade to think of the bright boy as some rich older woman's plaything. All Jade said to Lewis though was, "French lovers and scandal! Your nephew is experienced for one so young. He's a wonderful kid, Lewis. I'll certainly keep a close eye on him. Arielle told me she invited you and Scott to Merlin's birthday party tomorrow night. Will I be seeing you at The Castle?"

"Absolutely not," he scoffed. "I hate parties, and above all I hate you-know-who. I'm stunned the woman invited me."

"Don't call Arielle 'the woman'."

"I'll call her what I like. You know why."

Jade sighed. "I wish I hadn't agreed to her hosting the party at The Castle."

"Why did you?" asked Lewis.

"There is a simple answer, not grounded in reason or good judgment. I adore her."

They stood before Jade's front porch trimmed in gingerbread.

Jade looked up into Lewis' eyes. "I'd ask if you want to come in, but…"

"Leo still kicking?" Lewis asked.

"Yes thankfully!"

"Impossible then," he said.

"I know," said Jade. "Your allergies. I bid you farewell. Pray for my soul."

"The Castle will be fine," said Lewis. "Remember, historically speaking, it has withstood many a raucous party before."

Hands in the pockets of his coat, he ambled away down Jade's driveway, back towards High Dunsinane Road.

As Jade opened the door to her lamplit den, Leopold hobbled forward to greet her with a motorous purr. Jade wouldn't trade Leopold for anything, but oh how she wished Lewis could come inside too.

CHAPTER TWO

Saturday, April 1ˢᵗ - 9:00 a.m.

Carl paused from unpacking the boxes in the living room. Outside a mallard complained in the ice-laced stream where wet leaves clung to the rocks. Carl sympathized with the duck. April First, thirty degrees, and snow predicted later today.

"You got a text from Sal Marotta." Greta bustled into the room, holding Carl's phone out to him. "There you are, box cutter! I've been looking everywhere for you."

"What does Sal want?" Carl asked.

Greta peered at the phone's screen. "He wants to know if you will do him the honor of meeting him for a drink at one o'clock at a place called Thane's. You should go."

Carl cringed. "I don't think so. We need to focus on unpacking."

"You can take an hour or two off to meet with him I would think."

"What are you doing? Are you texting him?" He reached for the phone, as Greta swiveled away with a mischievous grin.

She hit send on the text to Sal: *Ok. See you then.*

"Confirmed," she said.

"Greta you didn't! And everyone thinks you're such an angel." He gave her his best "I mean business" police officer glare.

"Oh no! Not that look!" she laughed as he snatched her into his arms for a kiss. The phone pinged.

"Who could it be?" she said. Carl wrestled the phone away from her. "This man," he groaned. He showed Greta the screen with a row of thumbs up, followed by smiley faces with tongues out, a bursting champagne bottle, a glass of whiskey, a smoking cigar, concluding with a row of red hearts.

"Be nice. He's excited you're here," said Greta.

"I can see that." Carl gave Sal one thumbs up back.

Tires crunched up the gravel driveway outside.

"Must be them," Greta rushed to the window. "Yes, it is!"

They greeted their daughter Sarah, son-in-law Justin, and three-year-old granddaughter Rosie at the front door with hugs, ushering them inside.

"When did you arrive?" Justin helped little Rosie take off her red coat.

"Only two hours ago," said Greta. "The General has already put me to work. Thank you so much, Justin, for letting in the movers yesterday. I know you're busy at work. We appreciated the help. It made it so much easier for us this morning to have all the boxes and furniture waiting for us. Obviously, we have a million things to accomplish before this place is in order. It's worth it though. It's a dream come true to be closer to Rosie!"

"Ahem and?" Sarah said.

"And to you *all*," said Greta. "And we promise we won't annoy you."

"No, honey, we promise we will *try* not to annoy them. There is a difference," said Carl.

"Gammy!" Rosie lifted her arms to Greta who scooped her up.

"I missed you, darlin'. You know what Abuelo and Gammy brought all the way from Texas?"

"Pock-ess?" asked Rosie.

"Mommy's Polly Pocket toys, yes, munchkin. Do you want to play with them today?"

Rosie nodded.

"Good luck finding them right now, honey." Carl shook his head.

"I know where they are," said Greta. "Rosie, this is Gammy and Abuelo's new house, close to you. We can see you all the time, baby girl."

Rosie stared down her button nose at Greta. "I'm *not* a baby."

"Pardon me! That's right, you're a big girl now." Greta winked at Sarah.

"That's a hot button with her right now. She is *not* a baby."

"You only have to tell me once. You got that, Carl?" Greta laughed.

"I got it," Carl said. "She is a big girl!"

"So, you two are settling in nicely," said Sarah. "They say Glamis is the quintessential Connecticut town. I sound like the ad copy I've been writing at work. It is pretty cute around here though, isn't it?"

"*Glahms*," Carl practiced saying the name of the town. "It is hard for me to pronounce."

"For me too. It's Scottish. We'll get the hang of it with practice," said Greta. "Driving in this morning, it was all New England charm. On the way in we passed a Shad Shack—Carl and I had a laugh about that. And the liquor stores are called package stores up here for some reason? I love the colonial houses, the rocky outcrops, the romantic stone walls covered in brambles, the hilly lanes with names from Shakespeare plays. We drove through the village center with all those inviting shops and restaurants."

"And we haven't had a murder in 40 years," said Justin.

"That you know of," Carl said.

"Carl!" Greta gasped.

Carl suspected every town, even one as idyllic as Glamis, had its secrets and an underbelly if one knew how to look for it. He decided not to go into it. Greta would have a fit if he brought that kind of thing up when he was supposed to be enjoying his carefree retirement.

"I hear we will have snow later today," Carl changed the subject. "Is that normal for April?"

"Not unheard of," said Justin. "I'll tell you nobody is a fan of it this time of year."

"The snow will definitely be over soon," Sarah assured Carl.

"On the bright side, we will be able to enjoy some cozy nights by this fireplace," Greta said.

Using a fireplace in April? It's just wrong. Even if the weather was unappealing this time of year, he hopefully would be able to find some comfort food. "Any good Mexican restaurants in town?" Carl asked.

Sarah frowned, "You'll probably have to drive to one of the cities to get decent tacos. I don't know of any in Glamis."

"I will keep my eyes open," said Carl.

"If a good Mexican place around here exists, I'd put my money on you finding it," said Justin.

"Well yes, honey, Carl did have a 99 percent solve rate with the Houston PD," said Greta.

"If there is a taqueria within thirty miles of me, it is a *100 percent* chance I will find it," Carl interjected before Greta could go on. Justin probably didn't want to hear his mother-in-law going into rhapsodies about her husband's achievements. Carl loved how proud Greta was of him, but she could get carried away.

"We know we're going to have divine Italian food at Dolce Far Niente," said Greta.

"The best in the state," said Justin.

"It's too good. I'm eating pasta galore," Sarah said. "We could run together, Carl? I've got to get back to exercising for my own sanity. Justin, I used to run three miles with Carl each day before school. Remember, Carl?"

"Of course I do," said Carl.

"He would wake me up at five fifteen on the dot: 'Good morning, Sarah! We are leaving in ten minutes! Vamanos! Choo Choo!'"

Rosie laughed at her mother's enthusiastic imitation of her grandfather.

"You will see one day. It's not easy to wake up a teenager," said Carl. "But Sarah committed to running with me, and it was special to spend that time together."

"It was a turning point," Greta said. "Our household became a much happier place with you two all fired up on running endorphins."

"It definitely brought us closer," said Sarah. "Poor Carl had to listen to all my stories of high school drama."

"Come on. You know I enjoyed it," Carl said.

"I hate to say it, but we need to get going to work," said Justin. "Thank you so much for taking Rosie. I hope it's not too much with the move?"

"We're thrilled to have her with us," said Greta. "Do you two have a busy day?"

"Crazy. I've got a three hundred guest wedding today," said Sarah.

"Justin, tell us, what's it like to be married to the newly promoted Director of Weddings at The Lavender Inn and Spa?" Greta beamed.

"Not much fun so far," Justin said. "A lot of working at the dinner table. Last night, Sarah took a call at eleven after we'd already gone to bed."

Sarah blinked, holding back tears. If she had only one such overbearing client, she could handle it. But there were so many, and she was expected to take everything they dished out. She didn't want her parents to worry about her, but at this moment, Sarah felt overwhelmed, and Greta and Carl could see it.

"Darlin'," Greta rubbed Sarah's back.

Sarah hugged Rosie to her. "I'll be back at seven for her, if that sounds okay, Mom, Carl?"

"Fine by us. We'll take the best care of her," Greta reassured her.

Sarah wrapped her arms around her mother, "I'm so happy you and Carl are here."

"Hey," Greta looked into Sarah's eyes. "I'm glad we are too, sweetie."

"Ugh! I'm being silly. Sorry." Sarah's phone rang at full volume. "It's the bride. She's from New York. The CEO of a cosmetics company." She accepted the call. "Sarah speaking. Good morning, Ms. Payne. Oh no! Don't worry, I know how to fix this. I'm on my way to the Inn. I know a laundry company that works miracles. Yes, ma'am, I've seen them get tomato juice out of white satin before. Let me call them right now. I promise everything is going to be fine. See you at the suite in fifteen minutes. Come on, Justin, you need to drop me off now!" She raced out the door, cellphone to her ear.

After Sarah and Justin left, Greta turned to Carl, "How super is this going to be living here? We will see Rosie all the time."

"It's perfect," Carl said. "Well, it's almost perfect..."

"If the case of the hidden taqueria is the biggest mystery you have left to solve, life has definitely improved."

"Yes, it has," said Carl. "Sarah is stressed, honey."

"I could see that," said Greta.

"Was she nervous leaving Rosie with us do you think?" Carl asked.

"What's going on with her is bigger," said Greta. "She really needs us."

CHAPTER THREE

Saturday, April 1st - 9:30 a.m.

"Robin. The mail from yesterday?" Paul waved a stack of soggy envelopes.

"Shoot." Robin Glenmore stuck his coffee mug into the dishwasher, careful not to leave it in the sink this time. Paul hated when he did that. Paul also had told him there was a particular row of the top rack of the dishwasher where mugs should go. Robin could never remember if it was the outermost row or not. How could it possibly matter? Wouldn't the mug get clean either way? Sheesh.

A picture on the refrigerator held up by a lobster magnet caught Robin's eye. Paul and him, six years ago, both tan and smiling on a sailboat, the summer they fell in love in Newport, Rhode Island. Paul, newly arrived from London, worked at a restaurant on Bannister's Wharf. He was an ambitious, aspiring chef, intense, but radiating charm, a witty remark ever at the ready. In those days, Paul claimed to find what he called Robin's 'dreamy disposition' irresistible. "How's the view up there from the clouds, Oak King of Summer?" Paul would tease when he would catch Robin staring into space.

Paul hadn't used the expression for a couple of years now. Robin missed those words. In them, he heard Paul saying he accepted his quirks, even found them lovable. These days, Paul interpreted Robin's innate absent-mindedness as passive aggression.

"The mail is your one task, love," sighed Paul. "I'm doing all the other chores around here."

"I told you a chart would help me," said Robin. "I have so much on my mind."

"Fetching the mail once a day when you come home from work, doesn't warrant a chart system. And here is a package for you. What did you buy anyway?" Paul quirked an eyebrow.

"A new white button-down," said Robin. "All my other ones are ratty. Arrived just in time for me to wear to Merlin's party tonight. And I ordered two pairs of white gloves for us. What's that look? They'll be perfect with our costumes, and they'll keep our hands warm in the castle. The power's going to be turned off tonight apparently."

"I recall a recent mutual promise to pause the online shopping sprees. I'm holding up my end."

"Gee, I won't go buying anything without your written permission," said Robin.

"Don't make me the villain. You're the one keeping me in the dark. You tell me we can't afford the housekeeper anymore. We let her go. Last week at dinner, you propose a ski trip to the Alps for Christmas and show me pictures of a new sailboat you want to buy. Next, you drop the bomb we are on the verge of having to sell this house. What do you think I'm feeling? Complete bewilderment!"

"Fine, I'll return it all."

"Keep it. That's not the issue."

"What *is* your issue?" asked Robin.

"I want a clear understanding of our financial picture. Are we in trouble, or not? You can tell me the truth."

"It's too complicated for me to explain. Paul, don't walk away. I need to speak with my brother, but Merlin's been putting me off me. I've been trying to set up a time to meet with him all week."

"He won't be able to avoid you tonight," said Paul. "At his birthday party."

"I could do it then."

"You don't have a choice. We need clarity, Robin. Ask him for a word casually—"

"Thank you." Robin pulled a white glove onto his hand. "I know what I have to do."

CHAPTER FOUR

Saturday, April 1st - 10:30 a.m.

A Colonial Revival mansion housed Catia Boyd's Lavender Inn and Spa. From its deep porches, guests lounged in the plethora of white wicker furniture, savoring views of the Connecticut River. Inside, guests could relax in the massage room, as Catia was trying to do at this very moment. Lying face down on the padded table, she had her head turned to the side, as Trinity worked on the knots in her back. There were several, thanks to the never-ending to-do list running through Catia's head.

The setup of the wedding in the ballroom was at the top of the list. Sarah Marotta would have that under control. Sarah was one of the best hires Catia had ever made, a workhorse and smart too. Catia forced her focus back on Trinity, her new massage therapist. This was the young woman's first job after graduating from the top massage institute in the state. Catia wanted to ensure she had direction but also encouragement.

"Trinity, make sure to ask at the start of the treatment how much pressure the client prefers. People can be so timid until you ask them questions."

"Got it, Mrs. Boyd. How's the pressure for you?"

"Just right, thanks dear."

"So, do you and Doctor Boyd have fun plans this weekend?" Trinity asked.

"I am going to Merlin Glenmore's birthday party tonight at The Castle. Let's not have any more chit chat. I want to focus on what you're doing."

It was a good thing Catia could focus on more than one thing at a time, because her brain kept returning to that night's party. The invitation itself was full of what Catia assumed must be inside jokes and an odd three-line poem at the top. Attire: ill-fated lovers, the invite said. Catia would go as Elizabeth Taylor. People said she resembled Liz. Her husband Owen, as usual, said he would prefer to stay home and revel in re-runs of golf tournaments rather than get in a costume and hob nob. Knowing she wouldn't be able to change his mind, Catia hadn't tried. See how he felt when she paraded out the door tonight dressed to kill!

Her presence was sure to grate on the man of honor. Did Arielle love Merlin Glenmore? Catia had taken a liking to Arielle ever since she'd met her at one of The Castle fundraisers. She knew a hard worker when she saw one. Jade had glowing things to say about her too.

Arielle cared about making the museum a success and that was good for the town and, therefore, good for The Lavender Inn. Catia didn't have enough room in her schedule to nurture friendships. Whenever women got clingy or demanding with Catia's time she pulled away with "I'm too busy with work" texts until the friendship fizzled.

Arielle wasn't ruffled when weeks went by without a word between the two. They ran into each other around town, and once in a while would meet for lunch at Dolce Far Niente or go to Glamis' dive bar Puck's to share a bottle of sauvignon blanc and gossip in a shadowy alcove. Arielle did not strike Catia as a gold digger. As slimy and deceitful as Merlin was in her eyes, Catia could see how others, who had not come nose to nose with the man's evil, lying narcissism, might be taken in by him. Some people went mad for attention from men like Merlin. Arielle did confess to Catia she suspected her new husband of being a bit brutal at his core.

The young woman had no idea. Enlightening her on the subject would only make Catia feel pathetic. There were better ways than blabbing to find justice, and that was precisely what she needed. Even after all this time.

"That's nice," murmured Catia as Trinity massaged her hands with oil. "I love the smell of eucalyptus."

Chimes rang out, filling the room with noise. "That's my alarm on my phone in my purse over there. Alright. That's a wrap."

"Didn't you say you wanted me to do the hot stones?"

"No time. I've got a very important meeting with Housekeeping."

Catia's to-do list for today could fill a legal-sized piece of paper, but she could not help but be in a good mood. She really could not wait for the party tonight.

CHAPTER FIVE

Saturday, April 1st - 12:00 p.m.

Doctor Owen Boyd, general practitioner, left the Black Sheep Bakery on Main Street, clutching a brown bag containing his favorite meatloaf on brioche sandwich and a biscuit for Sibyl, his prized English Cream Dachshund. He strolled past a row of shops until they gave way to an old stone wall lining the sidewalk. It would be a light afternoon with only three more appointments. He looked forward to having tonight to himself.

While Catia was off socializing, his evening's entertainment would include a screening of the 2005 Masters, starring Tiger Woods. The glory of his hero's miraculous chip shot off the green at 16 made Owen tear up every time he rewatched the final round. On the menu for one and a half (counting Sibyl) tonight: pimento cheese sandwiches, pulled pork sliders, an Azalea cocktail (or four), followed by peach ice cream sandwiches, all in the comfort of his living room, without anyone around to grouse about any of it. He would be comatose by the time the car service brought Catia home after the party, and he would be out the door to golf before she awoke Sunday morning. Hopefully the snow predicted would only be a few flurries.

He felt a vibration and fished out his cellphone from his coat pocket.

"Doctor Boyd speaking." He pushed open the low wooden gate with his foot.

"Hello, Owen."

"Oh it's you! Give me a second," he said. "Let me get somewhere I can talk."

He bolted up the walkway to the front door of his practice, a prim, white colonial. Inside, he hustled into his office and shut the door. "I can talk now. How are you?" he asked.

"I'll just get right to it, Owen. I can't be your patient anymore."

"What? May I ask why?" His armpits dampened. He dropped the brown bag on his desk, shifting the phone to his other ear, as he struggled out of his stifling coat.

"I had a dream about you," she said. "A romantic dream...I won't go into it."

He could barely breathe.

"Do patients fall in love with you all the time?" she asked.

"Why no," he tried to make a joke of it in case this was a prank. "Not *all* the time."

"Anyway, it's not right for me to come to you and have these feelings for you...But you are a wonderful doctor. This is embarrassing. I should go."

She was serious.

"I have to say," Owen said. "The feelings you mention... might not be one-sided."

Sibyl, lying in Owen's desk chair, raised her narrow head to give him an unsettling frown.

"My heart is pounding," she said. "What am I doing calling you like this? I'll say goodbye."

"After this declaration, you're just going to hang up and run away?" He shooed Sibyl down from his chair.

"I hope it's enough for you to know how I feel," she said. "And I hope you will be there tonight. I heard you weren't coming. Won't you please change your mind? We could talk more at the party."

"I'll be there, alright," he said.

"I'm so glad. Don't tell Catia about this call, okay? She would murder me."

"Never, my darling."

"You called me your darling," she said.

"Do you like that?"

"It's delightful how you say it."

Sibyl let out a whine, her feathery tail swishing. Owen took the biscuit from the paper bag and handed it down to her.

He glanced at the clock on the wall. "Why don't we see each other *before* the party? Where are you right now?"

"I have so much to do to get ready. I wouldn't have time to meet before. And if I did, I wouldn't dare, Owen."

"Wouldn't dare?" he asked.

"I can't actually *do* anything bad."

"But you already are."

"What do you mean?" she asked.

"This call."

"It's just like Great Aunt Harriett used to say 'Crack the door for the devil, and he'll come bounding in.' *You* must be the morally superior one. If you so much as touch my hand, I would abandon myself totally to you. We can't ever be alone. I have to go. Just know I'll be thinking about you all the time...and in my dreams..."

"I can hardly believe this," said Owen.

"Is it good news?" she asked.

"It's fantastic news," he said.

"I can't wait to see you tonight. I must say goodbye."

"Must you, *my darling*?"

"Stop it—I'll melt," she giggled. "Goodbye."

"Goodbye," he said.

"Goodbye, Owen."

"Wait! This isn't an April Fool's joke, is it? Merlin's not behind this? I know he's the master prankster."

"How could you ask that? I'm stung." She hung up.

He put his hand to his chest and breathed deeply. What had just happened? Could she...?

If you so much as touch my hand, I would abandon myself totally to you.

He'd never had an affair before, never really had the opportunity if he was being honest with himself. He couldn't wait to see her tonight. He informed Catia in a text he had changed his mind about Merlin's party. He was going.

CHAPTER SIX

Saturday, April 1st

Chère Faustine,

How are things in Paris? Or have you retreated elsewhere? I write you from chilly, gray Glamis, the town in Connecticut The Waterhouses have called home since the 1700s. I never had a chance to tell you about my family and where we come from—you and I had much more urgent business to attend to.

I miss France desperately, but I am falling into step with life in this sleepy hamlet, nestled among the hills above the lower Connecticut River. Growing up, my mother took me to visit only a handful of times. You may have heard Mother is causing a stir, starring in the West End revival of Lady of the Camellias. She trusts her brother, the author Lewis Waterhouse (is he known in France?), will look after me.

I have thrown myself into my work at The Glenmore-Pace Castle, an operating museum, since mov-

ing here. I did not expect my life to change with a small-town internship, but it already has only a few weeks in. Being interested in history yourself, I know you would love the place. Ernest G. Glenmore (my boss Jade Glenmore's great-great grandfather) built Glenhurst, as he named it.

The Castle's interior evokes a moody English monastery as imagined by Glenmore. He loved the works of Tennyson and Poe. Pointed arches in the Gothic style frame the doors and windows. There is much very good stained-glass dating from Medieval, Renaissance, and 18th century (someone dear taught me to have an eye for such things...). One wanders shadowy, gloomy passages, comes upon chambers flooded with celestial light, nearly a whole wall a window. The effect is abbatial tinged with the profane. It is so you, ma divine.

Glenhurst fell into disrepair in the 1990s. The ancestral castle called to Jade Glenmore, despite the upkeep and renovations required. Through a private foundation she established and herculean efforts to secure grants and donations, she purchased The Castle from The Pace Family and saved it from demolition. Jade as Executive Director of The Glenmore-Pace Castle perpetually fundraises. The southwest tower needs to be rebuilt and the entire roof needs replacing. The Castle desperately needs an updated security system. I don't *need to tell you it all adds up to millions of dollars to keep the place in decent shape.*

Jade's father made a killing in finance and real estate but never had interest in The Castle and expressly did not want his fortune exhausted on "the extravagant money pit" (his words according to Jade). The old man died last July, but the loot has been inaccessible, due to several drawn-out lawsuits, until now...

Jade's younger brother, Merlin Glenmore, gained access to the fortune this week. It will be a happy 50th birthday for him indeed. The museum's fate rests on him. Otherwise, it likely must be sold to a local college and become an academic building. I have little faith Merlin will rise to the occasion. I will add, for completeness, Merlin was married to my late aunt Maeve Waterhouse, which technically makes him my uncle. I never felt any familial connection to him.

Now we come upon the most interesting aspect of my internship. There works at the museum a lady named Arielle, Merlin's second wife. How this goddess came to be employed doing grunt work at a museum in these remote environs remains a mystery to me. Arielle is the Director of Collections and her fascination with The Castle is infectious. She has a playful intelligence—the trait I rank highest in the category of charm. She is fair-haired, tall, and lithe. She is fifteen years older and five inches taller than your humble correspondent. But—as I hope you would agree—my height has yet to limit me romantically speaking.

I am baffled the bewitching Arielle fell for Merlin Glenmore of the snooty fox face. He refers to his ancestors' magnificent castle as "The Pile". It's unbearable hearing a man from Connecticut use the expression, the airs, ridiculous! I have never forgotten how you scolded me when I was trying to be a cynic like you. You said sincerity is the most attractive attitude for the American male under thirty.

Last fall, Arielle finished translating the diaries of Celestin Mabille, the French valet who served the Castle's builder Ernest Glenmore. She told me Celestin wrote scintillating entries about Ernest and his wife Catherine's unseemly passion. I assured Arielle the diaries couldn't offend me.

On my first day at the museum, Arielle the Exquisite instructed me on The Castle's most interesting objects and features. She described for me about a hundred architectural highlights, as I pointed to distinct parts of ornaments on the walls and asked what this was and what about this thingy inside that thingy.

Have you ever heard of a hunky punk? It's a gargoyle but with no functional purpose such as water drainage. All the gargoyles on The Castle are really hunky punks, except for those on the fountain in The Prior's Garden.

She also taught me about "quotations" which is using architectural details from another famous building. This can be done "wittily" as it is at The Castle, or in complete distaste as is more often the case in American architecture. Ernest Glenmore's castle contains "quotations" from Fonthill Abbey, Inverary Castle, Warwick Castle, Strawberry Hill (castle of Horace Walpole, author of the first Gothic novel The Castle of Otranto), and Abbotsford (home of Sir Walter Scott).

I hope to dazzle Arielle with my powerful absorption rate. That did not come out as sexy as I hoped. Makes my brain sound like three-ply toilet paper. Sometimes when I try to be too clever it just comes out bizarre.

During my lunch break on one of my first days as intern, I explored The Prior's Garden in the fog. I walked the labyrinth round and round to the center, and all the way back stone by stone to the beginning. Mary, the Queen of Heaven, is who I contemplated in the labyrinth. All this medieval religious imagery must be seeping in. Refreshingly mystical themes to ponder and relieve my mind from its anxious retracings of how things fell apart with us.

I found a secluded corner past The Prior's Garden and settled on a stone bench in front of The Glenmore Mausoleum for a light collation and one of my precious few remaining Gauloise. The lintel above the metal doors bears the Latin phrase "Nil Admirari" (trans-

lation: Let Nothing Astonish You), a steely attitude towards both life and the afterlife, whatever they hold. This stoic motto appears inside The Castle engraved over two fireplaces. Perhaps Ernest Glenmore offered these words to his descendants as a kind of protection spell against psychological pain. When you possess a nature that inclines towards trust, believing the best in people, as I do, it's advice you might appreciate but find impossible to fully embrace. I doubt I could embrace any philosophy fully. Eclecticism is my way. Adopt all that appeals, disregard what doesn't, allow myself to be guided exclusively by nothing.

I contemplated what words to have etched on my own gravestone one day. A phrase thought-provoking to the living, I decided, yet suitably reverent to the inhumed. As my mind lightbulbed on the title of a poem by a Decadent English poet, Arielle Glenmore emerged through the mist. She asked what I found to be so amusing. I told her I'd discovered the right words for my final place of rest. I spoke them in Latin (thinking of you, at that point, I confess...): *Non Sum Qualis eram Bonae Sub Regno Cynarae* ("I am not as I was in the reign of good Cynara").

I nearly fell off the bench when she said, "Dowson's poem. I love that one." Excitement shimmered in her eyes. "You're an unusual nineteen-year-old."

That's when things started to shift. She recognized herself in me. Here is a new friend who sees into my soul, with all its eccentricities mirroring her own. I can only describe the sensation as a (charged!) spiritual homecoming.

I performed for Arielle the entire Dowson poem from memory. She roared when I grabbed brown leaves from the ground and "flung roses, roses riotously with the throng" and when I did an impish dance as I "put thy pale, lost lilies out of mind".

Kneeling before her, I uttered the final sentence: "I have been faithful to thee, Cynara!" (dramatic pause, mischievously) "in my fashion."

She gave me a sad look and said, "I hope, before I die, someone makes me the subject of a poem as saucy and despairing as Dowson's."

Here indeed is a kindred spirit, perhaps something more...

The next day, in the groove of her computer keyboard, I stuck an index card with an ode to my lady. She removed it, placed it inside her desk drawer. Two days passed. She spoke not of it. I received the invitation to Merlin's birthday party last week and would you believe my ode appeared on it at the very top.

I know it is a signal just for me.

I wonder if you feel the slightest pang of envy, minx. From your complete silence these past few weeks I suspect you've moved on. I swear if you don't reply to this, I will never write you again. I'd rather be dead than bore a woman.

  Your fond ex(ile),

Scott Waterhouse

  PS. Take pity on your devoted etc and mail me one more pack of Gauloises. I'm fiending. This is the last time I'll ask this favor; I swear. I am quitting smoking for good. Uncle Lewis and my boss Jade are on my case all the time sniffing me, telling me I'll die hooked up to machines gasping. Their disapproval stresses me out so much I need a cigarette right now just thinking about it. Fail me not, Faustine!

CHAPTER SEVEN

Saturday, April 1ˢᵗ - 12:45 p.m.

The modest clay-colored Cape Cod house dating from the 1770s had witnessed the births and deaths of centuries of Waterhouses. The family had wrestled ferociously through wars, depressions, illnesses, and divorces to keep the house in its grasp. So far, the Waterhouses had come out of every battle triumphant thanks to sheer determination, willingness to get creative, and the exuberant force of personality animating each of its clan.

Lewis split logs at the bottom of the hill near his writer's shed, painted the same shade of reddish brown as the main house. It was a moot point whether the structure suited Lewis as an individual. Some of his fans might have envisioned him in a sprawling Tudor manor like that of his hero Talon de Fey. No, what suited Lewis individually was beside the point. Moving from the place was out of the question. The house was symbolic of the force of will and grit that flowed in Lewis' veins and those of his ancestors before him.

He'd be damned if he would be the Waterhouse to sell it.

"Hello, Lewis!" a woman called to him from the top of the hill near the main house. Arielle Glenmore tiptoed past the clapboard siding and picked her way down the grassy slope holding a white rectangle above her head like a flag of truce.

Unbelievable. What is that homewrecking harlot doing on my land?

Lewis slammed his axe through a log. He tried to tolerate this young woman's presence whenever he ran into her flouncing around Main Street. He didn't think Arielle was to blame for what Merlin did to Maeve. But everyone in Glamis knew she and Merlin had begun an intense friendship before Maeve's death. Merlin, who normally avoided the Glenmore Pace Museum at all costs, developed an uncharacteristic interest in seeing the castle archives after he met Jade's new hire.

Lewis believed Arielle had a hand in the undoing of his sister's marriage, whether it had been an emotional, or physical affair didn't matter to him a whit. He could not forgive what had happened to his sister. This woman should not be trespassing on his property. As she neared, he could see she was attractive. Scott had gone into ecstasies describing her brain power. Well, Maeve had been a sight more beautiful and no doubt smarter too than this floozy and look how it ended for her. It was hard to really think this woman was an actual 'floozy', but he required some invective for her.

He could be civil to Arielle up to a point. The anger and resentment he felt towards Merlin and his new bride *that* could not be quelled. Lewis flung the two pieces of wood aside and wiped his brow with his flannel sleeve, a strand of silver coming loose from his ponytail. He heaved a new cut of wood onto the chopping stump.

"What are you doing on my property?" Lewis asked.

"I'm picking up your nephew! Sorry to interrupt your smashing. I wish to confer."

She 'wishes to confer'.

The woman was presumptuous, probably arrogant too, looking the way she did and thinking she was so smart and charming to boot. Lewis could feel himself softening towards her despite himself. He didn't like it one bit. She held the lustrous envelope out to him.

"Here is another invitation," said Arielle. "I heard you set fire to the first one I sent. I want to make one final appeal for you to come to the Castle tonight. Jade would love it. Scott would love it."

He stared at the envelope, unmoving. *The impertinence.* He hated how she was hitting him over the head about the intimacy she shared with Jade and his nephew—knowing what they would love. Those two knew him well enough not to 'love' the notion of him being anywhere near that party.

"Scott said he doubted he could convince you to go," she continued. "My turn to take a whack at it."

He set down the ax and crossed his arms. He had never stood this close to her before. The innocent freckles on her nose contrasted with a hedonistic scent of jasmine and amber.

"Would you consider it?" she asked.

"Trust me, it will be much better for everyone if I stay away from Merlin Glenmore."

"This rift is all a misunderstanding. My husband is a good man. I'm certain you are too. And for my part, I *try* to be a good person as best I can, which is why I am here to offer the olive branch. Besides, it's really on behalf of my dear sister-in-law that I'm here. Jade did say you have the biggest heart of any man she's ever met."

Lewis buried his hands in his jean pockets. "She did?"

Now he felt himself softening, slipping. His resolve was the cold pat of butter, her charm the hissing skillet. So Jade sent her. Was it possible? What was he thinking. Jade was out of the question. If it didn't work out, and odds are it probably wouldn't, he couldn't stand the thought of losing her friendship, of being awkward with her running into her in the town center. It was better to just be grateful for what they had, a decades-long friendship of gold enlivened with a morsel of banter and flirtation. It was enough to get by on. Losing Jade after having a wild, impulsive fling with her was too painful to contemplate. Besides, he didn't want any messy situations while Scott lived with him.

"It surprised me when Jade said that too," Arielle forged on. "You're so gruff. But I know you are brilliant. I've read all your books."

"Nah. You have?"

"I devoured them."

"You've really read one of my books?" he asked.

"I said I read them *all*. Your hero de Fey knows exactly what a woman wants, especially the way he…" Arielle looked down, smiling, leaving Lewis mad with curiosity to hear what she had stopped herself from saying aloud.

Lewis' eyes narrowed. Could the tease be playing with him for sport? "Which of my books is your favorite?"

"*The Sorcerer's Mirror*. The way you opened the first chapter. I have never encountered such an imaginative love scene before! Confession, I organized the séance tonight as an homage to you."

"You're planning a séance for Merlin's party? He'll hate that."

She leaned close to him and whispered more in his ear.

"You've got my attention," he said, as she stepped away. "This devilry I may oblige....Just after nine?"

"Say you'll be there," she pressed the invitation to his hand. This time he took it.

"Good! You're here!" Scott called down from the hilltop.

"Hi there! You're ready to go?" She turned back to Lewis. "Thank you for being kind to me just now. I was scared you would shout me off the premises at first. You're sort of intimidating with this sexy wizard look you have going on. Friends? Friends one day maybe?"

"You'll stay on my good side as long as you don't try to seduce my nephew."

"No," her smile fell. "How could you... I would never. Everyone knows I'm happily married. Why would you say that?"

"Why do you think?"

He lifted the ax above his head and smashed it through the log.

CHAPTER EIGHT

Saturday, April 1st - 1:00 p.m.

Upon entering Thane's, cigar smoke, whiskey, and the smell of leather engulfed Carl. Already at one o'clock on a Saturday, customers occupied every club chair in the lounge. No Sal in sight. Carl stood against the oak paneled wall to wait for a table.

A man of seventy with tufty gray hair and five o'clock shadow raised his hand to the bartender. "Hey Francis! The check please."

"You got it, Zip," the bartender replied. He brought the check over to Zip, who sat with two others, one a stylish man of fifty and the other an auburn-haired man in his thirties in a burnt orange vest and blue jeans. Carl noticed a glinting gold wedding band on the fifty-year-old and no rings on the hands of the other two.

Zip resumed his conversation, leaning towards the older of his two companions, "You're thinkin' about it, aren't you? If ya do, Merl, just think of the looks on those poor innocent souls' faces…I tell ya what—man, look at me, tears are brewin'. Shoot. Give me just a sip of that, Rex."

Zip grabbed the crystal tumbler of scotch out of the scowling younger man's hand.

"Francis," Zip said to the bartender who waited patiently while Zip fished out his wallet from his jacket hanging on the back of his chair. "You know how I volunteer at the Glamis Animal Rescue?"

"How could he not, Uncle Zip?" said the younger man. "You try to get this poor feller to adopt an animal every time we're in here."

"Rex, hush. Show some respect for your elders. I'm telling you, Francis, this dog is mighty special. He just came to us. An eight-year-old lab chow mix. Only eighty pounds. He's got an even temper, mostly. A good boy, but you can't offend his pride. Don't come near him when he's eating is all. You think you and your wife might want to come down and just take a look at him?"

"That's a definite no for us," said Francis. "My wife and I are cat people."

"We got felines coming out our ears at The Rescue too!" said Zip.

"No, we're good."

"What about a pink cockatoo? You could wear her on your shoulder."

"Leave the man alone for godsake," said Rex.

Carl was thinking the same thing. He hated pushy people.

"An exotic bird on a man's shoulder adds extra, what's the word, Merl?" Zip snapped towards his friend.

Merlin rolled his eyes. "Panache, I suppose."

"Ha! Give you some *panache*."

"I couldn't pull that off," Francis said. "Just say the word if you need me, Gents. And Happy Birthday, Mr. Glenmore. Hope you have a blast tonight up at The Castle."

Zip gestured to the iridescent paper on the black marble plinth around which the men were gathered.

"Explain your invitation to me before we part ways," Zip said. "It's got poetry, people's names I don't recognize…who is Ernest? Who is Catherine? Is this party for you or not, Merl?"

"Ernest Glenmore is my great-great grandfather, the one who built The Pile," said Merlin. "Shortly after it was finished, he married his niece, Catherine."

"Woah! Yick," gasped Zip.

"It's true. Arielle discovered in the Castle archives a letter giving special permission from The Church for them to marry. Catherine's parents, Ernest's sister and brother-in-law, could not object. They died before the union occurred. Ernest was a catch in his day, an industrialist and decorated Union Army veteran.

Catherine was by all accounts a beautiful young widow from Boston. The two shared a common interest in the occult, table turning, and séances. Their married life didn't last long. Catherine died at twenty while giving birth to my grandfather's father, before she and Ernest had been married a year."

"It'd be tragic if it weren't so disgusting," Zip said to Rex.

They offended the gods, Carl thought.

"Arielle is fascinated by my forebearers," said Merlin. "They have been a private joke between us. Perversely, she took them as her inspiration for my party, *her* party really. Ill-fated lovers for costumes, the dreaded séance, and the guest list comprised of...her admirers." Merlin's eyes fell on Rex.

"Come on, Merl. You got nothing to worry about my nephew," said Zip. "She ain't Rex's type, and he ain't hers."

"He's everyone's type. Our Rex here is in his prime," said Merlin.

"Stop it with that," Rex protested.

"Yeah, really, Merl," said Zip. "You'll give my nephew a bigger head than he already has."

Zip slapped a twenty on the plinth for Francis. He fixed his cowboy hat on his head and reached for his jean jacket. "Let's get on back to the boat, Rex. I need me a nap before tonight. Merl, you oughta take one too.

Give you a second chance to wake up on the right side of the bed."

"No time," said Merlin. "I'm meeting my sister for lunch, so she can petition me for Pile money."

"Don't take no bull on your birthday," said Zip.

"I never do."

"See you tonight," said Rex. "Tell Arielle we can't wait."

"Why do you need me to tell her?" Merlin asked.

Rex cocked his head, "I don't follow."

"What I mean is I know you have her number."

Merlin patted Rex on the shoulder.

"Excuse me. I see you are leaving. Could I have this table?" Carl asked.

"It's all yours. Where you from?" Zip asked.

Merlin hurried to the curtain covered front door. He despised meeting men he did not already know.

"I just moved here from Texas," Carl said.

"My nephew and I are from Fort Worth! Proud to be from The Lonestar State," said Zip.

"And proud to be Aggies too," said Rex.

"Oh, okay," said Carl with a vague smile. "Good to know my wife and I are not the only Texans here."

"Take care." Zip touched his hat brim and followed Rex to the door.

The invitation left behind on the table read:

the little flower
white in sun
violet in shadow
–Anonymous

Catherine Glenmore Invites You

To Celebrate the 50th Birthday

of

Ernest Glenmore

Saturday, April 1st

At 7 o'clock in the evening

The Glenmore-Pace Castle

Cocktails, Dinner, Séance, Dancing

Attire: Dress As Your Favorite Famous Ill-Fated Lover

"Carl!"

Carl gasped as his in-law Sal crushed him around the middle. "I'm so glad you're here and here for good. Sorry I'm a couple minutes late. We've been busy all day. We have an important catering job tonight. We'll head over to Dolce Far Niente after a quick drink here. Are you hungry? We have a meatball special today. Prepare for an explosion of love in your mouth!"

Carl flinched.

"Let's sit," said Sal.

"Drinks, gentlemen?" Francis asked.

"Two scotches—Macallan okay?" Sal asked Carl.

"Perfect," said Carl. "Neat for me."

"Coming up," Francis said. "Cigars?"

"Yes," said Sal. "You know the kind. One for you, Carl?"

"Not for me, thank you," Carl said.

Sal leaned forward, "The party we're catering tonight is across the river at The Glenmore-Pace Castle. It's for that man who was just sitting where I am. Salt and pepper hair, nose in the air. He was leaving as I came in?"

"I encountered him."

"Merlin Glenmore is his name. This week, he inherited forty mill. I got the intel from his brother-in-law, the chef at my restaurant across the street. I'll introduce you to Chef Paul when we go over there."

Carl gritted his teeth. Of course, Sal would try to take over the entire remainder of his day. He had boxes and boxes to unpack. He had to get the bedroom set up in some kind of order enough for him and Greta to sleep comfortably tonight. Maybe he had misunderstood Sal. Perhaps Sal meant he would meet the chef when he went over to the restaurant on a different day.

Francis delivered their glasses of scotch. Sal inched closer to Carl, as he started puffing away at his cigar, "Merlin's first wife, Maeve, died in an accident this past October. He remarried a much younger woman in January. People around here judge him for it. Being a widower myself, I sympathize. Ever since I lost my Melissa I've been so lonely. She told me she didn't want me to be single for the rest of my days. Spring is around the corner, flowers coming up, and, between you and me, I have my eye on a special lady, Merlin's sister actually, Jade Glenmore. I've known her for ages. She's trying to get her brother to use part of his inheritance to rescue the Castle. Chef Paul believes Merlin's not going to agree to that. Could be devastating for this community. The museum brings a lot of tourists to this town."

"A big attraction," said Carl.

"I'll say. I have got it bad for Jade. An empress among women."

"I meant The—"

"It's not easy to get out of what the kids call the 'friend zone', once you're in there, Car. All these things I never had to think about before. I am giving it a try with Jade."

"Does she inherit any of this family fortune for herself?" Carl asked.

"Only a few crumbs went to her and the youngest brother Robin when the father died. I wouldn't be thrilled about the arrangement if I were those two. Ah! I need to tell you something important. Every Sunday our whole family, which includes you and Greta now, everyone comes to my restaurant to our private room, we call it The Vault, to join us for a feast. In normal Italian families, this would be at my house, but I run a busy restaurant. There's no way I'd be able to take off Sundays, so you all have to come to me. All family is *required* to attend, got it?"

"I will have to speak to my wife, but thank you for the invitation," said Carl. He would not let Sal trap him into a weekly commitment. No way.

"Nonsense. You're coming! Why don't you call Greta on our way? She can meet you for lunch at Dolce Far Niente right now. I bet you're starved after the drive this morning."

"No thank you. I can't accept this time. Greta and I are babysitting Rosie until Sarah gets off work tonight. We're in the middle of moving into our new home. I should get back to help soon."

"What? You're retired, my friend. You've got plenty of time for unpacking another day. Francis, please come over here?" Francis set down the silver cocktail shaker he was rinsing and came out from behind the bar.

"This is important, so listen carefully. This man is my in-law, Sarah's stepfather, my new bestie," Sal said.

Carl couldn't help his eyes from drifting up to the coffered ceiling in exasperation at the word 'bestie' coming out of a grown man's mouth. Sal pointed at Carl.

"Treat Mr. Sarabia here like royalty when he comes in. I know I can count on you to remember. You're the best in the biz. Our drinks go on my tab."

"Yes, of course, Mr. Marotta," Francis gave the thumbs up.

"No, no," Carl reached for his wallet.

"Don't worry about it," said Francis. "You know Mr. Marotta is the owner of Thane's, right?"

Sal opened his hands and grinned at his in-law, "Pretty cool stuff, huh? I'm glad I can share my favorite hangout spot with you. We're going to be in here havin' laughs and tellin' tales all the time."

Carl was sure he hadn't laughed once yet. The scotch had done little to lift his mood. His back hurt from the car ride this morning. He was ready to go home. Before he could find a polite way to break the news, Sal hustled him out onto Main Street, pausing traffic with the palm of his hand as they crossed to the other side.

Carl came to a halt as they reached the ramp leading up to the restaurant entrance. "Give me a moment, please. I need to call Greta and tell her the plan."

"Get her over here. I'll go inside and prepare your table. Don't be too long." Sal patted Carl's shoulder as he headed for the door.

Unbelievable! Carl remained outside shivering in the cold gust whipping down Main as he called Greta. He needed a warmer coat than his brown leather bomber jacket for this climate. As the phone rang, Carl took in the street lined with parked cars. Every spot in front of Dolce Far Niente was taken. Visitors from out of town must be flocking to Glamis on their day off to enjoy the curated boutiques, cozy, lamplit restaurants, and soak up the New England atmosphere of the town center, charming even on this gloomy, gray day. The air felt heavy and expectant like snow would be falling soon. Across the street, customers crowded inside the Black Sheep Bakery for lunch. He would have to check that place out with Greta. She loved a good coffee, and he was eager to find out if the bakery had decent scones, Carl's favorite baked good.

"Hey Carl," Greta answered at last.

"Honey," Carl said. "I've been taken hostage by Sal Marotta. I can't be alone another minute with this man. Did you know about his mandatory Sunday feasts at the restaurant?"

"Sarah mentioned those, yes. She and Justin haven't been able to find a way out of getting ensnared week after week."

"I am not going to be this man's hostage every Sunday, I promise you that," Carl said. "We are busy tomorrow. I'm going to make tostadas for us. Were you able to find the ingredients?"

"Some bad news. I went to the grocery store, but I couldn't find any of the stuff on your list besides yogurt and cereal. They didn't have habaneros either. Only bell peppers."

"You are kidding me."

"Rosie and I will come to meet you at the restaurant. Just go along with it. I don't want to offend Justin's father on our first day here. We've got to strategize on how we're going to deal with him. We'll be there soon."

"I can't believe this."

"Carl, lighten up. If having lunch at a top-rated Italian restaurant is the worst of our troubles, that's a blessing we can't take for granted."

"I just want a sandwich. I don't want to stuff myself on Italian food in the middle of the day," Carl said.

"Coming, Carl?" Sal's head poked out from the entrance.

He put his hand on Carl's shoulder as he escorted him inside. "Um, I overheard you. I'm going to ask Chef to make you a taste of home. See if he can put together some tacos for you. Better than a sandwich at home," he winked. "How about it?"

"The chef is from where?" Carl asked.

"England. What are you giving me that face for? Trust me, tacos aren't going to stump my Chef Paul. The man is a genius at Italian cuisine. He's not from Italy."

"Alright," said Carl. "We'll see."

Greta arrived ten minutes later with Rosie. Sal greeted them at the entrance. Carl was sitting close enough that he could see and hear the whole exchange.

"Who's your favorite, Rosie?" Sal asked.

"Sa!"

"Ding ding ding! We have a winner!"

"What about Gammy? I thought she was your favorite?" Greta teased.

"Gammy!" Rosie shouted.

"No take backsies," Sal said. "You were right the first time, Rosie." He looked up at Greta. "She is the spitting image of Justin. But, when she gives me this mischievous smile, she looks just like Sa, doesn't she?"

Greta did not comment. Carl could imagine what she was thinking. She felt the same way he did about self-absorbed people.

Carl took a deep breath as his wife and granddaughter joined him at the table. Greta ordered the salmon special, and Carl consented to the off-menu tacos, which Sal and Chef Paul delivered personally.

"Allow me to present Chef Paul Krebbs," said Sal.

"I did my best with the tacos," said Paul. "We don't of course have any tortillas—"

"Stop it. He's gonna love it," said Sal. "He's never had tacos like these—he'll only want them this way going forward, and we'll have to add tacos to the menu. Don't let them get cold, Carl. Eat."

"Nice of you to make the effort," Carl peeked inside the folded flatbread at roasted chicken, red peppers, and onions. He lifted the suspect improvisation to his mouth and took a bite.

"Hmm," he managed. "A little mild, the flavor. But pretty good, thank you." Carl didn't know how he would manage to finish more than one bite of the bland creation. These were the most flavorless excuses for tacos he'd ever encountered in his lifetime—undeserving of the name.

Carl expected Sal to preen at the compliment, but instead, Sal's attention drifted. He straightened to his full height. Carl wondered about the elegant blonde woman entering the dining room, as well as the young man following her. The mismatched couple caught Carl's attention. The woman looked as if she belonged at a charity lunch on Park Avenue and the young man with dark wavy hair, five foot four and about twenty,

Carl guessed, carried himself with an urbanity and ease beyond his years. He wore a white t-shirt beneath his midnight blue suede jacket, black jeans, and black leather boots. He smelled of cigarettes and a light, sophisticated cologne as he walked by. Both had been smoking. Carl smelled the woman as she passed his table too, cigarettes and her intense perfume with notes of jasmine and amber.

"Mrs. Glenmore," Sal said, "Are you joining us for lunch? Sit. Sit."

"Sal, you know I don't stand on ceremony," the woman said. "Call me Arielle. And this is my new intern Scott Waterhouse."

"I know who he is!" Sal said. "He's got the Waterhouse jawline. This is Lewis' nephew from Paris."

"I'm not actually *from* Paris, Mr. Marotta. I lived there. I'm *from* New York," Scott said. "New York City," he added.

"Well, we're glad to have you in Glamis. You can bring The Hipness into our corner of Connecticut, huh?" Sal said. "Your Uncle Lewis is one of my favorite regulars. A good customer. I am sure you will be too. Welcome to Dolce Far Niente, which in Italian means—"

"The sweetness of doing nothing," said Scott. "I'm familiar with the expression. My mother and I spent many summers in Tuscany doing just that."

"Sal," said Arielle, "You'll find this young man is truly an encyclopedia. I couldn't ask for a better intern."

Carl rolled his eyes as Sal seated Arielle and Scott two tables down from Carl and Greta.

"Hey, Arielle," Paul waved. "Merlin's new car," Paul gave a chef's kiss.

"We saw it parked across the street last night. We were all drooling," said Sal.

"Beautiful color, isn't it?" Arielle held back laughter as Sal billowed a white linen napkin onto her lap—and only her lap. Scott was left to fend for himself. "Thank you, Sal. Are you all set for tonight?"

"Everything will be perfect for Merlin's party, I promise," said Sal.

"Are you sure that's okay?" Paul asked Carl, motioning to the tacos. "I can bring you a different entree. Pasta is our specialty."

"It's fine," said Carl. "Thank you for these…"

"Alright," said Paul. "I'm headed back to the kitchen. Nice to meet you."

"Right behind you, Chef," said Sal. "Liking those tacos, Car? Thumbs up, okay, excellent. Katie will take care of you," he motioned to the server handing menus to Arielle and Scott.

"Sa?" Rosie's eyes welled at Sal's departure.

"I'll take her for a walk outside," said Greta. "Be right back."

As Carl ate, he could not avoid overhearing the conversation between Arielle Glenmore and Scott Waterhouse.

"The poem means live in light and in shadow," said Scott. "Embrace your dark side too. Be fully you. If you don't want to be a mother, tell him."

"You make such wild assumptions, Scott." Arielle looked at her menu.

"What are you smiling about?" he asked.

"That beguiling beauty mark by the corner of your mouth. Is it the secret to your je ne sais quoi?"

Scott set his elbow on the table and shielded the freckle with his palm. "It's not nice to trifle with someone at risk of falling in love with you."

"This isn't love," she said. "This is *violet in shadow*."

Carl remembered those words from the invitation. Could this young man be the anonymous poet?

"Stop hiding it from me," Arielle said.

Scott kept his hand covering the freckle. "You don't deserve it," he teased.

"I know who you remind me of."

"Who?" Scott asked.

"Vronsky."

"As in Count Vronsky? From *Anna Karenina*? No, you have it all wrong. I would never let anything bad happen to you. I'm marvelously discreet."

"No, you're not. You have one of those faces that betray all. Like right now!" They both laughed. "Jade warned me you have a crush on me."

"She ought to call Mount Everest a hill, or Versailles a hut, or *Anna Karenina* a novelette, before calling my feelings for you a mere crush."

Oh boy, Carl thought. The kid was half her age, and Arielle seemed to be enjoying his attention far too much.

"How long are you doing the internship with us?" she asked.

"You know the song '*If Ever I Would Leave You, It Wouldn't be in Springtime?*'"

Carl recognized the song from *Camelot*, one of his mother's favorite musicals.

"It's too easy for me to visualize you in a suit of armor," Arielle said.

"I am going as Sir Lancelot tonight," he said.

"Guinevere's another one we can add to the list of ruined married women."

"No, *she* has a happy ending."

"Wasn't she burned at the stake?" Arielle asked.

"No! Lancelot saves her," said Scott. "Remember? They ride off into the sunset. You have nothing to fear. I'll restrain myself from leaping across the table and kissing you. It will be 'at last,' as you commanded. See I listen."

"Then why are you hiding your beauty mark from me?"

"Answer my question about why you used the poem first," Scott insisted.

Katie appeared at their side. "Any questions for me? Or, are you two ready to order?"

"Why don't you go first, Scott. You look ravenous."

Money could not buy Merlin Glenmore a loyal wife, apparently. Carl felt a renewed appreciation for Greta, as she came back to the table with Rosie. He put his arm around his wife and kissed her hand.

"Wow, you must have enjoyed those tacos after all. They seem to have buoyed you," said Greta.

"It is my wife who buoys me," he replied. "And you know as well as I do those were not tacos, honey."

Greta's attention shifted. "A police officer," she said as a tall, built, bald man in uniform came towards them with a serious expression.

"I'm Dominic Marotta. Sal's brother. He told me you were here. I'm sorry to interrupt your meal. I couldn't wait to meet you, Lieutenant. It's an honor."

Dominic shook hands with Carl with a tough guy grip. "The pleasure is mine," Carl said.

Dominic turned to Greta. "And you must be Sarah's sister." Clearly, Dominic Marotta had a gentler approach with women.

"I'm her *mother*." Greta shook his hand warmly.

"Glad to meet you both. I'm sorry I couldn't make it to Sarah and Justin's wedding a few years back down in Texas. Lieutenant, please come visit us at the station soon. I told the other officers Carl Sarabia, the HPD legend who worked over 400 cases with a 99% solve rate is going to be living right here in Glamis! Incredible."

"It's kind of you to say," said Carl. "But I would never claim I did it alone."

"You have so much knowledge the officers here could benefit from," said Dominic. "Though, we're proud to say we haven't had a homicide in Glamis for forty years."

Greta squeezed Carl's leg under the table, knowing what he was on the cusp of saying.

"I will be happy to come by the station, as soon as Greta and I are settled in," said Carl.

"Perfect. Here's my information." Dominic handed Carl his card.

Sal fizzed into the dining room bearing meatballs bedecked in red sauce with finely shaved Parmesan on top. He brought them straight to Carl and Greta.

More food? Carl thought. Weren't the so-called "tacos" enough?

"You have to taste these!" Sal lightly slapped away his brother's hand. "Dom, hold off . First Carl and Greta."

Reluctantly, Carl picked up his fork and tried one. Greta did too, though she looked more eager than he felt.

"Best thing you've ever tasted?" Sal asked.

"No," said Carl.

"Carl," scolded Greta. "They're delicious! The best meatballs I have ever had, Sal."

Sal looked down at the meatballs. "He doesn't like it."

"I did not say that," Carl objected. "It's just not the *best* thing I ever tasted. That's a big statement, man."

"Hmm," Sal fed a piece to Rosie. Her eyes widened as the taste hit her.

"Ooh la la!" she exclaimed.

"Ooh la la is right. Hear that? Rosie girl loves them," Sal tapped his granddaughter on her nose. "Grandpa Sa has the best restaurant with the best food in the world. Don't you listen to what grumpy abooboo says."

Carl couldn't believe Sal was painting him in a negative light as the grouchy grandfather to his granddaughter. These meatballs, as admittedly delicious as they were, even from Carl's point of view, would probably give him and Greta both heartburn. Just what they needed as they worked on unpacking the house this afternoon.

As soon as they could politely leave, Carl ushered Greta and Rosie out the door. "I don't know how I'm going to live in the same town as that man," Carl said to Greta, on their walk home. "I really don't."

"Come on," said Greta. "He's a hoot."

"A hoot? At lunch, each bite I take— 'How is it? Is it good? Is it the best thing you ever had in your life?' I want to tell him the best thing I ever tasted are the carnitas tacos in Querétaro, Mexico. They blow your meatballs out of the water, buddy."

"They were delicious, *I* thought."

"Traitor."

"He's intimidated and trying to impress you," said Greta.

"Why are you taking his side?" Carl asked.

"I just want this to work. Can't you imagine this place as being a lovely home for us?"

"Not yet, I cannot. I'm sorry. That is the truth."

"It's only our first day here," said Greta. "Give it time."

Flurries started to fall as they marched up the incline of Great Birnam Wood Road, Carl pushing Rosie in her stroller.

"Snowing in April," he muttered.

"Spring is around the corner," said Greta. "This is a spectacular place to be in the summertime. Sarah says it rarely gets above eighty-five in August. Are you listening to me? Can you slow down? Why don't you visit the station like Dominic said? I bet you could teach the officers a lot. They've never had a homicide here."

"They are sure going to need me if there ever is one."

"And you'll have to remind them you're retired, Carl."

"I know that." He took her hand.

"It will feel better once we get our new home all set up."

"That is correct. Verdad, Rosie?" She giggled. "She's pretty cute, honey."

"She sure is. I don't care what anyone says, Rosie looks like Sarah to me," said Greta.

"And definitely not a thing like Sal."

"Sa?!" Rosie searched around for him.

"No, that man is not here. Thank God," Carl said under his breath.

CHAPTER NINE

Saturday, April 1st - 4:00 p.m.

The icy wind bit through the suede jacket Faustine had bought him in Paris. She loved to take him shopping. Because of his slenderness and shorter stature, it had been a challenge throughout his older teen years to find fashionable clothing that fit him. It was a relief to be taken in hand by Faustine with her exceptional sartorial style. He cringed more than a little though when she would introduce him to the salespeople as her 'baby brother'. He doubted if any of the salespeople believed it. He gladly suffered the indignity for her attention.

When Scott tried on an outfit where the pants were too long or the cuffs of the shirt went to his knuckles, Faustine would reassure him: 'You are perfect the way you are. I wouldn't change a thing. Marcel will make it fit you precisely'. Marcel was her go-to tailor who worked at a highly regarded bespoke men's boutique on the Place Vendome. Scott loved the way she would look at him from every angle in a new outfit. She had fiery opinions on buttons, collars, cuts of clothes, what stories colors told. He liked the way she ruffled his hair or tickled him when he acted restless. He loved the rare occasions when she would break her all-business attitude to give him a secret kiss inside a dressing room.

He tried not to shiver or let his teeth chatter. Now that he lived in Glamis, he should reevaluate his commitment to the 'suffer for fashion' attitude he'd learned from New York, London, and Paris. He leaned against the base of a lead figure of a satyr in the walled garden, admiring Arielle. He couldn't wait until she dumped her poor excuse for a husband. How had his old uncle Merlin, that arrogant creep, ever won her heart in the first place?

"Check it out," Arielle said as she blew smoke rings at him. He had just taught her how, and it excited him that she was game for anything—well, almost anything. So far, at least.

"Have you always been such a quick study in the debauched arts?" Scott asked.

"No, each one has required lots of practice," she said. "Here," she passed the cigarette back to him as her oval rings dissipated.

"Wait," said Scott. "Be amazed."

He blew a perfect O-shaped ring. As it floated towards her in the frigid air, he sang, "*A smoke ring for your finger...*"

"*I fashioned in the blue,*" she crooned back.

"You're un-stumpable."

"Doesn't everyone know Al Bowlly's hits from the '30s?" Arielle asked.

"Which reminds me. I have a gift for you slightly more substantial than a smoke ring." Scott pulled a leather box from his pocket and opened it.

"Tell me you're not." Arielle's eyebrows drew together in panic.

Scott forged on. "Don't freak out. It's a poison ring. I think it will fit your pinky. If I may." He took her right hand and slid the ring onto it. He delicately unlatched the top of the ring with its ruby set in silver to reveal a compartment inside. "This top bit opens like so. Decorative *and* useful for destroying one's enemies."

"Pre-owned by Lucrezia Borgia?" Arielle asked.

"Honestly maybe." Scott swayed on the balls of his feet inside his leather boots. "I'm glad it fits. You like it?"

"I adore it. Where did you get it?"

"It was a gift someone in Paris gave me, and now I'm giving it to you. You should have seen the look on your face. Trust me, when I propose, it won't be here, and it won't be with a poison ring."

"I hope not for the woman's sake," said Arielle, still gazing down at the ring with pleasure.

She can demur all she wants, Scott thought. Sooner or later, he would wear down her defenses, just as he had with Faustine. Arielle ceded ground to him every time they hung out together alone. "I think...a rose cut diamond for you," he teased, "when the second time comes around."

"Stop with that, Scott," Arielle said in a severe tone.

"Stop what?" he laughed. Of course, he knew what.

"You'll break your own heart, stupid boy. You will. I'm warning you."

"Don't call me a stupid boy," Scott protested.

"It's freezing out here," she said in a gentler tone. "Let's get inside."

He followed her into the shadowy cloister attached to the southern side of The Castle.

"Are you excited for the party?" Scott asked. He wasn't. Merlin being there (it being a celebration for *him*) put a damper on the prospect of much worthwhile happening with Arielle. Scott wished he could go to a real party with Arielle where they didn't know a soul. Where his uncle and bosses (Robin Glenmore would be there too) wouldn't be hovering around. Where he could dance with Arielle, get tipsy with her, sneak her back to his bedroom afterwards and at least hold her in his arms and whisper to her all the wonderful things he thought about her. All that was impossible tonight. So why not tell her *now* before the party some of the delicious fantasies he had about her. Why not push it just a bit further and see if she wouldn't be intoxicated by what he told her?

"Am I excited," Arielle said. She tried to block the panicky feeling flooding her mind. All three of them in the same room. No, all *four* of them now after that phone call. One who put her on a pedestal, one who made her feel like an adored little girl, one who had her eating out of his hand switching from cruelty to tenderness all the time, and one who might lose his mind and charge at her like a bull. How would she manage? "I'm nervous," she finally answered. "I hope Merlin allows himself to have fun. I can't believe Jade said yes to having the party here." Arielle unlocked a wooden door leading inside. "Our boss had lunch with Merlin today. She wanted to talk to him privately. She needs money. I wonder how that went. He's been in a hateful mood lately."

"Beast!" Scott imitated Jade.

Arielle laughed, how good it felt to laugh off some of her nerves! Scott was always good for that. She followed him out of the windowless gloom of the stone passageway into the sun-dappled hall past the grand staircase. Continuing eastward, they reached the Library, the most colorful, ornately Gothic chamber in the castle. Diamond panes of citrine, crimson, and emerald stained-glass shot playful light across the walnut floor. Murals depicted scenes from the legend of Robin Hood and Maid Marian between arched bookshelves, while across the ceiling Robin's Merry Men peered through branches in an enchanted Sherwood Forest.

"How could Merlin be in a hateful mood?" Scott asked. "If I inherited millions, I would throw a few bones to the museum. But first, we'd get you rapidly divorced."

"Scott, stop with comments like that. I'm not kidding." She slid back the pocket doors, opening onto the Music Room, which contained an Apollo Player Piano with foot pumps, a 17th century organ with ivory and ebony-covered oak pipes, and a glass-encased, seven-foot tall tromba marina. Off the dance floor, stood a table covered in white linen, loaded with red wine and spirits.

"It being your second wedding, we'll have a modest affair," continued Scott. "We won't skimp on the honeymoon. Was that a sigh? Of feverish anticipation, I hope."

"Scott, stop. You're mad," she giggled. He was distracting her at least.

Scott crossed his arms and shook his head. Amusement shone in his eyes. "I don't believe you. I don't think you want me to stop for a second. You're laughing! How can I stop? I'm just getting started. I've got to tell you everything I've dreamed up for us. At least three months cavorting through Greece, Italy, France. Imagine mornings breakfasting at sidewalk cafes, meandering around cathedrals and châteaux, venturing into every museum that piques our interest, savoring a lively muscadet in a Loire Valley vineyard. On our way to a candlelit dinner, holding hands as we traverse cobblestones, passing a street musician—"

"An accordion player," said Arielle.

Now she was relenting. Scott pressed on, "We pass a gifted accordion player—"

"Guillaume," said Arielle.

Scott loved it. "He has a name, does he? Alright, Guillaume, the gifted accordion player."

"Dark hair and a debonair mustache," Arielle embellished.

"Don't stare at him too long," said Scott. "You'll make me jealous. Guillaume, who is talented with music but sadly unblessed in the looks department—"

"No, Scott, he *is* blessed," Arielle giggled. "He looks just like a young Alain Delon."

"If not for his piggy eyes, unmitigated unibrow, and unforgivable halitosis," Scott said.

"No, no!" Arielle objected, tears of laughter rolling down her cheeks.

"The severest case in the history of France," Scott added mercilessly. He lived to make her laugh like this. "But how beautifully Guillaume serenades us with *La Vie en Rose*—"

"Too obvious," Arielle wiped at her eyes. "He's playing the sultry 'Habanera' from *Carmen*. That's my favorite."

"I know it's your favorite. But on the accordion? Fine. Somehow, Guillaume, whose musical talent is nothing short of miraculous, manages a stirring rendition of the 'Habanera'. Full of joie de vivre and sparkling, just as you are now, I can't resist pulling you close—"

"Shh stop," said Arielle. "I hear someone."

Jade loomed into the Library in black, a fuzzy hat on her head and puffer jacket covering her from chin to boots. "Afternoon," she said crisply. She carried a cumbersome box in her arms.

"Let me help," Arielle rushed to Jade, relieving her of the rented glassware.

"How was lunch with Merlin?" Arielle asked.

"His mood. You could have warned me."

"Did he come here with you?"

"No, he didn't," said Jade. "He said to expect him at six thirty. Scott, you reek of cigarettes. You must stop that awful habit. It cheapens you. Help me carry in the plates and cutlery from my car before your lungs fail. Didn't they teach you at school smoking kills?"

"Yes, no smoking. But most of all beware of women who only want to use me for my body."

"Beast!" said Jade.

Arielle and Scott locked eyes and tried to stifle their laughter. No one could deliver the word quite like Jade.

"And you," Jade sniffed at Arielle. "*You* have been smoking as well. Nothing escapes my notice."

Scott followed Jade into the entry hall and out the front doors. Halfway up a gravel path screened by columnar evergreens, Jade halted, "I want to speak with you privately. It's advice more than anything."

"Ask away," said Scott.

"No, I mean advice *for you*. This infatuation...let it go. Arielle is married. To my brother."

"Not happily."

"Scott! Enough. When a couple struggles to conceive—"

Scott winced. "Oh God, Boss, please stop."

"They are in love," Jade insisted. "Merlin is her perfect match."

"He's not," Scott interrupted. "He's monstrously old."

"He is five years younger than me, you pip!"

"I mean old for *her*. You're not old, Jade. Your beauty grows with every day!"

"Save your breath. Why not date someone your own age?"

There could be no inquiry he despised more. His mother suggested the same when she found out about his affair with Faustine. Why not date girls his own age? Because he loved older women. Faustine had taught him about Life and Style and how to beguile a woman. Faustine fawned over him the way girls his age never would. She regarded him as a rare, magical creature she couldn't fully possess. She adored him, but she was always lamenting he would not be hers forever, even when he swore he would be. She insisted their time together was finite, for a season. They should enjoy their affair all the more, she had insisted, knowing it was like the fragile beauty of autumn. It could not last.

"Arielle and I are only friends. Don't be absurd," said Scott.

Jade shook her head. "One day you will want to tell her your true feelings. When you do, you will witness how fast she flies away. Don't do that to yourself. There is only one man she is serious about. And he isn't a teenager."

How he hated being treated like a child. He was no common teenager. "As I said, she is just my friend. You are really embarrassing yourself."

"I am trying to spare *you* from embarrassment. And danger too," said Jade.

"How exciting. What danger?" Scott asked.

"Aren't you familiar with the perils of involving yourself with a married woman?"

Scott rolled his eyes. "Uncle Lewis. A real steel trap."

"I hope I have communicated my point."

Girls my own age. How stupid! There aren't any like Her. I would do what Richard III said he did out of passion for Lady Anne. "He that hath bereft thee, lady, of thy husband, Did it to help thee to a better husband."

Jade spun around to face him, "What on earth did you just say?"

"That was Shakespeare. I used to run lines with my mom when she was in *Richard III* and some of it stuck."

Jade gave Scott her sternest glare as she opened the cast iron gate to the staff parking lot.

***

Catia Boyd examined herself in her gilded bedroom mirror from side to side. She looked the spitting image of Elizabeth Taylor.

Owen set down an ugly, brown cardboard box on her vanity. "A package for you."

"The violet-colored contacts!" She purchased the non-prescription lenses online. "I didn't know if they would arrive in time. Delightful!"

"I've got to scrounge a costume from my closet," said Owen. "Probably just go with what I wore for Halloween."

"That's a good idea," she applied red lipstick and blotted on a tissue. "What made you change your mind, darling?"

"Huh?" Owen asked.

"I thought you were keen on having a night in," she said. "You bought the peach ice cream and everything for your Owen home-alone snack while you watch whatever Masters rerun you had planned. Now you want to come with me?"

"I feel like getting out," Owen said, annoyed at this interrogation. As if Catia cared that he was coming with her. It seemed she minded he *was* going. "How was your day?" he switched topics.

"Oh busy. We have a wedding tonight. Sarah's running it like a champ."

"Send me your latest P&L when you have a chance," said Owen. "That golf simulator is going to be a money maker for the Inn."

Owen was so proud of installing the golf simulator in a former storage shed in the garden of the Inn. Catia wanted to tell him no one except Owen himself used it for the entire month of March. She decided to hold her tongue. It ate at Catia that she had Owen to thank for the Inn. Initially, he doubted any likelihood of her business succeeding. He said she was out of her depth. Catia argued she had twenty years working her way up at various spas and hotels, gaining management experience. Owen insisted it was not the same thing.

Faced with her unwavering determination, he wrote her a check which allowed her to begin the project. Open now for two and a half years, The Lavender Inn and Spa was profitable, even in Owen's estimation. Catia felt a surge of triumph every time she entered the charming yet spotless lobby or the sanctuary of the immaculate spa. She involved herself in all aspects of the operation, training and supervising housekeeping, maintenance, the front desk, the massage therapists, the manicurists, the never-ending cycle of weddings, the chef, kitchen staff, waitstaff, and gardeners. Each employee received regular feedback and face time with Catia. She implemented quarterly meetings to go over the mission statement the staff had crafted together. She wanted her employees to feel pride in the Inn and invested in creating a superb experience for their customers.

The Inn staff continually surprised her with how far they took service for the guests. It had become a competition among the front desk associates as to whom could take their service the furthest. One of the front desk staffers had gone missing for an hour but Catia later found out he had offered to bathe and blow dry one of the guests' dogs who had gotten muddy on a hike. She told him he'd gone a bit overboard on that one. Later he showed her the guest left a five star rave mentioning "The Lavender Inn's crazy good attentiveness—you kind of feel like the staff is obsessed with your happiness. I mean that in the BEST way. I will be recommending a getaway here to all my friends and clients!".

Catia was proud of what she was building at the Inn. She knew she should apply a similar hands-on approach to sustaining her marriage. She resented Owen for doubting her abilities. Of course, she proved him wrong, but she could not let it go. It shattered her view of the purity of their partnership. She upheld total faith in his ability as a physician. Why did he doubt her own competence? Owen's discouraging remarks lessened once Catia discovered the effectiveness of sending him detailed spreadsheets showing the Inn's growing financial success. She wrote him a check to start paying him back for his investment, but he tore it up and told her "None of this. My money is your money."

"You haven't told me how I look," Catia said.

"Great, hon." Owen slipped out of his loafers and padded into the closet. He wasn't even looking.

CHAPTER TEN

Saturday, April 1st - 7:00 p.m.

In The Castle entry hall, Jade, dressed as Josephine Bonaparte, held up an electric candle to better see the new arrivals.

"I know who you are, Phantom," Jade said.

Zip Davis reached up his knobby knuckled hand to recenter the plastic half-mask on his face. Jade turned to the younger man beside him. "But who are you in this cape?"

"How do you do, Empress?" Rex leered at her with an open-mouthed grin, revealing fanged teeth.

"Ah ha," said Jade. "Good evening, Count Dracula."

"Everyone looks marvelous!" Arielle strutted into the entry hall dressed as Catherine Glenmore in a midnight blue taffeta gown and black gloves, bearing a candelabra in one hand. Jade thought it was about time. Arielle had taken a full hour to get dressed for the party, leaving Jade no choice but to handle finishing the party set-up, greeting the brooding Birthday Boy, serving him his favorite scotch, and now making sure the guests were greeted as they arrived. Arielle did look stunning of course, but Jade thought her make-up anachronistic, more suited for the red carpet than for a Victorian lady like Catherine Glenmore. Jade's great-great grandmother would never have worn eye liner or red lipstick. In the mid-1800s, cosmetics of that ilk were reserved for actresses and women of unmentionable professions. Arielle knew this, Jade was sure.

"My word, don't you look like the belle of the ball, Ma'am," Zip kissed Arielle's hand. "Here we are," he said. "Two ill-fated lovers. And here comes a third!"

A burly man stepped inside wearing a blonde mullet wig with bangs, a collared shirt beneath a down jacket, sunglasses, a golf glove, and American flag pants.

"Who are you supposed to be?" Jade asked. As best as she could tell the fellow was dressed as an avid political rally-goer who got drunk and woke up the next morning on a golf course.

"Hope you've got plenty of beer in this joint," the man replied. "I've been known to say, 'One's too many, and ten just ain't enough'."

Jade knew this tidbit was supposed to be The Clue to tip her off. Well, she had been right at least to pick up this personage was an avid tippler. She still had no idea of the identity of the colorful, possibly patriotic fellow. Whoever he was, Jade thought, he had a tragic sense of fashion, even for the 1980s.

"Ooh ooh! He's my hero, the golfer John Daly!" Zip clapped Owen Boyd on the back as he shook his hand. "Well done, Doc."

"I did my best," said Owen. "Scrounged this get up from my closet. I remembered the costume requirement about an hour ago. Luckily, I dug up this outfit from Halloween."

"Ahem." Catia shrugged her leopard coat to reveal bare shoulders and struck a pose. She wore a purple gown, a turban studded with silk flowers, and white gloves with rhinestone jewels on her wrists and neck.

"Gaze into the windows of my soul, if you dare," Catia showed off her colored contacts to Arielle.

"Those famous violet eyes," Arielle replied. "Did you come alone or with Mr. Burton, Ms. Taylor?"

"Solo. I haven't seen Dick in a while."

"You're terrible," Arielle giggled. "Cocktails this way." She took Rex Davis' arm.

"Freezing in here," Catia said to Jade. "I can see my breath. No heat, no power at all?"

"That's right," Jade tried to give off a positive attitude. It was a struggle. She felt a headache coming on. "It's for atmosphere. Robin will turn the power back on once the séance is over."

Catia cocked an eyebrow at the news. She wasn't a fan of the dark. Well at least she would be able to keep her fabulous leopard coat on without overheating.

The Library's colorful stained-glass windows reflected the glow of flameless candles. Antique books lined arched shelves. The inviting velvet upholstery of the furniture welcomed the guests as they entered the room, and the marble fireplace engraved with the Glenmore motto 'Nil Admirari' crackled with a real fire for once. Jade would never tell anyone this lest they think she was crazy, but she could read the Castle's moods. To her relief, she could see having a real party here and using the rooms as they were intended might just be a treat for the Castle after all. Being put to real use seemed to make it merry. She had been a worry wart for nothing. As they entered the sumptuous room, a tinny melody played in the Music Room beyond.

"Easy on the pedals, Chef. It's not a bicycle!" Scott clad in chainmail and armored shoes, instructed Paul, dressed as Oscar Wilde, on how to work the player piano. Paul was a whiz in the kitchen, but a pianist, he was not.

"Merlin, please listen," Robin Glenmore's voice echoed in the hall outside the Library. Catia and Rex cringed at one another. Owen and Zip glanced uneasily towards the open door leading to the Hall. Jade prayed her younger brothers had outgrown their penchant for physical altercations now that they had reached middle age.

Merlin stormed into the Library, Robin at his heels. Both looked surprised to find the chamber populated with costumed guests. Merlin scowled as he registered Catia in her ridiculous, trashy get up. What was she supposed to be? A washed-up woman of the night? When he was a boy he had thought Catia was a pest, spying on him and his siblings from the garage apartment where she lived with her mother the Glenmore Family's maid. He couldn't remember the mother's name anymore. Not that it mattered.

Merlin's expression softened when he took in his wife. Arielle looked radiant in her blue taffeta gown. She had taken pains to drive all the way down to Greenwich to pick up their attire from a costume shop specializing in historic costume rentals. Instead of this ridiculous party, he wished the two of them could have driven to New York, gone out to dine at a Michelin star restaurant, taken in a show at the high-end jazz club at Lincoln Center, ended the evening with a passionate night spent at the Plaza or the Pierre, with coffee and pancakes in bed the next morning. That's what he really wanted. Just to share his celebration with her alone. He once felt Arielle could read his mind, but that must have been a delusion generated from the high of being wildly attracted to her, not anything reality based. They clearly shared no telepathy, otherwise she would not have designed this evening of torture for him. He sunk into a highbacked red velvet armchair before the fireplace and hoped Robin would have the sense not to question him any further in front of the others.

Arielle clasped her hands, marveling at Robin and Merlin's transformations. "Goodness, don't the Glenmore brothers look ravishing in these Victorian suits?"

"I tried," Robin whispered to Jade. "He's not going to share a penny with either of us. He's a sadistic miser like Dad."

"I wouldn't hound him anymore," said Jade. "He may turn vicious."

"I can hear you, Jade," Merlin said loudly.

Rex squeezed Jade's shoulder as he passed her, acting as if he would handle the situation.

"I know Merl is Ernest Glenmore, but who are you supposed to be, Sir?" Rex asked Robin.

"I'm Alfred, Lord Douglas, the ill-fated lover of Oscar Wilde," Robin gestured to Paul in the Music Room.

Catia watched Merlin smirk as he looked into the fire. Was now the moment to go over and speak with him? She could drop ever so casually what she heard from Arielle. Maybe they would consider hiring a surrogate instead? She knew of a reputable service that helped a friend locate one and would be happy to pass that information along. The only thing stopping Catia was the thought of Arielle. It didn't seem fair to do this to another woman, to share her secret, but it was tempting to set in motion the end of Merlin's happiness. Catia would get a drink first before making the final decision on whether to ruin Merlin's life or not.

Jade turned to Arielle. "Are we all assembled?"

"This is everyone. Go on Merlin, tell them the rule and enforce it!"

"Fine," Merlin rose from his chair with a groan to make the announcement. "Honored guests," he began. "The time has come for the surrender of your cellphones. Place them in this box. They will be returned to you at the end of the evening."

"He is on such a power trip over this," Jade said. "You'd better explain to everyone, Arielle."

"We are going back in time this evening," Arielle said. "As you can see, we have shut off the power."

Catia rubbed her arms. "See and *feel*. It's freezing."

"Warm yourself by the fireplace, Liz dear," said Arielle. "We're going to be illuminated only by candlelight tonight—"

"*Flameless* candlelight," Jade indicated the flickering battery-powered candelabras stationed around the room.

"To achieve the atmosphere most conducive to communing with the spirits of the past, we free ourselves from the shackles of our modern devices," said Arielle.

"No shot. I have a wedding going on at the Inn tonight. Someone might need to reach me for an emergency," Catia bristled.

"Oh please, you know Sarah Marotta has it covered." Owen set his phone down inside the box. "Relax and enjoy your one night out this year."

"Surrender the goods, or leave the premises," said Merlin. Catia gave a loud sigh and forced herself to place her phone into the box, giving Merlin an 'I am not amused' eyebrow raise. The others complied with a few grunts of discontent as they gave up their phones.

A jaunty rendition of "Scotland the Brave" trilled from the player piano. "I've got the hang of it now," said Paul.

Scott held his hand out to Arielle with a flourish: "*Now tread we a measure!*"

"You've got me there. What's it from?"

"Yes! I stumped you. From the poem *Lochinvar* by Sir Walter Scott. Madame?"

As her gloved fingers descended towards his gauntlet-clad hand, the music roll flapped into itself.

"It's too early for dancing," said Jade.

"What would you care to drink, Ms. Taylor?" Rex called across the Music Room to Catia. "Champagne?!"

"Oh! The champagne is in the kitchen," said Arielle. "Would you help me?"

"Sure," said Rex and Scott at the same time.

Arielle flushed as her eyes darted between them. "You both can help. A guardian for either side of me. It's so spooky in these dark passages."

"Which I will remind you is exactly how you wanted them," said Jade.

"Arielle, are there any limes?" Owen asked from across the room.

"Oh certainly, Doctor Boyd. I'll get them for you. They're in the kitchen too."

"I'll join you," said Paul. "We'll bring out the appetizers."

Paul followed Scott, Rex, and Arielle into the entry hall and westward down the Castle's northern corridor, past the Armory and staff room, taking a left into the kitchen.

"'Certainly, Doctor Boyd. Limes? Oh, but certainly, doctor, dear doctor!' That's what you sounded like," said Rex.

"I hope you're not drunk already," said Arielle.

"Not nearly enough to stomach your foolishness. And at your own husband's birthday."

"One can never have too much ice at a party." Arielle knelt before a cooler and scooped cubes into a silver bucket.

"The snow is really coming down out there," said Paul.

"Have you heard if Sal and Justin are on the way?" Arielle asked.

"I'm sure they'll be here any minute with the main course and the cake. The appetizers are right here on these trays. Glad I brought them with me from the restaurant," said Paul. "Would you carry this one, Sir Lancelot? Hold it level. That one has the goat cheese and fig crostinis. Can't have them sliding all over the place."

"I've got them." Scott picked up the tray with care.

"I'll bring the champagne and our light source. Carry this ice, bloodsucker." Arielle shoved the bucket brimming with ice against Rex's chest.

Paul led the group into the corridor carrying two trays, Rex and Scott close behind him. Arielle trailed with a champagne bottle in one hand and the candelabra in the other.

"Scott," Arielle whispered. Scott turned around, as Rex and Paul continued down the passageway. "The limes. How could I forget?"

"My hands are full. *Oh.* Yes, let me help you."

Back in the kitchen, she set the champagne on the counter.

"Put down the tray. This way," she pointed to a closed wooden door.

Scott followed her back into the pantry. Snowfall dashed outside the lone window's leaded quarries. She shut the door, set the candelabra on the stone countertop. "Do you know why it's called a pantry? It comes from the French word for bread, pain. And the word parlor comes from parler, to talk."

"I already knew all that. My French is better than yours, remember," Scott said. He couldn't repress his nervous laughter. "Did you bring me in here to talk etymology?"

He stepped closer to her. Her satin-covered hands found either side of his face.

"So, this is 'at last'?" he murmured.

Her lips pressed against his in answer.

"We have to go back," she said. "I'll lose my head."

"I've already lost mine."

"*Arielle?*"

Scott and Arielle leapt apart as the pantry door swung open. Merlin stood tense with rage, in disbelief. He didn't need an explanation. It was obvious what was going on in here.

"Merlin! We have been looking everywhere for the limes," said Arielle.

Of course, there were no limes in the pantry, and Merlin knew it.

"I expected it would be Rex in here, but you can't rule out anyone with you apparently," Merlin said icily. "Not even my nephew."

Hearing Merlin use that word surprised Scott. When Merlin had been married to Aunt Maeve, he had never treated Scott like family, and Scott had never felt close to Merlin. It was yet another reason Scott was certain he would be a far better companion for Arielle than his heartless uncle.

"Go," Arielle urged Scott.

"Are you sure?" Scott asked, worried over leaving her with Merlin.

"Yes, of course. Don't be silly," she said.

Merlin stopped Scott at the door. "In days of old, do you know what a man of honor would do in this situation?"

"Challenge me to a duel? Up for one?"

"This is your final warning. Stay away from my wife," said Merlin.

"Swords or pistols?" asked Scott as the pantry door slammed in his face, Merlin sealing himself alone with Arielle.

Scott could not stop from grinning, remembering their kiss of just a few moments ago, their first kiss. He couldn't wait for the second and third, hopefully those would be uninterrupted. Yikes! Scott picked up the tray and started down the corridor to the Library. He knew the way in the dark.

In the Music Room, Scott set down the fig and goat cheese-bedecked crostinis in a space near the bucket of ice on the table.

"Looks delicious," said Catia. "Chef Paul, I can't stop eating these prosciutto and melon bites. Owen, try these!"

In the adjoining Library, Scott found Rex warming himself by the fire. Scott went to sit in the velvet armchair closest to the fireplace.

Rex tried to stop him. "That's Merl's chair."

Scott thunked down into it with a clank of chainmail. "Perfect."

"Find a gal your own age. That's my advice."

"I don't know what you're talking about," Scott said.

"I'll tell you this one time." Rex leaned forward. "She. Ain't. Yours. Pal."

"Your fangs really helped sell that," said Scott. "I'll say this, you're a good friend. Merlin doesn't deserve you. And he certainly doesn't deserve her."

Hearing Arielle's voice, Scott glanced around the wing of his armchair. Merlin made a show of kissing Arielle's hand as they re-entered the Library. She cooled Merlin down quickly, Scott thought. Arielle knew how to soothe tempers. He had seen her handle one particularly irritable, know-it-all visitor touring the castle. She had a talent for defusing tense situations and charming angry men.

"That's my chair," Merlin looked down his nose at Scott.

Rex yanked the young man to his feet. "Let's get that funny piano going, kid. I want to ask Liz Taylor to dance."

Scott reluctantly followed Rex to the cabinet displaying rows of piano rolls.

"*La Cumparsita*, the world's most famous tango. That's the one," Rex pointed out the song. Scott loaded it with utmost care onto the spool box. He sat down to the piano, pulled a lever, pumped the pedals. The music roll rotated. The strains of the famous tango filled the room, as Rex offered Catia his white-gloved hand.

"I don't know how to dance to this," she protested.

"Just follow me." Rex took her in his arms.

Catia struggled to keep up, tripping and halting. After stabbing Rex's feet twice with her stilettos, she waved him away laughing. "Enough! This is embarrassing. I can't keep up with you. Next victim!" She retreated from the dance floor.

"Arielle, let's see you try. Go on," Merlin nudged his wife towards the dance floor.

"I don't want to dance the tango," she protested.

"Too bad. It's my birthday," said Merlin.

The other guests circled around Rex and Arielle as they locked into frame. Her left hand latched beneath his upper arm, his right hand pressed beneath her left shoulder blade, her right hand in his left hand. The whirl of her gown and his cape obscured their footwork, as they moved together, pantherlike, peppering in staccato movements and swift dips as Rex stalked Arielle around the room, their bodies magnetized.

Merlin crossed his arms bracing himself for the truth he expected would reveal itself in the dance. Of all the men who admired his wife, handsome, vital, charismatic Rex threatened Merlin the most. Rex had a distinct ease with Arielle that disturbed Merlin. He wondered if he would pick up the truth observing them. Could you detect an affair just by watching two people move together long enough? If there was a truth to be gleaned from the dance, it was the undeniable one that they went well together physically. One might think they'd been dancing together their whole lives.

The music roll flapped up into itself, as the song ended.

"Thank God," said Jade, relieved the spectacle of the sensual tango was over.

Scott turned around on the piano bench to face the dancers, applauding with the others. Why hadn't he listened to his mother when she encouraged him to take up ballroom dance when he was younger? Scott keenly felt there was a gaping hole in his education as a worldly man not knowing how to tango. He knew just the woman he would ask to teach him. What fun they could have practicing during their lunch break.

"Who knew we had Ginger Rogers and Fred Astaire in our midst?" asked Robin.

"Enough showing off, you dumb clown." Zip scowled at Rex.

"How *did* you learn to dance like that?" Jade whispered to Arielle. "I would be impressed, if it wasn't so scandalous."

"It was only a dance," said Arielle.

"Not just any dance. *The tango*. The dips, the latching of legs, constant hip contact! With Merlin it would have been distasteful enough, but with Rex Davis, who dances alarmingly well, the tango is an act of indecency."

"You should let him take you for a spin next," said Arielle.

"I am not a motor vehicle." Jade straightened her tiara.

Owen sidled over to Arielle. "I loved watching you move out there. Try the stuffed shrimps yet? You haven't eaten a thing, have you," Owen fussed. "Come with me. Try some of these delicious Chef Paul creations. I want to ask you a rather burning question."

Arielle followed him to the hors d'oeuvres. "I was so thrilled by your call earlier." Owen made a show of examining the offerings. "Tell me when and where I can meet you in private, you naughty girl."

"Owen, you misunderstood. I could never," Arielle objected.

"Huh."

"I'm absolutely devoted to Merlin."

Owen scrutinized her. "I don't believe you for a second."

"You would have to be clever to persuade me to overcome my moral hesitations... I shall flee in fear of any man who charges me directly. You wouldn't have the patience required to woo someone of my unique temperament."

"Don't underestimate me." He licked aioli from his fingertip.

Zip reached between them for a shrimp. "Hey Doc, what do you call a worm on the green?"

"What's that?"

"A birdie opportunity!"

"Ha." Owen craned around Zip to address Arielle, but she was already fleeing across the room to talk with Jade. Bewildering. She'd come on so strong on the phone and now she was giving him the brush off. Had he read her interest in him wrong somehow? Owen felt foolish. He'd been willing for a few hours today to follow this woman right out of his marriage, trade Catia for a woman who didn't seem to care a whit about him now. Sibyl, his dachshund, had warned him. She knew what was best and would tell him if he would only pay attention. Now he felt he needed to make it up to Catia somehow. She was particularly beautiful tonight and keenly resembled Elizabeth Taylor, he had to admit.

"Dinner has arrived!" Sal Marotta swept into The Library brandishing a tray, followed by Justin laden with the rest of the catering.

"No, no! Not in here," said Jade. "The banqueting hall is where we'll dine."

"Hello, beautiful Josephine." Sal greeted Jade with a bow of his head. "Neither sleet, nor fog, nor driving snow could stand in the way of me reaching you with nourishment befitting an empress."

"You're too much," Jade blushed. "This way."

"Let me help carry some of this, Sal." Paul swooped in.

Arielle stood by the library door as the others filed out into the hall. Merlin rose from the chair and stretched out his arms. He crooked his finger at her, "A word."

Arielle went to him and swept her arms around his neck. "I can't tell, are you enjoying your birthday party?"

"No," Merlin buried his nose against her neck, smelling her familiar scent that still reduced him to a lustful mad man. "Ugh!" he stepped away before he *really* wanted her. "I just can't wait to escape with you. Get out of nasty cold New England. I'm sick of it. I want to go south with you and lock you away all for myself somewhere always warm with a high up ocean view."

"I'm imagining myself as Rapunzel in a Florida high rise," she said. "Which would make you—"

"Don't you dare say the old witch," said Merlin.

"I wasn't!" said Arielle. "I was going to say The Prince!"

"I've almost forgiven you for earlier. Don't upset me now," he said. "I know it wasn't your fault. It was that stupid boy. Forget a duel. Scott Waterhouse deserves to be horsewhipped. Would you enjoy watching me thrash the blaggard in the public square?"

"I'd never speak to you again if you did anything of the kind."

"You can't fool me," said Merlin. "You love it when 'history comes to life'. You would be totally fascinated to witness honor violence from The Age of Chivalry played out before your eyes. Wouldn't it be all the more thrilling that you yourself were the cause!"

"You don't know me at all if you think that," said Arielle. "You're all worked up when you have nothing to worry about, my love. It's such a waste of your energy. It is! Let's join the others. Shouldn't we invite the Marottas to stay for dinner with us?"

"Don't tell me one of them is another of your admirers. Or both father and son, you wanton wench. Am I supposed to accept the entire male population of Glamis is chasing you?"

"You're crazed!" Arielle laughed. "You should see this look in your eyes. Has the spirit of Ernest Glenmore possessed you?"

He captured her in his arms again. "Look at me. In the eyes. You love me, don't you?"

She nodded, giggling. "Of course, I love you, Merlin."

He brushed one of her bare shoulders reverently with his lips. He could hardly believe such a beautiful creature belonged to him. His first wife Maeve had been attractive in a pale, preppy, patrician way, but not gorgeous. Not like this dream girl who would fit right in on a Hollywood red carpet. His new wife. God help him, there was nothing Arielle could do to make him stop loving her. He prayed she would never discover the fact. The hold her physical beauty alone had over him ensured her complete possession of him. As callous as the wicked flirt could be, it made a man feel alive, young, and vital, to be madly in love.

"Will you be furious if I skip your séance?" he asked.

"Oh. It's your day," she sighed. "I can't say I'm surprised. Doctor Boyd didn't seem particularly interested in my séance either. After dinner, you could take him to the Conservatory. Play chess?"

"Not a bad idea. Or...I could take you away instead for a game of..."

"Excuse us." Sal poked his head into the room holding a glowing flameless candelabra. "I'll set this down, leave this precious light source with you two. Justin and I are on our way out the front. We wanted to say our goodbyes. Wish you a Happy Birthday, Mr. Glenmore."

"Yep, Happy Birthday, Mr. Glenmore," echoed Justin. "Also, dinner's ready and the others are ready. Don't want the food to get cold."

"Don't go just yet," said Arielle. "Let the snow die down. Would you stay and join us for dinner?"

"It's kind of you to ask, but we need to hit the road. Got a wife and baby at home," said Justin.

"Do we have to go?" Sal squinted at his son.

"Dad, we don't want to impose on their party."

"Oh my goodness, no, we would love to have you. Wouldn't we, Merlin? It's a once in a lifetime experience to dine in the Castle Banqueting Hall. Jade will never allow a real dinner to be eaten in there again."

"That's true." Sal raised his brows at his son.

"We know the food won't disappoint," Justin gave in. Sarah would hopefully understand it was a rare opportunity to enjoy the ambiance of the Castle in this way.

Sal gripped Merlin's shoulder. "Are you sure it's okay for us to crash your birthday party?"

"Fine! Join us," Merlin removed Sal Marotta's hand. It made his skin crawl when anyone except Arielle touched him without his permission.

Sal dug in his coat pocket. "Let me text Katie that we're not going back to Dolce tonight. We're closing soon anyway. She has it covered."

Sal messaged Katie. "And sent," he said.

Sal jumped at Merlin's hand, outstretched in front of his face.

"If you're going to stay, you will have to surrender your phones like everyone else."

"Seriously?" asked Sal.

"Seriously." Merlin grabbed the phone from Sal's hand. "Justin?"

"I didn't bring my phone," Justin said. "I forgot it at the restaurant." It was in his coat pocket, in fact, but he wanted to hang onto it in case Sarah needed to reach him. There was also the Yankees game to keep an eye on. He'd bet some real money on this one. It was a close one so far.

Merlin gave Justin a long stare. "Alright," he said. It wasn't as though he was prepared to pat the young man down. He would have to take his word for it, but he'd keep a sharp eye on him through dinner to make sure he wasn't lying.

II

Halfway through dinner, with the flameless candles casting shadows on the gold and burgundy damask covering the banquet table, the mood of the party was subdued. Everyone agreed the catered dinner of spinach and ricotta agnolotti and braised lamb shank from Dolce Far Niente was delicious, though not the perfect temperature, Paul fretted. Sal shushed him on that point. The castle's atmosphere was a novelty and perfect for a feast otherwise. Historic banners and pennants hung from the coffered ceiling. One felt Henry VIII and his retinue might parade into the hall at any moment. The enormous hearths with space inside enough to stand a war horse, framed both ends of the dining hall, but these fireplaces no longer worked. The guests kept on their jackets, and they continued imbibing with the excuse that it was helping them keep warm against the chill. In Robin's case, he consumed considerably more than his typical one glass of red a day. He was already two bottles deep, by Paul's count. He should say something again to him, but it was too late.

Robin wavered up from the banquet table, disentangling himself from his husband's grasp. "No, I *will* say this, Paul. My sister battled tirelessly for decades to preserve this historic place we're enjoying this evening. Certain people," he glared at Merlin, "can't seem to see the beauty and importance of it to our family personally and to History itself. They think it's a folly!"

"It is a folly." Merlin drummed his fingers next to his plate. "How about sitting down? Stop making an ass of yourself."

"I won't sit down, because I'm not finished," Robin said. "What can I say about you, Merlin? You refuse to speak to me in private. Fine. You force me to say it in front of everyone. To receive a fraction of what you inherited would mean salvation to me and our sister. I told you my business is struggling. Paul and I are on the verge of having to sell the house. Don't you remember Dad saying he trusted you to do what was right for me and Jade? To be a custodian of the wealth for the entire family's benefit? What did you do to deserve the honor anyway. I know. It's because you're the most like him, like Dad. *A toxic, malignant narcissist!*"

"How touching," Merlin dabbed his lips with his napkin. "I hope everyone will excuse this embarrassing outburst of jealousy from my dear little brother. Take a seat, Robin. We'll talk later. Lord, you can't even leave me alone on my birthday. Zero self-control."

"Please, sit, Robin. This isn't the way," said Paul. "We'll talk to him later. Together."

Robin sunk back into his chair defeated. He had only succeeded in looking pathetic, just as he did every time he came up against Merlin while growing up, trying to prove his case and getting smacked down by his cleverer, older brother. His parents had never taken his side, not even when Merlin would push him around when he was a tyke. He remembered Merlin shoving him to the floor, bumping his head, and when he cried and pointed at Merlin, his mother had believed Merlin when he said Robin had tripped. He must have been all of three, but he remembered as if it were happening to him now, the burning injustice of it.

Zip raised his glass as he stood. "I'd like to say I'm grateful to be here for the fiftieth birthday of a fine man who has become a dear friend of mine. This is a special place for a shindig, I will say. Who knew a poor boy from Texas would grow up to party in a palace like this with a bunch of Connecticut Yankees, enjoying an incredible feast prepared by Chef Paul and Dolce Far Niente. I'm lucky to be here celebrating my buddy today. Before I get emotional, cheers to you, Merl. Health and happiness. Here's hoping you have—how many children you want?"

"Five," said Merlin. "And that's only the boys." He winked at Arielle.

Zip gave a whoop sparking laughter from most of the guests. Catia blotted her mouth with her napkin to hide her grimace. Arielle gave a forced smile. Scott brushed her foot under the table to reassure her.

"Ooh doggie! I hope The Good Lord grants you all the offspring you can stand. On that note, cheers to you too, my dear," Zip toasted Arielle.

"My turn." Merlin gazed into his glass. "Thank you all for coming to my party. I'd like to think when it's your birthday you can take the opportunity to freely speak what's on your mind. I'd like to explain myself, in a way. There's been all kinds of buzz around town. Will I or won't I save this place?"

Jade sat up straighter, hands knotted in her lap. Could this be the moment her brother surprised her with by doing the right thing? Had Arielle worked her magic to convince Merlin, by showing him the museum in a special light this evening?

"Many of you," Merlin continued, "have remarked on The Castle's beauty and how lucky we are to be here enjoying it in this way. Unlike my romantically minded siblings and wife, I find no joy in the past. In fact, I frankly find it disgusting."

Jade slumped back in her chair. No, this wasn't Merlin having a change of heart. This was Merlin about to claw and slash at the meaning of Jade's life's work. Merlin's eyes settled on a distant corner of the grand hall. Jade thought he'd never looked so arrogant and cold.

"As I understand it," said Merlin, "After experiencing the horrors of war, our ancestor Ernest Glenmore wished to bury himself in a bygone day, where he could control his surroundings, be lord and master. He built these walls around himself and filled his dwelling with frivolous diversions. He cut himself off from the outside world to the degree that he married within his immediate gene pool. One shudders to think under what circumstances. I suspect Ernest lured his niece here and coerced Catherine by nefarious means to stay forever. Until, that is, she died nine months later giving birth to their spawn." His eyes fell on Arielle. "What a theme for my birthday, Sweetie."

"You read the valet's account," Arielle objected. "Ernest and Catherine were in love, according to him."

"No, I don't buy that. These rooms reek of bad deeds. Dad always said so too. And he also wisely observed that Glenhurst Castle leeches life from the present and the future. It wants us to stay here and commune with the dead, which is literally what you're proposing we do tonight, Arielle. You are giving it exactly what it wants. To be fretted over, kept alive, 'preserved' as some idiots call it. This place invites its servants to drink deeply of the esoteric, to fix one's eyes on the guttering flame and bathe in its darkness without shame. This is why I refuse to nourish this rotting cocoon.

"Beneath the façade and distractions of supposed 'cultural elevation', is an armored foot pushing the head of Humanity into the mud, where it believes it belongs. I feel its hatred emanating towards me. Fortunately, I remain immune to its infection. Here ends my speech and hopefully any further requests for funds to keep this stain on the name of Glenmore alive. I hope it is stuffed with whiteboards and desks by September. Or better yet demolished."

Jade cleared her throat, "I don't mean to provoke you, Merlin, not on your birthday, but when my life's work is so deeply misrepresented...I can't remain silent. The Castle to me represents beauty, transcendence, bold imagination. Catherine and Ernest Glenmore's romance, shall we say, is uncomfortable, but it is only one of many stories that happened here. These walls have witnessed sadness and grief, but also joy, life, and laughter. We safeguard important pieces of history here. The armor of knights who put duty, faith, and bravery above all. A lock of hair from a saint! The gloves worn by one of the greatest queens who ever ruled. Rare musical instruments that brought delight for centuries. And, if you refuse to acknowledge the historical or cultural value of the museum, you cannot deny its practical and economic importance to the Town of Glamis."

"It is a grotesque hunk of stucco or whatever it's built out of filled with junk," Merlin shot back. "You're deluded. It will never be practical or economical. If it was, you wouldn't be begging me for millions to keep it on life support for another two or three years. Then you'll come back with your guilt trips pleading for me to rescue it again. 'Oh, now the other tower is crumbling! That will be another million, please, Merlin'. I know it hurts you to hear it, but I'm right. You don't have the money to sustain it. So, sell it while you can, before it crumbles to pieces."

"I'm sorry," Justin raised his hand. "It is a fact that The Castle draws thousands of people every year to Glamis. The success of Thane's and Dolce Far Niente, the upswing of the entire village center, is thanks to the tourists who come to visit this attraction. Our town has thrived since Jade opened the museum."

"I might just leave," Merlin muttered.

"Everyone, please," said Arielle. "It's my husband's birthday. Who is ready for the séance portion of this evening's entertainment? Merlin and maybe you Doctor Boyd would like to do something else if that doesn't appeal? Then we'll be back down in a bit and recommence with the cake!"

"Doc, I don't expect you enjoy molesting the dead," said Merlin. "Care to join me for a game of chess instead?"

"Definitely," said Owen. "We'll leave the ghost hunting to the rest of you."

"God those pants are loud," Merlin mock shielded his eyes from the American flag themed pants worn by Owen.

"Wait up! I enjoy a game of chess." Justin was pretty sure he remembered how the pieces moved from when he was kid. Really he was dying to check on the Yankees' score and doubted he could get away with it sitting in a circle in a dark room. He'd be able to work around Merlin. The man of honor was well past his fourth scotch by now.

"Don't leave us, Justin," said Arielle. "Chef Paul is about to unveil a remarkable surprise."

"More silliness. Come with us, Justin," Merlin headed to the doors on the banquet hall's north side.

"Dad, you coming with us?" Justin asked Sal.

"No, you go on," said Sal. "I'd like to try to get in touch with your mother."

"After the séance, we'll reunite for cake and more dancing!" Arielle called after them.

"So, what is about to be unveiled?" Scott leaned into Arielle.

"Chef, would you kindly enlighten us?" Arielle asked.

"It's over here, I believe," Paul pointed to a sideboard. Arielle nodded.

Paul opened a drawer and lifted out a wooden box, a jar of sugar cubes, and an ornate slotted spoon in the shape of a leaf. He drew out a bottle from the box. "This is a pre-ban absinthe from before the turn of the twentieth century. Fewer than a hundred people living today have experienced this vintage. In keeping with some of the apparently controversial themes of this evening, we will taste history, specifically the Belle Epoque of Toulouse Lautrec and Rimbaud. This came into my possession when I worked at a famous cocktail bar in London, in the form of a gift from a regular who collected absinthe. I've saved it for a special occasion. I want to share it tonight with all of you as we embark on this spirited adventure."

"There isn't a chance it's so old it's poisonous?" Catia asked as Paul uncorked the bottle with the utmost care.

"Certainly not," Paul frowned. "It may however induce visions…or so they say." Paul set the slotted silver spoon across the top of Catia's glass, placed a sugar cube on top of it, and delicately poured the green liquid.

Rex moved his glass closer as Paul came around to him. "Fill 'er up."

Sal hoisted his glass up in the air. "Cheers, Chef."

Scott held his empty water glass up but Paul thought better of pouring him any. "None for the underaged,

I'm afraid," said Paul, moving on to pouring Zip a glass.

"Chef, honestly," Scott flushed with irritation. "I hope you haven't mistaken me for an average American nineteen-year-old. I was drinking Châteauneuf-du-Pape and Château Margaux on a weekly basis when I lived in Paris. I'm essentially a wine connoisseur." Thanks to Faustine, Scott silently acknowledged, who had lavished him with only the best for the blissful months he was her lover.

"Nice try," said Paul. "My policy is a firm no on serving the underaged and always has been."

Once everyone, except Scott, drained their glasses, Arielle began.

"We, Seekers having imbibed this sight-imbuing potion may now commence our quest into the psychic dimension. For those daring among you, follow me up to the Astral Chamber, where we will find out with which of us the dead desire to speak."

"I hope it's to me," mumbled Sal. "I hope she'll speak to me."

They stood from the table. As they progressed eastward past the darkened gift shop, they stayed silent, except for the rustling of costumes, until they emerged into the grand staircase hall.

"Bathed in sacred moonlight, we ascend to the plane above." Arielle led the party up the stairs, past an armored knight. They reached the upper landing and Arielle stopped before a grated metal door. During visiting hours at the Museum, the room remained locked, but its piercings allowed a glimpse of the octagonal study which once belonged to Ernest Glenmore. The metal barrier screeched as Arielle pushed it open and led the others inside the domed chamber. At the center of the vaulted ceiling a silvery pentagon-shape glittered above. Worn wooden planks made up the floor. Drawn velvet curtains masked the windows. The room was sparsely furnished, the walls without adornment, as if the space's only purpose was to provide a meeting place for secret deeds.

Along the western side of the room, a massive black lacquered cabinet with two doors towered, crowned with hooded arches. The right-hand door teemed with low relief figures, impossible to decipher clearly in the dim light. The upper half of the left-hand door held a diamond quarried window as if the cabinet kept one eye open.

Like the chamber itself, the mirrored table at the center of the room was octagonal, trimmed with a worn velvet bar. Spindly black chairs with triangular seats surrounded it.

Arielle invited them to take their places.

III

"Cigar anyone?" Merlin offered his leather case to Owen and Justin.

"Are you sure it's alright?" Owen asked.

"Won't Jade have a fit if we smoke in here?" asked Justin.

Owen squinted into The Conservatory's ceiling corners. "Cameras?"

Justin took the opportunity to glance down into his lap at the score, as Merlin turned to point out the single black bubble behind him. "The CCTV system needs electric power to work. These cameras are dead."

"Aw no!" Justin cringed.

Merlin turned back to face the younger man. "It's a good thing for us. That way we won't get caught smoking these in here. To state the obvious," he lifted his brows at Owen Boyd. Merlin had always thought the Marottas made up in boisterousness what they lacked in intelligence.

"Not that it's my business," said Owen, "but the current security situation seems feeble at best."

"Jade knows it's a problem," said Merlin. "A new system is on her list of urgent upgrades, but it's not cheap. As for the smoke detectors...here, some high-tech ventilation will do the trick." He passed the potted, young orange trees wintering inside, and opened a French door onto the snow-covered lawn.

"Merlin, you've told us what you're not going to do with your bounty. What *will* you do with it?" asked Owen.

"Move far away from here. There's a condo in Palm Beach I'm going to put an offer on next week. Twenty-second floor, beachfront view, two terraces, travertine floors, concrete accents. Four bedrooms, four bathrooms. And, my favorite feature of all: an in-unit car elevator for Hotspur. We'll spend winters there, and I'm thinking summer in San Sebastián, where we honeymooned."

"Well I don't like it," said Owen. "We'll miss you and your lovely wife too much. No chance you would keep a place in Glamis? Can't beat summer golf in Connecticut."

"No I'm done with it up here. It's not easy living in the same town as Lewis Waterhouse after all that happened. The man somehow blames me for Maeve…he's crazy anyway. The police thought so too."

"Tasty cigar. You sure this is okay?" Justin handed back the lighter.

Merlin slipped it into his pant pocket. "What would Jade do? Call us 'beasts'?"

"Anyone care to play?" Owen motioned to the chess board.

"Not yet," Merlin glanced at the watch on his wrist. "First my April Fool's prank. The ghost hunters upstairs will never see this coming. Keep your refuge from the idiots here. You two should play. Winner plays me next."

IV

"Spirit, we call you forth," said Arielle. "One dead longer than a century. A soul of renown whose name lives on."

A figure in a top hat stepped from behind the heavy curtains. His straight silver hair grazed the shoulders of his frock coat. He wore gold-rimmed goggles and held a contraption with a metal ball suspended from a wire hovering above a rounded base.

"What is that?" Sal yelped.

"Arielle, next to you!" said Catia. "Who is that?"

"Spirit, what is thy name?" Arielle asked.

"Talon de Fey," came the figure's familiar sonorous voice.

"It's Lewis," Jade sighed.

"You, sir, are not one of the dead," Arielle patted Lewis's shoulder. "You may be seated with the others."

"You nearly gave me a heart attack," said Sal.

"Pretty good, huh?" Lewis found an empty chair next to Jade and set his contraption down on the mirrored table.

"Beast," said Jade. "I thought you weren't coming."

"Arielle thought a surprise appearance might be fun, particularly for you. Yes, you heard right. Plus, she agreed to let me run the séance. How could I pass that up in this kind of atmosphere? But where's the 'man of honor'?"

Everyone jumped at a loud wooden *knock, knock, knock*.

"Oh no," groaned Sal. "No more scares!"

"What was that?" said Rex.

"A poltergeist?" joked Paul. Robin reached for his hand under the table.

The knocking continued to fill the room.

"Whoever is doing that, stop it at once," said Jade.

"What if this is wrong?" Sal asked. "What if we summoned an actual evil spirit?"

V

"God only knows what awful joke Merlin has up his sleeve." Owen rose to close the door opening onto the lawn. "I hate pranks."

"I do too," said Justin. "It's already a quarter past nine? Shoot. Excuse me, Doc. I forgot. Sarah's working late on a wedding tonight. I need to make a quick call to my mother-in-law. See if she can keep Rosie for a bit longer before Merlin comes back."

"Oh you still have your phone," Owen noted.

"Yeah, I told Merlin I forgot it at the restaurant. Please don't mention it to him. Wish me luck."

"Good luck. That game of chess when you get back?"

"Uh, sure. Count me in."

Justin set his cigar in a brass indent on the table.

"Oh here, take one of these." Owen held out an electric candle to Justin.

"Good thinking." Justin shut the door to the Conservatory behind him, as he stepped into the icy darkness of the Castle's northern corridor. He was grateful for the light in his hand.

VI

"We conjure in good faith one with a message to share tonight. We invite you, Spirit, to speak," said Lewis. "To help us understand you more clearly, we will use this oracle pendulum which swings to the word 'yes' or the word 'no' seemingly by its own volition, but we will know you, Spirit, are moving it." He slid the mechanism in front of Jade and said to her, "Kindly read out the answers to us. We'll go around the table and ask Spirit questions. Let's begin with you, Zip."

"With me? Alright. Spirit, are you a man or a woman?" Zip asked.

"It has to be a yes or no question," said Lewis.

"Oh," Zip frowned. "Are you a man, Spirit?"

The pendulum swung to 'No', eliciting gasps around the room.

"This is freaky! Spirit, are you a woman?" Catia asked.

The pendulum swung to 'yes'.

"Have you been dead long?" Arielle asked.

The pendulum swung to 'no'.

"Let me go next!" said Sal. "Did you live in Glamis when you were alive, Spirit?"

The pendulum swung to 'yes'.

"Did *I* know you?" asked Robin.

The pendulum swung to 'yes'.

"Yipes," Robin looked at Paul.

"Were you over the age of forty when you died, Spirit?" asked Paul.

The pendulum swung to 'yes'.

"Oh my God. It might be my Melissa. Is it you, Honey?" Sal leaned towards the contraption.

"It says no," said Jade. "Sorry, Sal."

"Did you know anyone here tonight besides Robin?" asked Rex.

The pendulum swung to 'yes' repeatedly.

"Did you know Merlin?" Lewis asked.

It swung to yes. Jade flinched, "I think that's enough—"

"Are you Aunt Maeve? It says yes," said Scott.

"That's it. No more." Jade seized the pendulum in her fist.

"A face!" Scott sprang to his feet, staring in terror at the looming, hearse-like cabinet against the wall. "A face. I saw it! There's someone inside!"

"Criminy. Nobody panic." Zip strode over to the hulking cabinet, Arielle close behind him. Zip grasped the handle and wrenched open the windowed cabinet door with a noisy rattle. Cold, stale air drifted out of the space.

"Is someone inside?" Sal yelped from the far wall, where the others huddled.

"Merl!" Zip gasped. His hands shook as he knelt into the cabinet.

"Help him!" Arielle shouted.

"I'm checking his pulse."

"Oh my God, oh my God," Arielle reeled away.

"There's blood all over him. Merlin! Merlin! He's got no pulse. Jesus, there's a knife in him. Oh, I can't look no more." Zip slammed the cabinet door shut. "Rex, get downstairs right now. Bring the doc up here. I think he's past saving but go on quick."

"A knife in him?" Robin looked at Paul.

"That's what I heard as well," Paul nodded.

"Come away, Arielle." Jade steered her sister-in-law towards the door. "Everyone, we need to leave the room immediately. We need to call the police. Don't touch anything." Jade would not allow herself to think about the horror inside the cabinet. The thing was to get out, get away from the body.

They fled the room into the hall. Zip spoke up, "Lewis, you got a phone on you, brother?"

"He doesn't," said Jade.

"No, I don't," said Lewis.

"Now do you see how a cell phone might be useful in emergencies?" asked Scott.

"Damn Luddite," said Sal. "How do you not have a cell phone—are you crazy?"

"No one here has one?" Lewis demanded.

"No!" the others chorused in a shout.

"Enough," Zip cut in. "Any idea where Merlin hid our phones?"

"The Library, I think," Arielle said. "I don't feel well. I might faint."

Scott sprang to her side. "I've got you. Deep breaths."

"We'll go to the Library now and search for the phones," said Zip. "Lock ourselves in there. Stay alert. This killer could be hiding anywhere. Who knows how to get the dang electricity back on?"

"I do. I turned it off earlier," said Robin. "I can get it back on. But the main power box is in the vaults."

"Let's go," Paul said.

The two men vanished down the stairs.

"Everyone else, to the Library. Hold on to the railing. Keep calm and stay on high alert," Zip's head swiveled left and right.

VII

"Doc!" Rex burst into the Conservatory.

Owen glanced up from the chess game. "Yes?"

"Hurry, follow me. Merlin's been stabbed. We found him just now. Come on!"

"Stabbed, is he?" Owen winked at Justin as he slid a bishop across the board.

"What are you doing just sitting there?" Rex demanded, his frustration growing with every second. "Didn't you hear what I said?"

Owen chuckled. "I'll guarantee you he's not dead. Merlin said he was going to pull an April Fool's Day prank on all of you. Looks like he succeeded."

"I don't think so," said Rex. "The man doesn't have a pulse. Come on, Doc, this is real serious!"

"I'll go with you. There is no need to shout at me," said Owen, the playfulness leaving his voice as he switched into physician mode. He lifted the itchy, blonde mullet wig off his head and set it on the table. "After you, Rex."

Owen and Justin followed Rex, still wearing his long black cape, up the back stairs, down the second-floor hallway to Ernest's Study. Rex pushed open the grated door. Along the study walls, sconces flickered on, dimly illuminating the mirrored table, chairs, and black cabinet.

"Well, that's good. The power is back," said Owen.

"He's in there." Rex pointed to the cabinet.

"Is this a joke? Is he going to jump out and scare me?" Owen asked.

"No," said Rex. "I certainly doubt it."

"Alright," sighed Owen, still not so sure. He creaked open the cabinet door with the window and peered inside. "Convincing. Merlin, you had your fun. Get up. Strange, he doesn't have any pants on."

Owen glanced into Rex and Justin's frightened faces. Owen peeled off the golf glove from his right hand and stuffed it into his back pocket. He knelt further into the cabinet to inspect something protruding from Merlin's chest.

"Oh God. He *has* been stabbed."

CHAPTER ELEVEN

Saturday, April 1ˢᵗ - 9:45 p.m.

"Lieutenant, I believe we have a homicide on our hands," Dominic Marotta said over the phone. "This is not an April Fool's joke. A Glamis local, Merlin Glenmore, appears to have been killed. His body was just found at The Glenmore-Pace Castle while they were celebrating his birthday. Detective Bell, from The Connecticut State Police, is on the way, driving down now. Can you meet me here?"

As Carl knew, a lot of small towns, like Glamis, weren't big enough to have a department devoted to major crimes or homicide, so they worked with the state police on violent crimes.

"Dominic, one moment." Carl muted the phone and spoke quietly to Greta, hoping not to wake Rosie asleep in her arms. "There was a murder tonight. He's asking for my help."

"No. You promised," Greta whispered.

Carl took the phone into the bathroom and shut the door.

"Hello Dominic," Carl said. "I'm retired. I made a commitment to my wife. You said the state police are on the way. They will know exactly what to do. Let's talk more tomorrow morning, if you think it's necessary."

Carl returned to the bedroom with a frown. Not acting in a situation like this was torture for him. In fact, it was incredibly frustrating not to be able to help in a situation where he knew he would be at the height of his powers to help. But a promise was a promise in Carl's book.

"Thank you, Carl," Greta said, as he climbed back into bed.

Carl's phone chimed once more.

"It's Justin. Justin, are you alright?" Carl asked.

"Did you hear what happened here at The Castle?" Justin asked.

"I did just now from Dominic, your uncle. You're still there now?"

"Yes, Dad and I both are. It was crazy. One minute I was talking to Merlin with Doctor Boyd. He was telling us about wanting to move to Florida. Then he goes to play a joke on the other guests. The next thing I know Rex Davis comes running in to tell me and Doctor Boyd he had been stabbed. Anyway, I'll tell you everything I know when you get here. Are you on the road yet, Carl?"

"I made a promise to Greta. The days of me leaving our house in the middle of the night to go to a crime scene are over. Your uncle and the Glamis police should be arriving now."

"So, you're not coming?" Justin said, surprise and an edge of disappointment in his voice. "I've got to go. The officers just walked in."

"Please call me on your way home," said Carl.

"Yeah. Bye." Justin hung up.

Carl set his phone on the bedside table. "He is upset I'm not going there."

"Well let him be. You're not getting involved and that's all there is to it," said Greta. "You're not the only person in the world who knows how to investigate a homicide. We can be supportive without you leaping into the fray. We need to check on Sarah too."

Greta dialed Sarah and put her on speaker phone.

"We heard what happened. Are you holding up alright?" asked Greta.

"I'm leaving the Inn right now," said Sarah. "I can't believe someone would kill Merlin Glenmore. I'm worried about Justin and Sal. And my boss Catia! They were right there during the murder. It's so frightening to think. Carl, I am so glad you're here to help. Are you going over there now?"

"I am retired now, Sarah. I made a promise to your mother—"

"But they'll need you," Sarah cut in.

"The police from the state have jurisdiction," said Carl. "What can I do?"

"Everything!" said Sarah. "I can't believe you're just going to stand by and not help. I wish you would rethink this."

"You can ask your mother but…"

"No, I'm not budging on this," said Greta. "This man has been through enough. And so have I."

"Mom, Justin is there at the castle. With a murderer possibly loose there!"

While Carl nodded in agreement, Greta rolled her eyes. "Sarah, I didn't know Merlin, but I am near certain no one wants to kill Justin Marotta. I do not think he is in danger, especially with law enforcement there. Rosie's asleep, so is it okay if she just stays with us overnight?"

"Yes, that would be good, Mom," said Sarah. "I'm heading to the Castle now to pick Justin up, once the police are done interviewing him. If something urgent comes up, Carl, can I count on you?"

"You are my daughter. I would give my life for you. If it is urgent, I will be there to help you always."

After the call, Greta switched off her lamp. She looked over at Carl, staring up at the ceiling, hands folded on his stomach. "Thank you for being a man of your word. I know staying out of this isn't easy."

"This is more difficult for me than you know." Carl stared into the dark, forcing himself to lie still.

II

"We won't keep you here much longer," said Dominic Marotta. "You may come up and collect your cellphones. Officer Timmons and I were able to locate them in a room called..." he referenced the Castle floor plan map designed for visitors, which Jade had given the officers upon their arrival. "The Oratory, whatever that is."

Catia raised her hand, "Are we considered suspects?"

"At this time, you are considered a witness, Mrs. Boyd," said Dominic.

Catia crossed her arms. "Then explain why Officer Keane asked us to prepare to give DNA swabs and fingerprints. Every single one of us who was here tonight is a suspect. I don't care what you say, Dominic Marotta. If the police require any biological matter from me, they can go through my attorney."

"Darn right," said Lewis.

"Amen, Sister," said Zip.

"You are all considered witnesses at this time," Dominic repeated firmly. "Law enforcement asks for your cooperation to help us solve this murder. Is there anyone here who will volunteer to give fingerprints and take a DNA swab to assist us as we analyze the crime scene, so we can catch the dangerous criminal who did this. Come on."

Only two of the witnesses raised their hands.

"Thank you, Sal and Justin. Now, who can tell me what time everyone went upstairs?"

"It was about nine o'clock when they went up," said Justin.

"You weren't with them?" asked Dominic.

"Justin and I joined Merlin in the Conservatory for a game of chess instead," said Owen.

"I see," Dominic jotted in his notepad. "The rest of you went upstairs?"

"Yes, Sir, that's right," said Zip.

"No, Zip, that is not exactly correct," said Jade. "Lewis, you made your presence known a few minutes after we sat down in the upstairs study for the séance."

"That's good to know. Thank you, Jade. Can you describe your movements prior to your appearance, Lewis?" Dominic asked.

"Sure can," said Lewis. "I came in through the front door a little before nine o'clock. I went up the main stairwell and into the study, where I hid behind these long heavy curtains. Arielle thought it would give the other guests a thrill if I surprised them once they were seated around the table in there."

"Did you see anyone on your way upstairs?" Dominic asked.

"Not a soul," said Lewis. "I think they were all still having dinner at that point."

Dominic jotted down a note. "For those who were in the study, take me through how you discovered Merlin's body."

"I saw a face looking out through the cabinet window," said Scott. "It was while we were using this spirit-divining contraption Uncle Lewis brought with him. I didn't recognize who it was. It could have been Merlin's face. I can't say for sure. It was just for a second. The room was dark."

"Did anyone else see this face in the cabinet?" Dominic asked. "Nobody? After Scott saw the face what happened?"

"I opened the cabinet door," said Zip, "expecting it might be another prank. That's when I found Merl. Blood all over him and what looked like a knife stuck into his chest. I took his pulse. There weren't none."

"Did Mr. Glenmore have pants on at that time?" Dominic asked.

"Yes, Sir, I believe so," said Zip, but his voice didn't sound fully sure.

"He did," Jade spoke up. "His pants were on. I certainly would have noticed if they were not."

"Thank you for confirming, Jade," said Dominic. "What happened next?"

"I told Rex to run and bring Doctor Boyd right away," Zip said. "It's what they do in all them detective shows. Paul and Robin left to get the electricity back on. The rest of us went downstairs and locked ourselves inside the Library. We hunted all over for our phones to call the police but couldn't find them."

"Rex came into the Conservatory telling Justin and me that Merlin had been stabbed," said Owen. "We followed Rex upstairs to the cabinet where I examined the body."

"And you said for sure there were no pants on Merlin's body when you arrived?" Dominic asked.

"Correct. No pants. I remarked on it to Justin and Rex. At first, I thought this could all be an April Fool's prank. I checked Merlin for a pulse. It became apparent it was not a joke. Justin then called the police."

"I went downstairs and found the others in the Library," said Justin. "They were scared at first to open the door, but Dad recognized my voice. I assured them I had called the station already and you were on the way."

"How did you come to have a phone on you, when everyone else had to give them up?" Dominic asked.

"I told Merlin I didn't have it on me," said Justin. "I needed it so I could give my mother-in-law a call to let her know I wouldn't be on time to pick up Rosie."

"Excuse me. When will be free to go?" Catia asked. Sitting around this gloomy castle was wearing on her after tonight's ordeal. She wanted to make sure Arielle was alright and then retreat to the safety of her own bed.

"I understand you're ready to leave, Mrs. Boyd. You have all been through quite an experience," Dominic said. "You will be allowed to return home tonight, once someone from the State Police has had a chance to speak with you. You will all be asked to remain in Glamis while the investigation continues, and please refrain from speaking to members of the media. Someone from the Glamis Police Department will be in touch to schedule times for you to give us your formal statements. If you'll just wait here in the meantime."

"Can Arielle stay with us tonight?" Scott asked Lewis.

"That's a no," said Lewis.

"Fine, I'll stay with her at her place. It's wrong for her to be left alone."

Catia put her arm around Arielle. "She can stay with us tonight, right, Owen?"

"That'd be fine." Owen wasn't sure if he really wanted Arielle to after the exchanges of today. It wasn't as though he could say no. The woman's husband had just been murdered.

"Thank you so much, Catia, but I want to be in my own bed tonight," said Arielle.

"At least let us drop you at home?" Catia asked.

Arielle nodded, holding back an ugly storm of tears.

"I'd be happy to see *you* home tonight, Jade," said Sal.

"I could also," Lewis offered.

"No, but thank you," Jade avoided Lewis' eyes. "You and Scott should get home as soon as we're done here. I expect it might take some time before they let me go."

Dominic turned to Zip. "One more thing. Do you recall the time you discovered Merlin's body?"

"No, Sir, I do not," said Zip. "I wasn't wearing a watch and didn't have my cellular of course. I doubt I would have thought to look at either anyway in the moment."

"I might be able to help," Justin looked down at his phone. "I made the call to the police station at 9:36. You could work backwards from there?"

"I'd guess no more than six or seven minutes passed between when we found Merl and when Justin called the police," said Rex.

"How long do you think he'd been dead when you reached him, Doc?" asked Dominic.

"No longer than twenty minutes," said Owen.

Dom glanced up from his notepad at Justin, "Any idea what time Merlin left the Conservatory to go upstairs?"

"I called Greta at 9:15," said Justin. "He left a minute or two before that."

"That's very helpful," said Dominic. "I need your assistance on a few urgent matters, Jade. The rest of you please wait here for Officer Bell from the State Police. Officer Timmons," Dominic turned to his colleague, "go ahead and take the DNA swabs and fingerprints from Sal and Justin."

"I've got everything set up in the kitchen," Officer Victor Timmons said. Justin followed him, but Sal hung back.

"I'll be right with you, Victor," Sal said to Timmons, who had attended school with Justin. Sal had gotten to know Victor when he and Justin played on the same baseball team in high school. "Dominic," he said to his brother, "Could we speak somewhere in private?"

Dominic walked out into the hall with Sal.

As soon as the door to the library was shut Sal fired his first question at his brother. "Does Justin need an attorney?"

"I don't know how many times I have to say it. He's not a suspect, Sal."

"He and Owen Boyd were the only two people here tonight who weren't in the Study with us when Merlin was killed. See what I'm saying? When this state detective gets here, you'll get the boot from this case, Dom. He won't know Justin from Adam, and they're going to make my son the lead suspect. He was one of only two who had the opportunity."

"You're letting your imagination run wild."

"Make sure they know it couldn't have been my son who did this," said Sal.

Dominic couldn't believe Sal was trying to boss him around even now during a homicide investigation. He wanted to let his older brother have it, but instead he said firmly, "Back off, Sal. You need to let me do my job."

III

While the newly arrived Detective Nemo Bell from the State Police spoke to witnesses downstairs, Officer Andrew Keane led Dominic Marotta to the Study at the top of the grand staircase.

"From what we've gathered so far, Glenmore was stabbed in there," Keane nodded his head toward the opulent bed chamber, where two forensics specialists from New Haven worked. "He was found inside this cabinet in here. On the museum map this room, where the party guests did the séance, is called 'Ernest Glenmore's Study'."

The metal screen stood open. The two men passed through the graceful stone archway. Bright police lights flooded the octagon. Forensics had completed their work here already, taken photos and samples, and moved on to the bedroom next door. Dominic pulled on a pair of blue plastic gloves and leaned into the musty cabinet to examine the body.

Keane shone a flashlight for Dominic over the corpse of Merlin Glenmore. The expensive leather loafers with gold horse bit ornaments on his feet. Bony, bare ankles. Hairy, pale muscular calves and vulnerable, white thighs extended from black silk boxers.

Dominic turned over Merlin's white gloved hands, dried blood on the palm-sides. A weapon hilt protruded from the starched shirtfront stained with blood.

"Distinctive sort of blade," Dominic said. "Could have come from the castle's collection. I hate to put her through this, but I think Jade Glenmore would be the best person to confirm if it's a museum piece or not."

"I'll make a note for us to ask her. What do you think about the pants going missing?" Keane asked. "We haven't been able to locate them. When the witnesses first discovered the body, he had the pants on. But, when Doctor Boyd came in to look a few minutes later, the body is bare-legged like this, his pants nowhere to be seen. Any hunches on that?"

"Very odd. We'll have to look into that more," Dominic said.

"Got any idea why—"

"No, I don't. Not yet anyway," Dom snapped.

If Carl Sarabia hadn't made that promise to his wife, he would be here now. Dom had no doubt *he* would be well on his way to solving the entire case before the state police arrived. Before retiring, Sarabia had been a chief homicide investigator in Houston for years and would certainly figure out why a killer would be willing to take the risk of coming back to remove pants from a corpse. "Jerk," muttered Dominic. Keane gave him a startled look. "No, not you, Keane. Let's go to the bedroom next door. What does the map call it?"

"Ernest Glenmore's Bedchamber," said Keane. "Sounds fancy."

Dom greeted the two forensic specialists decked out from head to toe in personal protective equipment. They crouched in front of a gilded stone fireplace. Ernest's Bedchamber, in contrast to the sparse study, was decorated in a manner befitting a Tudor royal. Purple curtains threaded with silver draped a four-poster bed. Portraits of nobles framed in black and gold adorned the emerald silk covered walls. Opposite the fireplace, leather bound volumes lined a built-in bookcase topped with the ubiquitous gothic arch. Between the lancet windows facing north, a mannequin of a young woman with dark hair in a braided bun sat at a dressing table looking at a crystal ball mounted on an ornate silver base. A brooding, bearded gentleman mannequin stood beside her wearing a cravat and formal suit.

"Any idea who they are?" Dominic asked. "Oh it says here on the plaque. Ernest and Catherine Glenmore. Ernest Glenmore's the one who built the Castle."

Dominic and Keane visited the bedroom's two ancillary chambers, a white subway-tiled bathroom with a clawfoot tub and a windowless dressing room with the mannequin of Ernest's valet Celestin Mabille in livery inside. They returned to the bedroom to speak to the two specialists huddled over a taped off section of the wooden floor in front of the fireplace.

"Blood spatter," Dom observed.

"Yes, indeed," one of the specialists replied. "We found something interesting. A charred piece of fabric in the fireplace." She held up the bagged evidence. "And," she handed him another bag. "Four metal pieces."

Dominic examined them. "They look like snaps. Very interesting. I'll make sure to tell Detective Bell about this right away when we speak to him downstairs. I hope we're not getting in your way."

"No worries," she said. "Thanks for being mindful wearing your PPE both of you. We've seen it all from local police. They usually remember the gloves and shoe covers, but get all prickly when we ask them to wear hair nets, coveralls and masks. It gets awkward when we have to remind them."

"We do our best," said Dominic, feeling a bit patronized. He had a feeling he and the Glamis PD officers were going to be at the bottom of the food chain in this investigation. It would be a victory if he could find something everyone else missed.

"It doesn't add up, does it," said Keane. "Merlin is stabbed by the fireplace. How does he end up in the cabinet without anyone seeing him get put inside there?"

"Hard to make sense of it," said Dominic. "Let's head back downstairs. We'll see if Jade Glenmore can identify the murder weapon. You took photos, right?"

Keane nodded.

As they descended the grand staircase, Timmons called to them from the ground floor. "Dom, Detective Bell wants to see you right away."

IV

Dom entered the staff room to find the Detective seated with Sal and Jade at the round table. Nemo Bell stood up to shake Dom's hand. Bell had considerable good looks, and he wasn't above using them to his advantage if it helped propel a case. He had aquiline features and brilliant green eyes that could hypnotize anyone if he wore a shirt in a color close to them. His easy smile radiated know-it-all-ness and in-charge-ness. Dom disliked him immediately.

"I'd like to ask Ms. Glenmore to have a look at the murder weapon to see if she can identify it," said Dominic. "Then it would be good to let her go for the night."

"Think again," said Bell.

"It can't wait until tomorrow?" asked Jade. "I'm in shock. I would like to go home."

"Ms. Glenmore," Nemo Bell turned his full attention on her, "I am acutely aware of what you've been through this evening. I'm an empath. I feel your pain more than you can imagine. But, I do need a walk-through *tonight*. I will rely on you to tell me if there is something that is odd or out of place. I would not ask you, except there is no one else who would be better able to do this. Unless there is someone else?"

"No," she shook her head. "Well, Arielle perhaps, but she's in a worse state than I am. She loved my brother very much. I'll help you."

"Thank you," said Bell. "If an object is missing from this museum, it is extremely important for us to know about it. Let's see if you can identify the murder weapon first. Bring up the photo please. Show it to me first."

Andrew Keane brought the image up on a tablet and showed it to Bell.

"This will not be easy to look at, Ms. Glenmore," said Bell. "If you can try to put your emotions aside, and look at the image analytically... Keane, go ahead and show it to her. Is this weapon part of the museum's collection?"

"I do recognize it," Jade averted her eyes from the screen. "It's a fine example of a late 17th-Century English plug bayonet. It's a weapon that could be used in battle if a soldier ran out of gunpowder. The bayonet inserts into a musket barrel, or one could use it alone as a dagger. Someone must have taken it from The Castle's Armory tonight."

"Let's go there now to confirm," said Bell.

Jade led the police down the corridor. She stopped in front of the roped-off room filled with antique weapons, heraldic shields, and armor.

Jade pointed, "Yes, there! You can see where it is missing in the glass case. Oh, the carpet in front of it looks wet. See those dark spots? Is it a leak?"

Detective Bell unhooked the rope and bent over the four dark splotches on the red carpet.

"It's not blood, is it?" Jade asked.

"Water, I believe," said Bell. "I don't see any signs of the ceiling leaking. Keane, bring the photographer down here to get a shot of this rug. Also make sure we get a moisture sample right away." He stood back up to his full height and stared up at the black bubble on the ceiling. "You have a security camera in here I see,

Ms. Glenmore. We need to review the footage. You have someone on that already, Officer Marotta?"

"The cameras weren't on tonight," said Dominic. "Intentionally."

"Oh that's odd," frowned Bell. He spun around to look at Jade. "Can you explain why that would be?"

"I regret it deeply now," said Jade. "We shut off the power for the evening."

"For what purpose?" asked Bell.

"Atmosphere," Jade threw her hands in the air. "The main entertainment tonight was a séance."

"You couldn't just turn off the lights and leave them off?" Bell asked.

"It was a reckless, stupid thing to do. I never should have allowed it. If the killer stole the plug bayonet from The Armory after we shut off the power, I'm sorry to say there will be no camera footage to show who took it."

"I find this most irritating," said Bell. "When did you last see the plug bayonet in the Armory, Ms. Glenmore?"

"Yesterday."

"Hmm," Bell frowned. "Keane, take a note if you would. I'll need to see footage of the Armory before the electricity was turned off. At least we'll see if it was here right before the party or if it had already been taken. If so, that would be lucky. We could go back on the tape and possibly see who took it. We'll start the walk-through, Ms. Glenmore. I know you're tired. We need to go over the entire property. Let's start in the basement and work our way up."

"You mean the vaults," Jade rubbed her temples. "One wouldn't call it a basement...not with any accuracy."

Sal locked eyes with Dominic and gestured with a tilt of his head towards Jade.

"Doing alright, Jade? Need a break?" Dominic asked.

"I'm fine. No, I'm not fine. But I understand why it's necessary. Let's get this over with quickly. Your brother is kind to wait for me."

"I'm here for you, Jade," said Sal.

Bell turned around to take in Sal. "Why are you still here? You're free to leave like the others."

"He won't do any harm," said Dominic. "Sal here is my brother. He's here for moral support. He's going to take Jade home."

Bell's eyes darted between Dominic and Sal. "That may be the case, but he needs to wait outside the crime scene."

"You've got to be kidding me," Sal scoffed. "Fine, I'll go. Jade, I'll be in the car in the parking lot, assuming they let me wait for you *there*." Sal huffed out the front door.

"Officer," Bell pointed at Dominic. "I need to speak with you in private. We will just be a second, Ms. Glenmore. Please wait here."

He ushered Dominic into the Small Parlor, next to the Armory, and shut the door.

"Sal Marotta is your brother. And Justin Marotta, is also your relative, I assume?"

"Sal's son. My nephew."

"Doctor Owen Boyd and Justin Marotta were not in the room with the others when the body of Merlin Glenmore was discovered."

"That's right. They were not," said Dominic.

"I understand they were not together the whole time either in the lead up to the body being discovered," said Bell. "These two men have no one to vouch for them for at least thirteen minutes during the probable window of time when the murder occurred."

"Alright," said Dom. "But there's no way it was my nephew."

Bell shook his head in disgust. "At this point, he can't be ruled out."

Dominic glared down at Bell, "And I'm telling you, yes, he can."

"Officer Marotta, you have what is known as a 'conflict of interest'. It could harm the credibility of this investigation, which is now under my direction."

"I know these people, Detective," said Dominic. "I think this is most likely a robbery gone wrong—"

"I'm sorry. You need to recuse yourself, Marotta," said Bell. "If you don't believe me, call Colonel Evans and hear it from him."

"I will. I'll call him."

"Go ahead," said Bell. "I'll continue with Ms. Glenmore."

Dominic avoided Jade as he passed through the entry hall out the front door. He hoped to God he didn't run into Sal now. He just might explode.

CHAPTER TWELVE

Sunday, April 2nd - 8:00 a.m.

In the front windows of the Black Sheep Bakery, Sal clasped Jade against him as her body shook with sobs. Lewis bounded inside, ignoring the aromas of fresh baked banana nut muffins and coffee. Jade brushed away tears from her red-rimmed eyes, as Lewis approached.

"Guessing you didn't sleep much last night," Lewis said.

"She's going to be okay," Sal rubbed her shoulder.

"The loss of a sibling is terrible," Lewis said.

"I'm not crying about that," Jade wiped her eyes with a napkin. "It's Leopold!"

Lewis blinked. "Your cat? Oh, Jade."

"Let it all out, my dear," Sal croaked. "I took her home last night. We found he had passed on to kitty heaven. He lived a good long life, but it's never easy."

Abby Upham, the owner of the Black Sheep, came out from behind the counter with warm muffins on a plate. "I'm so sorry about Leopold, Jade. And your brother as well," she added though she certainly felt worse about the cat.

"Thank you," said Jade. "I apologize for the scene. This can't be good for business, me sobbing away in the corner."

"You just try to drive them away," Abby smirked. "I'm the only public establishment in this town that serves coffee before ten on a Sunday. These are sick and addicted caffeine fiends we're talking about. They wake up with only one thought: their morning brew and how quickly they can get it down their gullets. They won't think twice about a woman crying her eyes out in the corner. Look, there's one of the worst standing right there." She motioned with her chin to a man in a pale-yellow sweater in tortoise shell glasses helping himself at the row of coffee dispensers.

The man turned, stirring sugar into his coffee, "I can hear you, Abby. Your library books are two days overdue." He secured the lid on his cup and gave her a mock glare. "I'm going to have to fine you terribly."

Abby rolled her eyes at Jade. "He's not going to fine me. He thinks I'm cute. I'll be with you in two seconds, Peter," Abby said to her friend the librarian who had turned bright red. "You feel any better?" she squeezed Jade's hand.

"I'm embarrassed." Jade dabbed at her nose.

"Don't be. Half the people in this town have bawled in here at one time or another. Including a man in close proximity to you. Not saying who."

"Not me," said Sal.

"Certainly wasn't—oh," said Lewis remembering. "Right. You brought me muffins when my first novel got rejected for the hundredth time. I was here. Yes, have no shame, Jade."

"Do what you need to do," Abby said. "I wish I had more soothing words, but there's nothing I can say that'll provide more comfort than what The Black Sheep's world-famous banana nut muffins can provide."

"Thank you, Abby. I'm going to bury him. My cat, I mean," Jade said.

"Woah woah, why not just cremate him?" Sal asked. "We'll buy a nice urn."

"He'll be buried in my backyard. Today."

Abby retreated behind the counter to ring Peter up.

"You're exhausted, Jade," Sal frowned. "After all you went through last night with your brother—"

"You don't have to help me," said Jade. "Leopold was my friend for twenty years. I'll bury him myself. Alone, if I have to!"

"I think—"

Jade cut him off, "In this matter, I don't care what you think *or* what you do."

"You sound determined," said Sal. "How about I hire someone to do the burial? Tell her, Lewis, she shouldn't—"

"I don't want to hire anyone," said Jade. She appreciated the friendship and comfort Sal had shown her, but his bossiness was starting to rear its head. She had no patience for that today.

"I'll help," said Lewis. "Assuming the ground is soft enough to dig a grave. I'm willing to give it my best effort. If you don't mind, I would like to get a coffee first. I'm one of those desperate caffeine fiends Abby was talking about. I'll just be a second. Eat some of that goodness. You need your strength."

Jade nodded and took a bite of the muffin.

"My brother's calling," said Sal. "Dom? What's up?" Sal leapt to his feet. "That doesn't sound good at all. I'll be right there. I'm calling Carl."

CHAPTER THIRTEEN

Sunday, April 2nd - 8:30 a.m.

"Why did you leave the Conservatory immediately after Merlin Glenmore?" Detective Bell kept his eyes locked on Justin as he took a sip of black coffee from a Glamis PD mug. He had only slept three hours last night, but he felt wide awake, agitated inside, itching to uncover who had killed Merlin Glenmore and above all how.

Justin, who had also only gotten three hours of sleep but was not buzzing with energy, quite the contrary, leaned back in his metal folding chair with his arms crossed. "I remembered I needed to call my mother-in-law Greta and tell her my change of plans. I was supposed to be to her house to pick my daughter Rosie up around eight thirty last night, but my dad and I ended up staying for dinner with everyone at the Castle. I stepped into the hallway outside to make the call. I didn't want Doctor Boyd to have to listen to me on the phone."

"The call with your mother-in-law lasted thirteen minutes. What did you two talk about for so long?"

"We were debating if it would be best if Rosie just spent the night at their house, since it would be pretty late by the time I got there. Sarah, my wife, wouldn't be done at work until about midnight. She runs weddings at The Lavender Inn. Anyway, Rosie is having trouble falling asleep at night. She was waiting for me to tuck her in like I usually do. Greta asked me to help convince Rosie to go to bed. With three-year-olds that can take a while."

"Was the door to the Conservatory open or shut when you were having this call?" asked Bell.

"It was closed the entire time," Justin said.

"Did you see anyone else while you were in the hall?"

"No one," said Justin. "Everybody was upstairs, except for me and Doctor Boyd."

"After your call, did you go anywhere? Wander around a little?"

"No, not at all. I went right back into the Conservatory. Doctor Boyd and I started a game of chess. We played about four or five moves each, until Rex Davis ran into the room to get The Doc."

"According to another witness, you made a comment last night about how important The Castle is to your family businesses," said Bell. "Do you remember that?"

"I do," Justin said. "It's true for the whole town."

"Merlin Glenmore wasn't going to help rescue The Castle, was he? He made a speech about it, I understand. Hard to take from your perspective."

"Sure, it was," Justin crossed his arms.

"He wasn't a very nice fellow, Merlin Glenmore?"

"Nah, not at all. He was pretty much an arrogant jerk. Hate to speak ill of the dead, but I'm supposed to tell you the truth, aren't I?"

"And nothing but ideally," Bell grinned. "So you really couldn't stand the man, huh?"

"No," Justin said. "Wait, you don't think I was the one who killed Merlin Glenmore?"

"What the devil—" Bell exclaimed as the door to the office opened.

"Excuse me," Carl stepped inside.

"Good lord. Lieutenant Carl Sarabia?" Bell leapt to his feet. "What are you doing here? You wouldn't recognize me, I'm sure. I attended your seminar at the IACP convention in Dallas last year. I'm honored to make your acquaintance. I'm Detective Nemo Bell with The Connecticut State Police, Eastern District Major Crime Squad. I'm in charge of this investigation."

"This is my son-in-law," said Carl putting his hands on Justin's shoulders. "I came to remind him that it's never advisable to speak to the police in a homicide investigation without an attorney present."

Bell paused for a moment in shock, as Carl's unexpected advice and the detail about who Justin was related to sank in.

"Oh dear, you misunderstand," said Bell. "This is an interview with a witness. I'm getting the facts. You would say he *shouldn't* cooperate?"

"I repeat not without his attorney. Justin, come on, let's go."

"Is that allowed?" Justin asked.

"Of course. You are under no obligation to stay."

"Oh, I thought I had to. Sorry for the awkwardness," he muttered to Bell not making eye contact with him as he left the office, Carl right behind him.

As Carl and Justin exited the station, the sun hit their eyes. The snow was beginning to melt along the sides of the plowed street. Sarah ran over the salt strewn sidewalk in her duck boots, hurtling her arms around Justin.

"Wow! Did you think they had me behind bars?" Justin laughed.

"I didn't know what was going on in there. Sal and Carl had a bad feeling. That's why Carl went in to get you."

"Guys, I can fend for myself, you know," said Justin. "Detective Bell said I was being questioned as a witness. Dad, you're here too?"

"Your son is trying to play it so cool, as usual," Sarah said.

Sal stormed past Justin, and gripped Carl by the shoulders. "Car, you need to go back in there and tell them you will help with this case."

Carl wrenched himself away from Sal's grasp. Who did this man think he was, ordering him around and handling him like this?

"How many times do I have to repeat myself to you? I am retired," said Carl.

Sal narrowed his eyes at him, "Your family needs you. I know about your promise to Greta. I can convince her to change her mind about this, when you two come to brunch today at Dolce Far Niente. She's a reasonable person—"

"We are not coming to your brunch today," said Carl. He had to establish the boundary with Sal. There was no way he was fighting this battle every week.

"What? Really?" Sal's eyes shone with moisture. "You don't see why it might be important to come together as a family after all that happened last night? You're starting to tick me off, Carl. Justin, Sarah, if you're coming to Sunday brunch, let's go."

They followed Sal to his SUV. In the back seat, Sarah avoided Carl's eyes as they drove away. He hated that his daughter was under this pushy tyrant's thumb. Justin clearly wasn't standing up to his father either.

He didn't want to create bad blood with his in-law, but he was certainly not going to be bullied into a gathering he didn't care to attend. Greta would have to stand her ground too. It irked Carl that she seemed to be giving Sal the benefit of the doubt. Carl needed her on his side in this matter. They needed a unified front. You could not give this man an inch.

Back home, Carl noticed the Jeep missing in the driveway. He gave Greta a call.

"Where are you, Honey?" he asked.

"I'm headed to Dolce Far Niente for brunch. I've got Rosie with me. Sarah called and begged me to go. I know you probably don't want to."

"So, you left without me? Without telling me the plan?"

"Don't be mad," said Greta. "I need to be there for Sarah, and you need to calm down. You're all wound up for no reason. I'm pulling into Dolce's parking lot. I'll only stay for a bit."

"Next time, can you please share your plans with me *before* you jump forward with them, as I would have the courtesy to do for you? And explain this to me, how does a Sunday dinner start before ten am?"

"It's a brunch this week. He wanted to be with us all right away this morning to talk about what happened."

"That's worse! He just changes the plan and expects us to free up our schedule to be there at this new time. It's incredible. I can't stand him."

"I don't want to start World War III in Sarah's backyard. But it's okay that you don't want to go. You don't have to. Lie down. I know you didn't sleep a wink last night. I love you. I'll be home later. Bye, hon."

"Unbelievable," said Carl.

CHAPTER FOURTEEN

Sunday, April 2nd - 9:30 a.m.

"No," Greta sipped a delicious espresso, glaring at a gold-framed poster of a voluptuous Sophia Loren and the famous quote "Everything You See I Owe to Spaghetti". They were gathered inside The Vault, Dolce Far Niente's private dining room. The room had formerly served as an actual bank vault when the building housed the old Glamis Savings Bank.

"Carl is retired," Greta insisted. "We put those days behind us when we left Texas."

"For Justin's sake, Mom," Sarah said. "Please hear us out. There might be a way for Carl to solve the case without being involved directly. He can use the information we get for him from the witnesses. We'll casually drop key evidence on him. He won't be able to help but put the solution together and deliver it with a tidy bow to the police, maybe even anonymously, if you think that's better! You know him, Mom. He can do it!"

"You would be tampering with witnesses, Sarah," Greta said.

"No, we would not," said Sal. "Tampering would be *influencing* witnesses. There's no law against having social conversations with our friends and neighbors."

"Come on, Sal. They'll see right through your attempts to pump them for information," said Greta.

"That's where you come in, Mom," said Sarah. "You were an investigative reporter for twenty-seven years. You know how to get people to spill their guts without them being aware of it. Teach us your finesse."

"Greta," said Sal. "For Justin's sake. The father of your own granddaughter."

"That Detective Bell was asking me some pretty intense questions," said Justin. "I answered them truthfully, but it was like he was trying to see if I was hiding something. There is no way though that they actually think I killed Merlin Glenmore. I mean why? Plus I'm a family man, a nice guy. Everybody in town would vouch for me, right? Anyway, I hope you help us, Greta."

Greta puffed out her cheeks and sighed with exasperation. It concerned her that her son-in-law was turning out to be so naïve. Well, as long as Carl didn't come out of retirement, what harm could it do for her to help as much as she could.

"Love you, Gammy," whispered Rosie.

"Mm!" Greta made an exasperated sound and smoothed her hair behind her ears. She pointed at Sal. "First of all, no one is going to breathe a word of this to Carl. I can't have my husband thinking he has the green light to spring headlong into this case. If he solves it from the information we informally give him, I suppose it can't do much harm. You all need coaching, that's for sure. I'll share with you my interviewing approach."

"Excuse me," said Sal. "Nobody knows how to charm gossip out of a customer better than," he touched his chest. "Give pointers to Justin and Sarah of course, but I don't think I personally need coaching." Greta clenched her jaw and gathered her purse as if to leave. "I meant—listen, Greta! Let me rephrase. I was going to say I'm going to be your star pupil. Stay, please. We all have so much to learn from you."

An inner fire lit up Greta's amber eyes, "The most common motivation for homicide according to Carl is money. We have to find out who all will benefit financially from Merlin Glenmore's death, directly or indirectly. And it's not always the person who gets the most money either. It can be somebody who gets what seems like a pittance, but that amount means the world to them."

"In this particular case, what about the motive of lust?" Sal asked. "What? I'm not joking! Couldn't it be someone had a thing for Merlin's wife and wanted him out of the way plain and simple. There's also the motive of revenge...Maeve Glenmore..."

"I like the way you're thinking Dad," said Justin. "The man who did it really hated Merlin."

"It could be a woman," Sarah said.

"Nah, not what my gut tells me," said Justin. "The man hated Merlin enough to kill him and then risk coming back to the scene of the crime to take the pants off the corpse. To leave the body even more humiliated. That's hatred with a dash of recklessness right there."

"Wait, back up. He didn't have pants when exactly?" Greta asked.

"It's the oddest thing of all," said Sal. "Merlin *did* have pants on it when we first found him you know *dead* in the cabinet. Then we all left the room to go downstairs. Only a few minutes later, when Justin, Doctor Boyd, and Rex Davis came to the study so Boyd could take a look, the pants were gone from Merlin's body."

"Somebody went to the trouble of coming back and taking them off in that tiny window of time. Huh. Why?" Greta pondered.

"Someone sending a message?" Sarah asked.

"An expression of hate or revenge, I'm telling you," Justin said. "It wasn't enough to leave the corpse the way it was. He had to make the sight even worse."

"I'm making a list of everyone who was at the party. Our list of suspects. Tell me the name of each person who was there and how they knew Merlin. I want to make sure I've got down who is who."

Sal, Sarah, and Justin eagerly filled her in on each guest and gave a brief sketch of their relationship to Merlin and to each other.

"Doctor Boyd is a top suspect," said Sal. "He was the only one besides Justin who *could* have done it, right?"

"I doubt it was Doctor Boyd, Dad," said Justin. "He wasn't out of breath when I came back into the room after my phone call. Wouldn't he be gasping if he'd run through the french doors outside in the snow, all the way around the Castle, upstairs, committed murder, ran back downstairs, out the front entrance, back around the Castle and to the Conservatory? When I came back in, he was relaxed waiting for me at the chess board. Oh, and he would need to somehow steal Merlin's pants between when everyone left the study and when we went upstairs to see if Dr. Boyd could give medical aid. I don't see how it would be possible."

"It sounds risky too," said Sarah. "You might have come back into the room at any time. And the pants bit would have required an accomplice. What do we think about Lewis Waterhouse?"

"Speaking of accomplices, I thought of him too," said Sal. "Scott might not have been telling the truth about seeing the face in the cabinet. To cover for his uncle. Lewis might have been able to do it before he entered the Study." Sal rubbed the stubble on his cheek and shook his head. "Nah, I've known the guy my whole life. It wasn't Lewis."

"Speculation is not going to get us anywhere at this stage," said Greta. "We need to gather facts first. Facts will point us to the truth. Let's talk about my method to get the suspects we want to question to open up. Everyone remember the word for sun in Spanish, SOL."

"SOL is an acronym for quite a different expression in English," said Justin.

"Very funny," said Greta. "But we do want to use it as an acronym. The S is for silence—don't fear a pause after asking a difficult question. I've found it's after enduring the longer silences that the best information comes out. The O is for open-ended questions, which will obtain more information than ones only requiring a 'yes' or a 'no'. The L is loosen them up with casual kind remarks or a low-key topic they will enjoy—"

"Or with an alcoholic beverage!" Justin chimed in.

Greta continued, "It's important to remember if someone is catching on to what you're doing, you need to make your excuses and leave. Alright, we don't have time to waste."

"After all this preparation, we're ready for the field," said Sal. "Armed with the Greta Klein SOL Technique. It's time to make these canaries sing!"

"This isn't a game, Sal," said Greta. "And we will get just one chance at this. Now, let's talk assignments and get interviewing suspects. We'll stay in touch and reconvene here later to review what we've learned. I can't emphasize enough how important it is that the information we gather does not leave our circle. No one outside of this room can find out what we're up to. Most of all Carl."

CHAPTER FIFTEEN

Sunday, April 2nd - 10:45 a.m.

As she waited for her boss Catia Boyd to arrive, Sarah sat on a lacquered chair facing the view of the moving river and the bare maples dripping in the sunlight as the snow melted. Inside, leafy tropical plants and wallpaper picturing green and white trailing succulents enlivened The Lavender Inn & Spa's tearoom.

Catia clacked around a palm tree, wearing a pale pink suit with a floral pocket square. "I'm here. Running on adrenaline and Nitro. Officer Keane made the simplest question sound like a murder accusation. He was just hoping I slipped up and confessed. Absurd. Not that I have anything to worry about. *I* have no secrets."

Considering how fast Catia was talking, Sarah doubted that. She didn't know what Catia was hiding, but she intended to find out.

Catia continued, as if she hadn't taken a breath. "I saw the mother of the bride in the lobby just now. She was delighted with how the wedding turned out and specifically mentioned how you came to the rescue when the maid of honor spilled her bloody mary all over the bride's gown. Excellent work, Sarah. But it's your day off today. What couldn't wait until Monday? Please don't tell me you're quitting."

"No, no! Not that. It's an advertising question. The deadline is tomorrow. I didn't want to waste a whole day to ask you about it."

"That's a relief." Catia uncapped her fountain pen and wrote Sarah/Weddings at the top of a clean page in her notebook.

"And most importantly, I wanted to check on you, Catia. How are you doing after last night?"

"You're such a sweetheart, Sarah. I'm alright. It's Arielle Glenmore we should all be worried about. Poor thing. I offered to sleep over last night. I thought it wouldn't be right for us to leave her. She insisted I go home with Owen. I suppose everyone reacts differently in tragic circumstances like this. Today could be harder for her than yesterday. I'm taking her lunch when you and I are through here."

"I can't imagine what she's feeling," said Sarah. "I would be out of my mind. Does she have any family nearby?"

"One aunt I think, but they're not close."

"I don't know about yours, but my husband was pretty shaken up," Sarah said. "The police questioned Justin this morning."

"They asked Owen to go into the station today too," said Catia. "I insisted they send the officer here to take my statement."

"Did it go alright for Owen? They weren't trying to accuse him too, I hope?"

"Must have gone fine enough. He texted me he's coming to use the golf simulator here. Glamis Hills is closed because of the snow, so he can't golf there."

"Do you know what sounds really good?" Sarah asked. "A Bloody Mary."

"Ooh yes. Might be just the cure to kick my gruesome champagne hangover." Catia hailed the server and ordered the drinks. She introduced Sarah to her new hire.

"This is Hazel. She started yesterday. She worked at some high-end bars in New York before moving here recently. Now we can say we have a brilliant mixologist at The Inn."

Three minutes later Hazel delivered the icy, murky-red drinks. "Here you are, Mrs. Boyd, Sarah."

"Record time. I applaud you," said Catia.

"Told you I was fast," Hazel smiled. "Enjoy."

"Patting myself on the back. She was a good hire. This is just the restorative we need, Sarah."

"Agreed. I'm worried sick. I don't know how you're staying calm. Neither of our husbands have alibis."

"They don't have motives either. At least mine doesn't. Does yours?"

"Of course not," said Sarah. "Not Justin. But some people hated Merlin in this town." She waited. Sarah knew Catia had not been fond of Merlin. She wondered if she could get Catia to admit anything about their history. She hoped Catia would reveal Owen's feelings about Merlin too. Sarah didn't love the idea of putting her job in jeopardy by prying into her boss' personal life, but she would do anything for Justin. Besides, she thought, if she followed her mother's guidance, Catia would never know why Sarah was asking about Owen's motive.

"Some had good reason to hate that man," said Catia. "Most people in town knew about his birthday party. If you think about it, anyone could have gotten inside The Castle last night. Logically, I don't think it could have been a party guest. The police are fools if they think so. The front doors weren't locked. The place has an infinite number of hiding places. It was so dark in there. It would be easy to creep around undetected. Lewis Waterhouse snuck in with no problem—no one saw him, until he popped out and scared us in the Study. We were distracted, drinking, caught up in the festivities, not to mention witnessing some remarkable grievances being vented by all the three Glenmore siblings at dinner. We wouldn't have noticed when the killer came in. It's all too disturbing to dwell on." She tapped her manicured nails on the marble tabletop and sighed. "What's this advertising opportunity you want to meet so urgently about?"

"Right," said Sarah. "I want to know if I've got the green light to move forward with a sponsored article in *New England Bride*. The deadline to reserve is tomorrow. Sorry for the short notice. My father-in-law Sal just proposed we go in with him on this. Our headline would be something like 'Why Glamis is the Next Top Wedding Destination in New England'. We would spotlight Dolce Far Niente as a prime spot for a rehearsal dinner, The Lavender Inn and Spa as a premier venue for a wedding, and Thane's to rent out for a wedding after-party."

"How much for our share of the ad?"

"It would be one thousand. The Marotta Group will cover the rest. I think this would be great exposure for the three businesses."

"I'm glad you brought this to me. I am interested, but I need to check what we have remaining in our marketing budget for this quarter. I don't think it will be a problem. You've barely touched your drink."

"Getting heartburn," Sarah said. "I'm so jittery after what happened last night. Thinking about a murderer being on the loose. Maybe someone we know."

Catia sucked up the last of the peppery liquid and slid her glass away. She checked her watch, "I do need to run. I have an hour to bring Arielle her lunch before my meeting with the gardening staff. Some impending hydrangea catastrophe with this late snowfall. Thank you, Sarah, my dear. I want you to know I notice your dedication. I appreciate how you give your all. Girl after my own heart. I'll call you about the ad tonight. Maybe around eight-ish, nine-ish. I've got a packed day."

Catia hustled out to the lobby. Just great, thought Sarah. Nothing more relaxing than expecting a call from your boss at an indeterminate time on a Sunday night.

Sarah visited the ladies room on her way out. Gilded swan faucets decorated rose quartz sinks. The powder room glowed pink warmth and the golden lighting was flattering, even when you were operating on three hours sleep as Sarah was. The bags under her eyes didn't stand out for once as she looked in the mirror. She hadn't gotten much of importance out of Catia. Sarah was starting to wonder if it had been worth coming here on her day off. Maybe her mother could have gotten more out of her boss. As Sarah dried her hands, Wilma, a woman in her late sixties wearing a uniform patterned with sprigs of lavender rolled in her cleaning cart.

"What are you doing here today, Miss Sarah? You don't work Sundays." Wilma started spraying the mirrors above the sinks and wiping them down.

"I had to meet Ms. Boyd," said Sarah. "So, that was a lively wedding last night! Hats off to you and the housekeeping team, everything looks immaculately clean today."

"It's a beautiful place here. Beats the last hotel I used to work at by a mile," Wilma said.

"Ms. Boyd has impeccable taste. Though she can be a stickler, huh?" Sarah applied her pink lipstick in the mirror.

"She is, ma'am, but she's a good boss. She's fair, and she listens to us. I've known her since she was a little thing. Ms. Boyd's mother Inez was in my women's prayer group at Our Lady of Fatima. Inez was a housekeeper. Maybe you already know all about that."

"I don't! I didn't. That's interesting," said Sarah.

"Explains a lot about how she operates this place. Inez worked for The Glenmore Family when Catia was a youngster. She saw exactly how not to treat staff in that home."

"They weren't good employers?" asked Sarah.

"Didn't have common sense or common decency. The oldest boy Merlin made up a story about a stolen watch that belonged to Mr. Glenmore, his father. The boy stole it himself! They took his word over Inez's, and she had twenty years working for them and not one single incident."

"That's terrible. Inez was fired?"

"Fired and worse!" said Wilma. "Mrs. Glenmore told all the other muckety-mucks Inez was a thief. She couldn't get another job in Glamis. No husband in the picture. Inez went through a rough time. For all Ms. Boyd's toughness, she cares, wants us to feel pride in where we work, and we do, don't we? We're part of her dream. She's moved on from the past with her head held high. And Merlin Glenmore will soon be rotting beneath a stone. What goes around, comes around."

"Tenfold apparently," said Sarah.

"No, ma'am. Merlin got exactly what he gave. His fortune taken away, that's the price for what he did to Inez. His life taken away, that's the price for what he did to his wife. *The first one.* Fair, no?"

CHAPTER SIXTEEN

Sunday, April 2nd - 10:45 a.m.

Scott closed his notebook and set his pen down on the varnished wood counter inside the boathouse of Robin's Marina. "Robin isn't in today."

"I see," said Greta. "Is he offering tours tomorrow? Everything seems to be thawing around here in all this sunshine. I could do the morning anytime. Can you take down my information and find out if he is available?"

"You're probably not aware that Robin Glenmore's brother died yesterday," said Scott.

"Yes, I did hear that. I thought he might be here. Work is the best distraction during times of grief. Did you know the man who died?"

"I knew him. I was there at the party when it happened."

"My heavens! I overheard something about this at The Black Sheep this morning. He died last night up at The Castle, didn't he? If you don't mind me asking, how did it happen?"

"Interested in all the gory tidbits, huh?" Scott swiveled from side to side on his barstool. "We found Merlin stabbed to death. And I'm sure I'll be a leading suspect. I'm in love with his wife, his widow. We kissed last night for the first time. You want the salacious details on that too?"

Actually, Greta did want the salacious details, but she couldn't admit it outright. "I didn't mean to pry. Has anyone bothered to ask you how you are doing? No. Well, are you alright?"

He tapped his phone in front of him. "She won't return my calls or texts. Like some kind of pathetic crazy person I went to her apartment this morning. She wouldn't open the door. I don't know what more to do without seeming like a stalker."

"She just lost her husband," said Greta. "Whatever you may think about him, she is grieving right now. I guess you might be a reminder to her of some behavior that felt like heaven at the time but stings the conscience like hell in retrospect."

"I want her to know she's not alone," said Scott. "I don't know why I'm telling this to a stranger."

"You need someone to talk to. May I sit for a moment? I walked from the village center. These heels weren't the best choice." Greta hoisted herself onto a bar stool and set her purse on the counter.

"We recommend boat shoes or sneakers for our tours. It's not dressy. Did you come from church?"

"What a keen eye you have. I did go to mass this morning," said Greta. "Are you religious?"

"No," he said, "but I am doing advanced Jungian shadow work. Self-guided. Spiritually it is high stakes. The Shadow resents being repressed and if left unexamined may wreak havoc. I am trying to be more myself and spend time in meditation, compromising with my inner demons. If I can't assimilate my shadow, it could consume me. Like demonic possession. On the other hand, if I succeed, I'll be much improved. It's worth the risk. My judgment can be off, despite my best intentions." Scott gazed down at the varnished wood counter. He said in a voice strangled with emotion. "I thought Arielle was worth the risk too."

"I fell madly in love when I was about your age," said Greta. "He was a literature professor at my college. He would do all kinds of wild stunts. He climbed through the window of our third-floor classroom to deliver Romeo's lines. One afternoon, I was helping him gather wildflowers in a field about half a mile from the college. The plan was to decorate the classroom as Titania's Bower for our unit on *A Midsummer Night's Dream*. I had hair back then to rival Farrah Fawcett's. The professor and I got caught in a thunderstorm and took refuge in a garden shed. He put his arms around me to warm me up. Before I knew it, we were kissing passionately. In the words of Titania, 'Methought I was enamor'd of an ass'. The next day, the rogue announced his engagement to a fellow senior, one of my closest sorority sisters. They'd been having a secret affair all semester. I felt so angry, so used, so devastated. Does that sound familiar?" Greta asked.

"It would be more relatable to my situation if the sorority sister turned up dead and the professor ghosted you," said Scott.

"I have to ask," said Greta. "You're at this party with a lot of people around. How did it happen that you and she had the opportunity to...?"

"You *do* want the lurid details, don't you, Ma'am? She stopped me while we were on our way to the Library bringing champagne and appetizers from the kitchen. The other two men with us, Chef Paul and Rex Davis, continued on. Arielle beckoned me back to the kitchen and into the pantry. That's when it happened, the kiss. The moment was cruelly cut short. By her husband."

"Oh dear."

"Merlin banished me after a few nasty words. I don't know what Arielle said to him in there alone. They rejoined the party as if nothing happened."

"And not too long afterwards, Merlin was found dead," Greta said.

"If I hadn't been with the others the entire night, I would probably be behind bars right now."

Greta smiled kindly at him. "I don't see you as a killer. You're sort of..."

"You can say it. Puny?" he asked.

"No, I was going to say sweet," she said. "You're cringing. Well, it's not the worst quality. It's a winning one in fact. You should find someone who is as excited about you as you are about them. It took me time to learn that lesson myself. Now I'm married to a wonderful man, almost eighteen years we've spent together. It's my greatest joy to love him and feel the love he has for me."

"You're lucky you dodged the scoundrel professor," said Scott. "You've been kind to me. Thank you. What's your name?"

"Greta Klein."

"I'm Scott Waterhouse. Alright, Greta, you want to see the legendary birds of the Connecticut River?"

"Very much. I'm crazy about eagles and ospreys."

"I'll talk to Robin and see if he's up for doing a tour with you. Write your name and number down here. You can do ten tomorrow morning, Milady?"

"That should be fine," Greta laughed. "Thank you. Be careful, Scott."

"You mean because there's a killer on the loose?" he asked.

"Well certainly that, but it was the self-guided shadow work I was referring to, dear."

CHAPTER SEVENTEEN

Sunday, April 2nd - 10:45 a.m.

"Clean and tidy is how we keep it here at the rescue," Zip escorted Sal past the rows of kennels. "You said on the phone you want to adopt a kitten?"

"Yes," said Sal. "Take me to the cutest one you've got."

"Ain't a one won't melt your heart. See for yourself."

Zip unlatched a Dutch door and showed Sal into a stall where five kittens roamed and played on fresh woodchips covering the floor. One white Siamese kitten rolled onto her back and looked up at Sal. An orange and white tabby lapped out of a water dish daintily.

"I have a confession," said Sal. "The kitten isn't for me exactly. It's a gift for Jade Glenmore."

"Hold your horses, partner. We don't do live animals as gifts. What you should do is bring Jade here so she can decide if she wants the cat and which one. Just take a couple of pics for now and see what she thinks."

"Fine, yes, you're right. Just some photos for now. She needs a new furry friend. She's been through so much loss in the past twenty-four hours. Her brother's death, and the same night she loses her beloved cat. Unreal what happened last night at the Castle. You and your nephew Rex were close friends with Merlin. How are you two holding up?" asked Sal.

"We hadn't known him for long, but he was a fast friend. I hope they find his killer soon. I ain't ever come across anything like what I saw done to him in that cabinet. I told the police the same this morning at the station. In a world full of chaos, caring for these animals comforts me. I came down here right after I finished my chat with that Detective Bell. Jiminy, he believes the killer was someone who was a guest at the party. I'm thinking Catia Boyd was dead on when she said we're being regarded as suspects, all of us."

"Do you have any hunches on who could have done it?" Sal asked.

Zip jingled a ball for a fluffy black kitten with paws poised to bat. "I got theories. I ain't sharin' them. Especially not with somebody who loves to gossip as much I know you do, Sal Marotta. Sorry, but at my age I call it like I see it."

Sal was offended but determined not to show it. "I'm talkative, sure," Sal said, "but when it comes to important matters, I can keep my mouth shut. I'm only curious about your opinion. You're the perceptive type, and I'd love any insight I could get. They took my brother Dom off the case you know. The state detective suspects my son, Justin."

"Ha. That's a good one. That kid couldn't hurt a fly. Doctor Boyd may be another story. He could have slipped outside when your son was making his phone call. Wouldn't have taken more than a few minutes. Stuck Merlin, shoved him in the cabinet, run back before Justin comes in. It's possible."

"Why would he have done something so awful though?" Sal asked.

"Merlin's wife," Zip whispered. "Owen Boyd's eyes barely left her last night. I overheard them, a pretty suggestive conversation before dinner."

"*Really*," said Sal. "Wow, you could be right."

"I seen it happen before. A feller who wants what he can't have, then he goes and removes the obstacle to his happiness so to speak."

"Did you share your suspicions about Doctor Boyd with the police?" Sal asked.

"No, Sir, just pure speculation. I wouldn't air my thoughts to the police unless I had actual proof. There's someone else it might be too."

Sal waited, remembering Greta's SOL Method.

"Scott Waterhouse," said Zip. "You notice what was going on at my end of the table at dinner? The boy was shamelessly cooing over Merlin's wife. Same motive as Doctor Boyd. Merl hated the pipsqueak following her around. He even had words with Scott last night. It's not hard to imagine what could ensue when an imbalanced teenager gets lovestruck, the next thing you know..."

"Just a second. Why do you say Scott is imbalanced?" Sal asked.

"It's there for any soul to read on the internet. A French news story—you hit translate and you can read the whole thing in English. A Parisian woman's husband was murdered while she was having an affair with Scott Waterhouse. They were both under suspicion for some time. The article claims it was the Corsican Mob behind the man's killing, drug-related, so the reporter said. All I'm saying is this woman's husband was stabbed to death, just like Merl. Look it up." He gestured to the kittens. "Any of these float your boat?"

"I'll definitely get a picture of these two."

"The black fluffy one is a male about five months old named Bartlett. He's affectionate as you can see. Has good hunting instincts too." The kitten rubbed his head against Zip's hand. "And the white one is a prissy little thing named Bluebell. See she's got the blue eyes."

Sal snapped photos of the two kittens. "I can't wait to show these to Jade and see what she thinks. I'm going to lift her right out of her grief."

CHAPTER EIGHTEEN

Sunday, April 2nd - 11:30 a.m.

Sarah looked for Owen inside The Lavender Inn's new golf simulator shed, installed at the far end of the brick garden path. "Doctor Boyd, are you in here?" She fought against the weighty green curtain across the entrance until she found the opening.

"Who's that?" he asked.

"Sarah," she waved.

"I reserved the simulator until one." He glanced at the clock. "I've got another hour and a half."

"Oh that's fine! No problem. Actually Catia mentioned you were here. I wanted to pop in and say hello. See how you are doing. I can't believe what happened last night to Merlin Glenmore."

"Ugh, let's not talk about that," said Owen. "I came here to clear my head. I had my interview with the detective at the police station. I'm praying the course at Glamis Hills will open by next weekend, so I can get some real golf in. The weather is supposed to improve drastically. I drove by just now and most of the snow had melted. I could have played, but they have the golf pro out there holding the line. Some nonsense about the 'health of the course'. Hopefully next weekend. I'm sick of being cooped up. Sibyl and I can't wait. She rides in the cart with me." Owen glanced behind him at a leather armchair, where Sibyl resembled a blonde loaf of bread wedged against one arm.

"Oh dear. No no no no. Dogs are not allowed in the simulator, Doctor Boyd."

"Why?"

"Well that's the rule your wife set. Only service animals."

Owen waved Sarah away.

"Is Catia worried about someone having an allergy to dogs? Listen, I paid thousands for this top of the line golf simulator to be installed. I think I have some patron's rights. Why don't you stop being rude to Sibyl and say hello. She likes you. Look, her tail is wagging! Isn't she cute?"

"I wasn't here. I never saw this." Sarah went to Sibyl and stroked her bony head and silky ears. "It's scary to think Merlin's killer could be someone we know."

"It might be, it might not," said Owen. "I haven't the faintest idea why anyone would want him dead. The people who have the most to gain from his death have irrefutable alibis."

"What kind of a person kills by stabbing?" Sarah mused.

"I'm not a criminal psychologist, but I would have to say the killer was powerful, quick, and knew the environment of The Castle well. I'd guess it was someone close to Merlin unless the killer somehow snuck up on him. This person apparently had the opportunity to get into the Armory and take the weapon while the cameras were off."

"The murder weapon was from The Castle's collection?"

"That's what I gleaned from being interrogated today by Detective Bell. Apparently, it was taken from a display case in the Armory. Some kind of bayonet."

"What do you make of Merlin's wife Arielle? You know there are rumors flying around."

Owen yanked the pitching wedge from his golf bag. "I hate gossip."

"Oh, me too," Sarah agreed.

Owen turned back to the screen lining up his chip shot onto the virtual turtle backed green surrounded by bunkers. "In my professional opinion, Arielle Glenmore is a harmless tease," Owen said, "not a murderer. She's not a rule breaker when it comes down to it. I don't think she would have an affair. Not even if the man was irresistible."

"I didn't realize you knew Arielle so well."

"I don't really. I've always been a keen observer," said Owen. He needed to be careful what he said to Sarah. She was sharper and more curious than he first realized. "Arielle is Catia's friend. One perceives things. As a doctor I know people, and I've seen a lot of human behavior."

He chipped the plastic ball with smooth finesse into the screen and watched the digital ball roll into the cup.

"Birdie. What else can I clear up for you, my dear?"

"I hope the police find out who really did it soon and leave innocent people like you and Justin alone."

"They will," said Owen. "I'm sure you have better things to do than sitting in the dark watching me play virtual golf. Not that I would ever object to the company of such a lovely woman."

"I should be going, you're right."

"Sarah," he said, as she reached the curtained doorway. "They can't accuse either of us without evidence. I guarantee you there is none."

CHAPTER NINETEEN

Sunday, April 2nd - 11:30 a.m.

"Oh Leopold," Jade choked. The bundled blanket rested at the bottom of the open grave. "Let's finish this now, before I lose it."

Lewis and Jade took up their shovels to fill the grave. They didn't break until they formed a compact mound. Jade rested a bouquet of white lilies on the fresh earth.

"I'm glad we did it this way for him, you know?" She wiped her nose with a handkerchief. "The physical labor did me good. Somehow, I knew it would. I certainly appreciated the assistance of *your* considerable strength. I don't know how to thank you for helping me."

"I've got an idea how. Could we go inside for a minute? I'd love something to drink," Lewis said.

Jade brushed the hair from her face. "Yes, yes, come in. I'll make some tea."

Lewis sat in the kitchen on a plaid cushioned chair, as Jade put the kettle on the stove.

"I have a confession for you," he said.

Jade gripped the counter with both hands, "Alright, go ahead."

"Now is as good a time as any to just go for it, I guess, and tell you. I suspect you already know the truth, deep down, but—"

The doorbell rang three times.

"Detective Bell said they wouldn't be coming by until three!" Relieved not to have to hear his confession, Jade rushed out of the kitchen to the front door. She peeked through the lace curtain. "What is Sal doing here?"

Sal held out his phone towards her face as she opened the door.

"Zip, put them on. We're doing a live video chat, Jade. Bartlett and Bluebell, meet your new mama," Sal beamed down at the alert, whiskered faces. "We can go pick them up from the animal rescue today."

"Have you lost your mind?" said Jade. "Absolutely not. Sal, I am not ready for this. You can't—" The two helpless orphans cut her off with indignant mews. "Oh, but they're darling—"

The kitchen door banged shut.

"Oh no- Lewis! Don't leave." But he had already gone. "This is beastly, Sal. Lewis has finally come into the house, and now he thinks I'm getting another cat. He is allergic," said Jade.

"Is he?" Sal feigned surprise. "Oh yes, that's right. What a shame. I love cats. I'm not allergic. Thanks,

Zip! Signing off! I'll hopefully be seeing you soon with this one," he gestured his thumb at Jade. He ended the video chat.

A loud whistle peeled from the kitchen.

"The tea," said Jade. "Come in, I suppose. You are too much, Sal Marotta!"

She ushered Sal into the sitting area. He plopped down on the sofa. As soon as Jade left the room, Sal leapt to his feet and went to the living room window. He saw Lewis heading away towards High Dunsinane. He slipped out his phone to text Greta:

> LW LEAVING JG's, GOING WESTWARD ON MAIN. CATCH HIM!

Jade carried in a tray with the tea and a plate of shortbread cookies. "I feel guilty about Lewis. He's been helping me all morning."

"Don't worry about that grump," said Sal. "After all you've been through. Today is about you. Deal with Lewis next week, next month."

"This was so presumptuous of you. I'm not ready for a new cat, let alone two! What were you thinking?"

"I was hoping to lift your spirits. How are you holding up, Jade?"

She slumped back against the sofa. "I'm drained, as you might expect. The lawyer who prepared Merlin's will is going to read it to our family in the next day or two. The police are requiring a copy of it. He thought we, the family, also have a right to know the contents. Though he did say it won't be official until it's proved by the judge. I don't have high hopes after the speech Merlin made last night at dinner. It could be that all the money was left to his wife."

"Have you spoken with Arielle?" Sal asked.

"I have not. I'll try her later, it's just...I'm a bit sickened by her at present. I can't help but think what if she encouraged someone too much—she can be quite the flirt—and he turned out to be homicidal, you know what I mean? You should have seen her dancing with Rex Davis before dinner last night—totally shocking, sort of impressive too I'll admit. You weren't there yet, but the way they tangoed—it was like they were on *Dancing with the Stars*. Next, I see her having an intimate conversation with Doctor Boyd, who was practically ravishing her with his eyes. Worst of all, there's young Scott, full of romantic sentiments. He has the worst crush. I'm sure he would do anything for her. I don't see how any of those men could have done it though. I should call Arielle. She's just the type to relish being foolish and free in the moment, then in the aftermath feel tortured over how she conducted herself. Especially now, with Merlin dead in the midst of her ridiculousness...I ought to call her. We'll have to plan the funeral together eventually."

They talked for a while longer. Sal delicately, in his estimation, elicited a few more details about the day of the party from Jade. He had a rough estimate now of the time each guest arrived at The Castle on Saturday night. He made a few quick notes in his phone. Jade gave him a quizzical look. "Are you putting together some kind of timeline, Sal? Do you think you are going to solve the murder?"

"No! Not at all. I have a curious mind. You know me. Well, I'm going to be late for my interview with Detective Bell. I've got to run. I'll come straight back afterwards. We can go to the animal rescue together and pick up those kitties."

"No kitties," Jade said. "I think your heart is in the right place, but I'm not ready, Sal. I'm just not."

"How about dinner together on Tuesday night?" Sal asked, front doorknob in hand.

"I just don't know. The lawyer might be reading Merlin's will that day."

"And after that, you'll want to unwind over a good meal with a friend who adores you, worships you, makes you laugh. Trust me you will. I'll call you to confirm!"

"Beast."

CHAPTER TWENTY

Sunday, April 2nd - 12:00 p.m.

"Excuse me, are you Lewis Waterhouse, the author?"

An elegant woman around Lewis's age stood on the steps of The Black Sheep holding a to-go cup.

"That's me," he replied.

"I'm Greta Klein. I'm a writer too. New to Glamis. I'm so sorry to ask. Could you spare a couple of minutes to tell me about your publishing experience? I'm about to begin negotiations for my first novel. I hear you are the most knowledgeable person in town about the literary world."

"You heard right, but you couldn't have caught me at a worse time," said Lewis.

"Drat," said Greta. "What about later in the day? I can see you're busy. I wouldn't pester you, but here's the thing. I've got meetings with three different agents tomorrow. They're all interested in representing me, and I'm a complete novice."

"You say your meetings with agents are tomorrow?" Lewis asked.

"I know having the right agent can make or break a writer's career. I would love to know what to ask, what to watch out for, that kind of thing." Greta gave him her most innocent, babe in the woods eyes.

"Which agents? Maybe I know of them."

Greta thought fast and rattled off three names she made up on the spot.

"Nope, never heard of them, but that doesn't mean anything," said Lewis. "There are a million agents out there. Alright, come on, walk with me to my place."

Lewis expounded on his experience with his own agent, one of his favorite topics. He gave Greta his best advice during the walk down Main Street. Once they arrived in front of Lewis' front yard, he couldn't help but ask, "Just curious, have you read any of my de Fey novels?"

"I confess I haven't had the pleasure yet."

"Ah ha. I'll get you a copy of the first book. You'll want to read all nineteen in order. I'm toiling away on the twentieth book now. Care to come down and see my writer's lair?"

"Yes, please!" Greta took in the reddish-brown cape house as they walked past it. "When was it built? 1700s?"

"1772. It's never left the family. We Waterhouses are a stubborn, tenacious bunch. You would think we were hanging onto Mount Vernon, not a three thousand square foot two bedroom. I'd be lying if I said I wasn't madly attached to it myself. My grandparents lived here before me, and once they passed the house came to me."

Greta followed Lewis down the hill, past an axe lodged in a stump. "I can't stay too much longer. My husband is expecting me. Tomorrow I'm hoping we'll get to go on the eagle watching boat tour with Robin Glenmore. Before my meetings," she added.

Lewis crossed his arms, "You know someone murdered Robin's brother Merlin yesterday at The Castle. I was there."

"I did hear about the murder. Just too awful for words. I assume you must have been acquainted with the man who was killed?" Greta asked.

"Oh, was I ever. He was the worst human being I've had the misfortune of knowing."

"Really? Why would you go to his birthday party?" Greta asked.

"His new wife Arielle came here yesterday and practically begged me to. She laid on the charm and claimed to be a fan of my books. That alone wouldn't have tipped the scales. What did it was when she suggested I could play a prank at his party. She thought it would add to the atmosphere to have me conduct the seance. I was banking on Merlin being in the room when I showed up, but he wasn't."

"What was the prank?"

"I snuck into The Castle when everyone was at dinner and during the séance in the upstairs study I materialized next to Arielle. My main prank, an admittedly malicious one, involved a psychic contraption that 'communicates with the dead'. I could manipulate the pendulum to point to 'yes' or 'no' with the use of a magnet. I hoped if Merlin were spying on us, he'd be getting mighty uneasy when it became apparent Maeve was the spirit."

"Who was Maeve?" Greta asked.

"His first wife and she was—now don't let me get started on all of that! Here's The Shed."

Greta read the sign nailed to the door. "Beware Writer Bites. Ha?"

"Go on in," said Lewis.

Inside the shed, Greta touched the spines of the books lining the shelves along one wall, "You've written so many novels, Lewis. My."

A dusty photograph of Lewis with a woman caught Greta's eye. Lewis took down a copy of his first novel, grabbed a permanent marker from the desk drawer, and scribbled his signature inside, while holding the cap between his teeth. He held the book out to her. "For you."

"I can't wait to read this," said Greta. "The woman in this photograph caught my eye. May I ask who she is?"

"That's Maeve."

"Merlin's first wife you were just talking about," said Greta.

"My sister," Lewis said. "She was with me at my first book signing. She was the only one who showed up, besides the bookstore owner. I almost gave up on writing that very moment, but she convinced me to toughen up. We went down the street to a bar after I signed all five copies of my novel the bookstore brought in. She gave me a pep talk about how it might not happen at first, but if I kept going with de Fey's adventures, she believed I would have a line out the door for my signings one day. The next year, forty people showed for my second book's launch. The following year, for my third de Fey, folks spilled out of the store into the street, more than a hundred people showed. Nowadays there are so many fans who come to my events it freaks me out. They try to book me in arenas and auditoriums. Overwhelming. I come up with all kinds of excuses to get out of doing them. Anyway, Maeve's belief in me kept me going."

"I have to ask...Did I hear she died in a car accident?"

"Accident? Merlin was asking around town about a hit man in the weeks leading up to her death. I don't believe that could be a coincidence."

"He was? Did the police look into it?"

"They said they would, but they were never able to get anywhere. Thought I was mad with grief. I don't think they ever took me seriously."

Greta looked back at the photo of the striking woman in gold hoop earrings with a defiant expression, her arm around Lewis' shoulder. "Why would he ever do that to her?"

"He fell in love with a younger woman, but he didn't want to divorce my sister," said Lewis. "They'd been married a long time. She would have gotten half of everything he owned. He couldn't stand it, so..."

"He killed her? I'm so sorry. That breaks my heart for you," said Greta. "I can't believe the police weren't able to do more. Weren't there others who heard him talking about the hit man?"

"The only one I knew of, Rex Davis, was not willing to talk to the police. He said he couldn't rat out his friend."

"Sickening," said Greta.

"It is sickening. Merlin fell in love practically at first sight with this Arielle, the one who came here to convince me to go to his stupid party. She was working at the Castle with Jade, Merlin's sister, and that's how he got to know her so well. Things weren't great between him and Maeve at that point. My sister didn't take any of his crap anymore, rolled her eyes at Merlin. Arielle treated him like he was this larger-than-life romantic hero and clung to his every word. Add to this equation the fact that Maeve had never been able to have a child. Merlin decided to dispose of my sister, and that's what he did.

"There is no question in my mind he was behind it. I went to the police to tell them the truth when they declared her death an 'accident'. They didn't take me seriously, said something about did I know Maeve had been drinking heavily that day before she got behind the wheel. It was a cover up. Now, I have to meet with those same police officers later this afternoon at the station. I am not shedding any tears over someone ridding the world of Merlin Glenmore. I am sure whoever did it had a good reason."

"I can't say I blame you," said Greta.

"Blame *me*? It wasn't I who killed him. It was someone who has guts."

"Lewis, I came to apologize—oh." Jade stood in the doorway of the shed taking in Greta. "I didn't realize you had company. I'll go."

"Hang on, let me introduce you—wait, where are you going? Can you wait a minute?"

"No need, honestly," Jade waved him away as she climbed back up the hill to the road.

"Fine," said Lewis. "Let her think whatever she wants to."

"I better go too," said Greta. "Thank you for the book and all your advice."

"Um, Greta," he said. "You're not an undercover detective, are you?"

"Me? No, how funny."

"You asked me a lot of probing questions, but not too many that would be helpful to you in your 'negotiations' tomorrow," he said, using air quotes. "Journalist?"

"I'm a retired reporter. I am full of questions for people who interest me."

Lewis grunted. "Well, good luck with your meetings, Ms. Klein, if they are indeed real."

Greta thanked him and retreated up the hillside as fast as her legs would take her in heels.

CHAPTER TWENTY-ONE

Sunday, April 2nd - 1:30 p.m.

Busying himself with the boxes in his home office, Carl began to relax. Greta would be home soon. He would talk this through with her. She would tell him her side. He would tell her his. They would listen respectfully and work through the problem. This would not become a pattern that would unravel their relationship. Carl unwrapped the framed letter from a U.S. President commending his exceptional public service to the state of Texas. Though his politics differed from this President, he felt proud to be honored by the highest-ranking official in his country. He held the framed letter against one of the walls of the office to see where it would look best.

His phone pinged. Finally! A reply from Greta:

Bear with me. I'm going to spend the rest of the day with Sarah. We are going to some thrift shops. I think every New England home needs a wooden mallard, don't you? So we are on the hunt for one. I'll be home later. If you get hungry before I'm back, eat dinner without me. There are canned soups in the cupboard.

He tried calling her. He went to voicemail.

Can't talk right now, came a new text from Greta.

"Unbelievable," Carl said. She can't talk to her own husband? Canned soup for dinner? These wishy-washy plans on when she would be back. The need for a wooden mallard? What was this silliness she was talking about? What happened to his wife? What was she up to? He thought about texting her and demanding an explanation for her uncharacteristic behavior. No, on second thought.

He texted her back a simmering "Ok."

His phone buzzed, the caller id reading Glamis Police Department. "*Well,*" he thought, "*Looks like there is someone who wants to talk to me.*"

"Lieutenant," came an eager voice on the other end. "This is Detective Bell. I'm here with Officer Marotta. Is now a good time to talk?"

CHAPTER TWENTY-TWO

Sunday, April 2nd - 3:00 p.m.

Justin pushed through the aluminum doors into the busy kitchen of Dolce Far Niente, knowing he would find Chef Paul there. "Chef, stop whatever you are doing. Come across the street and have a drink with me. I need to talk to someone who was there last night. You know just to process."

"Fine, I can sneak off for a bit. I just survived an hourlong Q&A with Detective Bell."

Paul and Justin crossed the street to Thane's a few minutes later. Five men sat around a table playing a noisy game of dice, but the cigar bar was quiet otherwise.

"There's Rex. Let's sit with him," said Justin.

Rex sat alone at a table in the corner. He looked up from his phone as Justin and Paul joined him. "Hey there. Join me for a drink?"

Francis took their orders and left them alone after delivering their drinks.

"How were *your* interrogations?" Justin asked Rex and Paul.

"They fired off a bunch of questions about you, Bud," said Rex. "And just as many about the Doc. Your movements, all that."

"If only the cameras worked last night," said Justin.

Rex crunched on an ice cube, "I've got a theory."

"Oh?" said Justin.

"You and the Doc ain't the only ones without alibis. Didn't Lewis Waterhouse have a pretty good reason to want Merlin dead, and didn't he have the opportunity, if you think about it?" asked Rex. "Why couldn't he have gotten to Merl right before he went into the séance room? Scott says he saw someone in the cabinet. He can't say for sure who it was. It's possible the kid made up seeing the face to protect his uncle."

"Rex, did you know Merlin planned to be inside the cabinet? Did he let you in on his prank?" Justin asked.

"Heck no. I am sure Merl wanted to scare the bejesus out of me along with the rest of 'em," said Rex.

"Sounds like him," said Paul.

Rex's brow furrowed with offense. "He wasn't perfect, but he was my friend," said Rex.

"You were close to him. I apologize," said Paul.

"I've always wondered, Rex, how did you and Zip become friends with Merlin?" Justin asked.

"We met him here at Thane's. It was only a few weeks after we'd moved up last August. I spotted him across the room, sitting over there. We could tell right away he was some kind of uptight Connecticut Yankee all puffed up and full of himself. Remember how he would kinda look off into the distance when he talked to you? If he did deign to talk to you! Well, me and Zip made a bet on whether we could befriend him or not. Looked like a challenge alright. Zip bet he could pry him open. I thought we didn't have a prayer. Zip wore him down sure enough. Lost me fifty bucks on that bet, but I gained a good friend."

"And what about his wife, Arielle? You must know her well too," Justin said.

"Zip and I became acquainted with her before Merlin, actually. Zip took The Castle tour when we moved here. Arielle was his guide, and he met her then. We ran into her a few days later at The Black Sheep, and Zip said to her, 'You were the charmer who gave me a tour and didn't answer my question correctly.' That got her attention good, and she said, 'What question didn't I answer right?' all surprised. Zip said he'd asked her to get dinner with him after the Castle tour, and she'd said no. The old dog didn't stand a chance with her. Merl snatched her up instead."

"Did Merlin say to either of you anything about being concerned for his safety recently?" Justin asked.

"Don't look at me. My brother-in-law barely acknowledged my existence," said Paul.

"What about you, Rex? Did he say anything about being scared or...?"

"Hey, I already been interrogated once today."

"What I really want to know is did Merlin fear Lewis?" Despite what his father believed, Justin wasn't so sure Lewis couldn't be the killer.

"Shoulda." Rex took a sip of scotch. "Makes me queasy to remember it. Back in the fall of last year, Merl told me Lewis Waterhouse was writing a book about a hit man. He asked if I knew anyone in that line of work his brother-in-law could talk to off the record for research. Course I sure couldn't help him. I was honestly offended he thought I might be able to. Maybe I should have known better, but I asked Lewis one day in passing if he'd found a hit man to talk to yet. He looked at me like I'd sprouted nine heads. I explained I heard he was researching a book and wanted to find a real life hit man to interview. Woo doggie, did the man explode. Now, I never revealed it was Merlin who told me that. Lewis figured it out on his own. Paints an ugly picture, don't it? But I swear it couldn't have been Merlin behind his first wife's death."

"Oh no?" Paul asked. "Everything you just said would indicate he was. Why did he fish around about a hit man?"

"Could have been one of Merlin's innocent pranks to get Lewis riled and the timing of it turned out unfortunate. Gives Lewis a good motive to see Merl dead though, don't it? I sure hope the cops wise up and get *you* off their list, Justin."

"How can you be sure it wasn't Marotta?" Paul asked.

"Very funny," said Justin. He didn't find it funny. Paul really knew how to needle him after all these years working together.

"Just wasn't," Rex said. "Our pal Justin here don't have the temperament for killing."

"Thanks," Justin said, though he wasn't sure if that had been a compliment the way Rex had said it. "What about Paul here? Does he have the temperament?"

"Might could," said Rex. "If he had a good enough reason. I'd bet he'd do it real clever, so he wouldn't get caught neither."

"I," Paul touched his own chest, "am above suspicion with my perfect alibi. I shouldn't joke. I was not close to my brother-in-law, everyone knows that. He didn't give me the time of day except occasionally he would thank me for 'looking after his little brother'. He was vicious to Robin. I couldn't look past that."

"Well, his sense of humor weren't for everybody," said Rex. "Once I got to know him and he warmed to me, he cracked me up. Funny. Vicious kind of funny though, like you said."

"He never revealed his humorous side to *me*. Vicious I saw plenty of," said Paul. "Entitled and stingy, in abundance. We will see what happens with all the money he's leaving behind. Robin and I could use even a small windfall."

"I hope your husband gets his due," said Rex. "Jade, too. I tell you I wouldn't be surprised if Uncle Zip got Merl to will his entire fortune to the Glamis Animal Rescue."

"I'm not laughing." Paul drained the last of his drink.

"When do they read Merlin's will to the family?" Justin asked.

"The lawyer is reaching out to us tomorrow to set the meeting. Pray for us, if you two are the praying kind," said Paul.

"Sure am," said Rex.

"I'll say one for you too," Paul winked.

"For me. How come?" Rex smiled.

"For good luck with the widow. You know what I'm talking about. She's going to be a catch once a decent amount of time passes. You two are friendly. You can't deny it, my young friend. Don't you think a woman like that could fall for a buff, handsome fellow her own age? Might be a nice change for her."

"Chef, you got me all wrong," Rex said.

"Do I?" Paul asked. "Justin, you should have seen how beautifully those two danced the tango. They looked perfect together too—both so statuesque. How did you learn all those moves anyway? The way you danced with her—you can't say something electric wasn't happening between you two."

"I can. You're wrong wrong wrong."

"In what way?" asked Paul.

"I'm not attracted to the female of the species."

"Seriously?" Paul asked. "Huh. I had no idea. I was totally off."

"Yep," said Rex. "Francis, another round right here."

"I had it all wrong too," said Justin. "I thought you were in love with Arielle for sure."

"Naw," Rex said. "She's a beautiful woman alright, don't misunderstand me, but not my type."

"Funny. I was convinced you were jealous of Doctor Boyd and her," said Paul. "You made a big deal about Arielle being so solicitous towards him last night. Remember in the kitchen?"

"I got on her case somewhat, sure. It was because Merl deserved better on his birthday from his own wife," said Rex. "One thing about me ya'll might not realize is I am extremely loyal to my friends."

"That's not the only thing I didn't realize about you. Aren't you full of surprises, cowboy. You could knock me over with a feather," Paul laughed.

CHAPTER TWENTY-THREE

Sunday, April 2nd - 7:00 p.m.

Following a tip-off from Sal, Greta limped down High Dunsinane Road, cursing her choice of shoes. She trudged across the muddy gravel parking lot of Puck's Tavern, where Dominic Marotta watched from behind the wheel of his patrol car.

Dominic waited in his car outside for Arielle Glenmore to come out from the Irish pub. The woman could probably afford her own private security, but the Glamis Police Department was kissing her rich behind, having an officer watch out for her on every shift. He had to protect her but not invade her privacy at the same time by following her inside.

Greta noticed Dominic in the police car as she walked by but pretended otherwise. She didn't want anyone on the force to have any inkling she was involving herself in their investigation. She avoided eye contact with her in-law and pushed open the door to Puck's Tavern. The bar was quiet on a Sunday night. Greta scanned the faces of the handful of patrons inside. The smell of french fries and ketchup and a nearby cheeseburger made her stomach growl. She ordered a ginger ale and asked for it to be served in a wine glass, then headed to the back deck encased in plastic with a smudgy view of the river at dusk. Greta found Arielle at a wooden picnic table, bundled in a red puffy jacket, a glass of white and a half empty bottle in an ice bucket next to her.

"Nice spot out here," Greta said. "But you should never drink alone. Mind if I join you?" She sat down on the bench across from Arielle. Greta sighed as she slipped her feet out of the high heels. She focused her attention on Arielle. "Are you doing alright, honey?"

"No," Arielle said. "But I'm trying to fix that." She lifted the glass to her lips. "My husband was killed last night."

"I'm so sorry. He was the one...at The Castle? It's all over the news."

"You're not another reporter, are you?" Arielle asked.

"Oh no, darlin'. I'm a retired gal. I'm new to town. Justin Marotta is my son-in-law."

"I know him. He and his father Sal were there last night too."

"We're very concerned," said Greta. "The police seem to think poor Justin is a lead suspect."

"I don't see how they could," said Arielle. "He barely knew Merlin. But somebody did do it. I'm scared I was the reason."

"Why would *you* be the reason?" Greta took a sip of the sweet ginger ale.

Arielle looked out towards the river. "I think it was someone who wanted Merlin gone to get to me."

"There is a certain young man working at the Marina who declared enthusiastic feelings for you," said Greta. "Are you afraid it was him?"

Arielle lowered her eyes, wondering how this woman could know about Scott's crush. How often had he crowed about protecting her honor? This strange woman knew her business thanks to him. Laughable. "No, it couldn't be Scott. He was by my side all night."

"Who then?" Greta asked.

"I'll be in more danger if I say anything. I don't have proof. I'm frightened by what this man, whoever he may be, will do if I don't follow along with his plans. Maybe he would kill me too."

"I heard you will inherit a fortune from your husband," said Greta. "Won't that afford you a new life, if you need to get far away from this dangerous person?"

"I have no idea. I could never talk to my husband about money. He was touchy about the subject." Arielle drew hearts on the foggy sides of her wine glass, thinking. "He must have gained access to his inheritance money last week the way his siblings closed in on him. Merlin was bursting with new plans for us like he was scared any second everything might be taken away. He bought a flashy sports car last week. He wanted us to start a new life together in Florida. I didn't want to move away from my world here. Now I might. Or maybe not. I'm not in any state of mind to decide my future. I have no idea if he left me any money. He never told me he was going to. I can't believe he's gone."

"You must have loved your husband very much," said Greta seeing the tears well up in Arielle's eyes. "You two had a whirlwind romance from what people around here say. You were married recently, weren't you?"

Arielle wiped the wet smears beneath her eyes. "He proposed to me on December 28th. I hadn't seen him or heard a word from him in over a month. I assumed he'd been in mourning for his wife, Maeve. She was killed when her car left the road one night on her way home from Vermont. She'd been drinking apparently. Merlin said something to me the month before her death. I couldn't get it out of my head. It made me believe he would come back, to collect on my promise."

"I can't help but ask…what did he say to you, before her death?" Greta asked.

"I shouldn't be talking about this, but with Merlin gone, I guess it doesn't matter anymore. It would be a relief to tell someone." Arielle sighed. "It was several weeks before Maeve's accident. He flat out ignored me the night before at a fundraiser for The Castle. He treated me like a dull peon beneath his notice. It drove me crazy. I thought he had lost interest in me. Let me make it clear—we were not having an affair, at least not physically. I would never do that. But emotionally, it was another story. How can you turn off your heart?

"Merlin and I had such a connection. Anyway, the next day, it was a gorgeous October afternoon, warm enough for us to have the windows in the office open. I heard my favorite aria playing outside, 'The Seguidilla' from *Carmen*. I rushed outside, following the sound to Merlin's black convertible parked by the front gates. I couldn't see his eyes behind his dark sunglasses. He asked me to get in the car. He wasn't smiling. I obeyed, but I began to tremble uncontrollably as soon as I sat down. I remember my teeth were chattering away. I couldn't stop them. It was so embarrassing. I waited for him to speak first, in case he was going to say it was all finished between us, whatever 'it' was. He drove in silence. I remember worrying how I would find the moral strength to resist him if his plan was to bring me somewhere to make love to me. He was married, but I was so wild for him, awed by him, intimidated by him too."

Arielle emptied the rest of the bottle into her glass. "Eventually, Merlin slowed onto the shoulder of a lane. He shut off the car, took off his seat belt and his sunglasses and turned to fully face me saying, 'I'm certain by now you know I am in love with you.' He said I'd made it clear to him as long as he was married, things between us couldn't progress. He needed to know if I was using his marriage as a face-saving excuse to keep him at bay. I swore it wasn't true. He asked me one more question. He insisted I absolutely had to tell him the truth. I remember exactly what he said, 'Suppose Maeve was out of the picture. Let's say a grandfather clock collapses on her, killing her instantly…if I were free, would you be mine, fully mine, without any hesitation?'"

"How did you answer him?" Greta asked.

"Not the way he wanted at all. I started telling him I was *flattered*. He said 'flattered' was 'condescending and evasive' and exactly what he feared about me, that I was incapable of being serious and honest. I wasn't going to beg him to believe me. He hated groveling! 'I wouldn't hesitate,' I whispered to him before I left the car when he dropped me off back at the Castle. He said nothing in response. I thought it was all over. But I couldn't stop thinking about what he said. I had seen a ferocity in him for the first time. As awful as it sounds, this drew me to him more. Calling him would be wrong. I could only wait and hope this most captivating man would come back into my life and be my wicked playmate again. I couldn't believe it when I heard Merlin's wife died in a car accident a few weeks later. I wondered if it was all my fault."

"How could it be?"

"Well I had said to him I wouldn't hesitate if she were...dead."

"Lordy, and you ended up marrying the man? Weren't you frightened of him?"

"Well, in a way, but...how can I explain it? I knew all about Merlin's family history. I worked at the Castle, built by his great-great grandfather Ernest Glenmore. I knew about Ernest's character intimately from reading about him and from his own letters. It dawned on me Merlin *was* his ancestor Ernest Glenmore, passionate to the point of madness! I could hear Ernest speaking through him, sensual and ruthless. To be at the center of this kind of attention, not of our times, an all or nothing, life or death desire distinctly of the past...I knew now how Anne Boleyn felt when Henry the VIII overturned the world in pursuit of her! Does any of this make sense, or does it appall you?"

Greta could barely believe her ears hearing about the strange, disturbing bond Arielle described. There was something broken and warped in this woman. Greta pushed her moral judgment aside and encouraged Arielle to continue her story.

"I've loved some bad boys in my day too. I follow you all too well, Honey," Greta reassured her in true southern fashion.

"Here is Merlin." Arielle pulled out her phone from her purse and showed Greta a photo of him on their wedding day. "And this was Ernest." Arielle pulled up a photo of a 19th century man in formal attire, black hair swept back, with a dark mustache and beard, a white hat held by one gloved hand on his lap. "Those light, intense eyes, their expressions. They look identical, don't they? And their way of thinking, of loving—that's the irony of it all. Merlin never saw it. I saw it so intensely. As much as he hated the past and his ancestry and The Castle, here it all was *inhabiting* him without his even being aware of it. I couldn't look away."

"There is a resemblance between the two." Greta handed the phone back to Arielle. "Merlin came back into your life after his wife's death, and proposed? And you accepted? All fears he might be a man who killed his first wife evaporated?"

"It might sound like madness. As much as I feared what he may have done, I *longed* for his attention. I had endured two months of silence from him. He caught me by surprise showing up that December night at The Castle. It was after my last tour of the day. He stood there in the entry hall. I knew he'd come to collect on my promise to him. I took his hand without a word and led him into the Small Parlor. I shut the door. We kissed fiercely against it. An ecstatic energy filled me like I'd never experienced before. I knew from the look he gave me afterwards he felt the same magic coursing between us. We found his sister Jade at work in the staff room. Merlin told her we were in love, and we were going to be married. I must have looked stunned. Jade said to him: 'You haven't bothered to ask *her* yet?' He turned to me, 'You want to marry me, don't you?' We were married within a month."

"I'm sorry for you," said Greta. "It sounds like you were crazy about him. You must be devastated to lose him. And in such a sudden, horrible way."

"I can't let myself go there. I need more of this." Arielle returned a few moments later with a new bottle.

As she poured another glass, Greta asked, "Did you know Merlin would be inside the cabinet last night? Did you know he planned to play a prank?"

"I thought Merlin was downstairs with your son-in-law Justin and Doctor Boyd. Merlin was invincible, kingly, otherworldly in my eyes, to see him lying there, slain…"

"It's terrible what you've been through. I don't think drinking more wine will help at this point. How about a glass of water instead?"

"No. It's the only thing keeping me from being consumed by the sadness, the fear. Jade and Robin, Merlin's siblings, must know how deeply I loved their brother. Neither one called today. I'm scared they think I'm an evil woman and they won't love me anymore," she sobbed.

"Now of course not, Silly! You strike me as a romantic soul who was lured into a fantasy—"

"It wasn't a fantasy," Arielle sniffled.

"Some might say you built Merlin up to epic proportions, casting all moral considerations aside."

"No, didn't you hear what I said? I insisted we wait. I never let him do anything, until the time was right. He pushed me and pushed me, but I resisted him, really I did, until he was truly free. I can't believe he's gone. I feel like I did when I was a child, poor little Arielle Cook. Both my parents died when I was young. I was alone in the world for so long, until Merlin."

"How old were you when your parents died?" Greta asked.

"Six when my mother died. My memory of her is fuzzy, but I was extremely close to my father. He died when I was fifteen. He was a brilliant architect, a bookworm too."

"Where did you go after your father passed? Do you have other family?"

"Only Great Aunt Harriett. I moved in with her. I hated my teenage years."

"For many it is an era best left buried in the past," said Greta.

"I agree. I got an invitation to my high school reunion. It's later this week. I tore it up. The Cooks will never be darkening the doors of Woolsey High School again, I promise you that. I hate whoever has done this to Merlin and me. Taken away my chance to have a family. None of them really care about me I guess. Not Jade, or Robin, or Paul."

A question was at the tip of Greta's tongue, but she decided to ask a different one, "Who do you think could have done it? It sounds as though you might have an idea." She leaned forward and whispered, "You will be safer if you share your suspicions."

"What are you after?" Arielle asked in a raw, low voice. All inclinations she'd had to talk about Merlin were gone. "Get away from me, you stupid old snoop."

CHAPTER TWENTY-FOUR

Sunday, April 2nd - 9:45 p.m.

Worked up from the excitement of the day, Greta struggled to get the key into the lock as she let herself into the house. Her handwritten notes from the evening's secret conclave at Dolce Far Niente summarizing the information gathered by herself, Sal, Justin, and Sarah remained zipped inside her purse. On the kitchen counter she set down leftovers from dinner. The printer hummed in Carl's office.

"Carl, honey?" she knocked.

Carl swiveled around in his chair to face her and crossed his arms. "It is almost ten o'clock. Where have you been?"

"At Dolce Far Niente and then I ran a bunch of errands," she said. "I got hungry for a snack and went back to Dolce."

Carl's brow furrowed at this. "You forgot you had a husband?"

She went in to kiss his cheek. "No," he turned his face away, "You are in the dog house."

"Oh, Carl. I did not forget you," said Greta. "And I have proof. Sal sent me home with all kinds of goodies for you. They're in the kitchen. Come with me and have some."

"I will have to look at it. I'm starving. I ate only soup for dinner."

Carl shut the office door behind him and followed Greta.

She pulled back the aluminum foil to reveal ciabatta sandwiches filled with fresh prosciutto, mozzarella, and basil with pesto and two chocolate chip cannoli. "Dig in!" she said.

"What's this? I'll try it. How was the brunch at Sal's?" Carl tried to conceal his enjoyment of a ricotta-filled pastry.

"We couldn't stop talking about the murder," she said. "I heard all the gossip."

Carl dusted powdered sugar from his hands. "Did you hear anything interesting?"

"Where to begin," said Greta. "There's a well-known author who lives here in Glamis. His name is Lewis Waterhouse. He was there at The Castle during the murder. He was Merlin's first wife Maeve's brother. He is totally convinced his sister's death this past fall was no accident. He believes Merlin was behind it. He hated Merlin and with good reason."

Carl looked inside a ciabatta sandwich. "I'm listening. What else?"

"There's Catia Boyd, the owner of The Lavender Inn and Spa, who was also there last night. Her mother worked for Merlin Glenmore's parents as a housekeeper, until young Merlin falsely accused her of theft, and she was fired. She couldn't get a new job in Glamis. Another motive there."

Carl plucked the last sandwich half from the plate.

"And," said Greta, "Things get crazier when it comes to this other party guest, Scott Waterhouse. He is Lewis' nephew, a nineteen-year-old who interns at The Castle. He and Arielle Glenmore *kissed* last night!"

"Kissed?" asked Carl.

"You heard me right," said Greta. "Arielle brought him to the kitchen pantry and that's where it happened. Merlin came in and caught them."

"Who told you?"

Greta caught herself just in time. "Sal told me."

"And he heard it from who?" Carl asked.

"I can't remember. Sal knows everything," Greta picked up the empty paper plate, "including how to cook apparently. I'm glad to see you ate every crumb."

"Only because I was on the verge of starvation," Carl said. "I had to eat out of desperation. My wife abandoned me."

"You're so dramatic," said Greta.

"Did Sal ask why I wasn't there at the brunch?"

"Of course he did. I said I couldn't pry you away from unpacking. Everyone except Sal understood, but we eventually moved past the topic. The murder was what everyone wanted to talk about."

Greta continued to fill Carl in on what she learned, while setting up the coffee for the morning.

"Oh, tomorrow I have a surprise for you." She took her purse in hand.

"Tell me it does not involve Sal Marotta please," said Carl.

"It does not. You and I are going to take a boat ride at ten o'clock. We'll get to see eagles and ospreys out on the river."

Carl didn't look excited at all. "It will be freezing, honey," he said.

"Oh now, it's supposed to warm up to fifty-five," said Greta. "You know who is giving us the tour? Merlin's younger brother Robin Glenmore. He owns The Marina and does the boat tours himself."

Carl crossed his arms and leaned against the counter, "You tell me you want me to stay out of this investigation. Every word since you came through the door tonight has been about the homicide case. Tomorrow, you propose we go to see the murdered man's brother. What are you up to exactly?"

"For land's sakes, Carl," said Greta. "It's a coincidence Robin Glenmore runs the only bird watching boat tour in town. You spent the entire day cooped up in here. You need fresh air and a change of scenery tomorrow. I'm going upstairs. Are you coming?"

"A few more minutes to finish something, and I will be up."

"I'm glad you're not too annoyed with me," Greta kissed his cheek.

"Well, it was not right you going to Sal's without telling me your plan first," Carl said.

"I'll communicate better next time. We can talk more about it upstairs."

Carl noticed the black purse in Greta's hand traveling up the steps with her. Odd.

CHAPTER TWENTY-FIVE

Monday, April 3rd - 10:00 a.m.

"Who is ready to see some eagles?" Robin forced enthusiasm into his voice. He handed out his standard issue blankets and binoculars to Carl and Greta, who huddled together for warmth in the cockpit of the aluminum fishing boat. Lively river waves splashed against the side of the boat. The cold wind gusted Greta's hair into a wild tangle.

"So much for my do!" Greta laughed.

"Don't worry about it," Robin said. "Want a hat?" He tossed her a white cap with Robin's Marina logo on the front. She gratefully put it on. Carl came prepared wearing a wool beanie.

"This will be about a two hour tour. Bundle up! We always provide blankets because it is chilly out here on the water. Scott told me you two are new to town?"

"We are. Thrilled to be here. Glamis is such an adorable town," said Greta. "This is gonna be an adventure, Honey!" she squeezed Carl's hand.

"I'm freezing." Carl studied the blanket and smelled it. Satisfied it was clean enough, he wrapped it around himself.

"We are loving it here in Glamis," Greta said.

"I've lived here most of my life," said Robin. "It's definitely grown up to be a more happening place than when I was a kid. Lots going on for a small town. Especially in recent years with the push to revitalize the village center." Robin fired up the engine, untied the lines, and looking over his shoulder, carefully reversed the boat away from the dock. "If you look upriver that way, see the white mansion right by the bridge? That's The Opera House, built in 1877 in the Second Empire style. Broadway actors come all the way up here to perform. Paul and I used to have season tickets. Not this year, but that's another story. You'll have to check it out."

"We certainly will. Powerful current!" Greta shouted.

"Yes it is," Robin said. "So, now that you live here, you've got to learn how to be River People. What made you two pick Glamis?"

"Our daughter Sarah and son-in-law Justin live here with our three-year-old granddaughter," said Greta. "They lived in New York until about a year and a half ago, when they decided to move to Glamis, Justin's hometown. Do you know him? Justin Marotta? He was there at the party Saturday night. It was a relative of yours who died, wasn't it?"

"Ugh, gosh. Yes, my brother."

"Please accept our condolences."

Robin cleared his throat. "I do know Justin and Sarah. I see the resemblance between you and your daughter. I know sweet little Rosie too. My husband Paul is the chef at the Marottas' restaurant. We all get together and try out his new recipes. Sarah wants the dishes spicier."

"That's Carl's influence," said Greta. "Sarah didn't eat spicy food when Carl first moved in, after we got married. She said she despised Mexican food just to get his goat. But, once she and Carl started to bond, she began eating tacos, tamales, enchiladas."

"Now she loves them," said Carl. "That makes me happy. And Rosie is next."

"I'd heard from Justin his in-laws were moving to town. So it's you two," said Robin.

"You can tell us the truth, was he nervous about us moving here?" asked Greta.

"A little."

"In-laws can be tricky," said Greta. "Do you get along well with your in-laws?"

"Yep. I just have one in-law in town, my brother's second wife, Arielle. I get along with her fine." Robin scanned the bare tree branches above as they drifted down river through the waves.

"We heard your brother and his wife had a whirlwind romance right after his first wife's tragic death," said Greta.

Robin cut the motor. The waves lapped against the boat. He took up his binoculars. "Bingo, look up there, top of these branches."

"Oh, an eagle. See it, Carl? It's magnificent!"

Carl gazed up through his binoculars. "Ah yes, I see it! Incredible."

"You were going to tell us about your brother and sister-in-law, sorry for the interruption," said Greta.

"I was?" Robin asked.

"Honey," Carl scolded.

"That's okay. You're here to look at the birds and enjoy the sights of the river, not hear about my family. I think."

"I'm interested in hearing more," shrugged Greta. "I love stories about how people fall in love. How did it happen between Arielle and Merlin? It isn't difficult to imagine what drew Merlin to her. I've seen her. But what do you think drew *her* to him?"

"At first, it could have been our family's history, honestly. It fascinates Arielle. Merlin for once took an interest in it too, knowing it was a sort of an aphrodisiac for her."

"Family history an aphrodisiac?" Greta laughed.

"It's true. Arielle is an architecture and history nut. She works at the Castle and tells the history of the place in such a compelling way on her tours. The first day they met, Merlin went to The Castle so Jade, our sister, could sign some papers. He ended up having Arielle give him a private tour and spent an hour with her afterwards letting her read him letters from the archives. They became friends. Friends who bristled with excitement whenever the other one walked into the room."

"And was there a secret affair, while Merlin was married to Maeve?" Greta asked.

Carl stared at Greta, his eyes narrowing. *What was she up to?* "Forgive my wife, please," Carl said. "She is being so nosy."

"You look like an angry hoot owl wrapped up in that hat and blanket scowling," Greta said. "I give people the benefit of the doubt. If the rumors are not true, Robin will clear it up for us."

"As far as I know, they did not have an affair, at least physically speaking. Merlin was right where you're sitting on this boat, a week before Maeve died, and he was in knots over the situation. I was surprised he confided in me. We weren't close, but he wanted my opinion. He wanted Arielle, but he would never divorce his wife. He was convinced Maeve would take half the fortune. He was losing his mind over what to do. He said he didn't think he could let her go. Arielle bewitched him."

"Wow. Did you think the timing of Maeve's death was...*convenient* in light of your brother's dilemma?" asked Greta.

Carl covered his face with his hand. Good Lord, had she no shame?

"Many people thought so," Robin said. "I'm sure Merlin wouldn't have been capable of harming Maeve or having her harmed. I do truly think it was an accident. The police found out Maeve drank a cocktail in the late afternoon and two glasses of wine at dinner that night before she started her drive home."

"That's really sad." Greta shook her head. "But it's good I suppose Merlin wasn't alone for long. Were you surprised when Arielle and Merlin got together so quickly after the death?"

"They were crazy about each other, and he wanted children badly. Maeve didn't want them, or couldn't have them. That was never clear to me. Anyway, this was his chance."

"Was the marriage between Arielle and Merlin a happy one as far as you could tell?"

"At first, and you'd think it would be. They were in their honeymoon period—not married three months. Tension started between the two. Merlin kept her in the dark on the details of his finances. I didn't know the details either. My guess? She is about to become a rich woman. We'll find out tomorrow, when my sister, Arielle, and I meet with the lawyer to hear the details of the will. My brother and I weren't on the best terms. It will be a shame to see our father's entire fortune leave the family if that's what happens."

"Why weren't you on good terms with your brother?" Greta asked.

"Greta, stop," Carl said.

"It's alright. At the end of the day, I've found money soils everything," said Robin. "Even what should be the purest things." He turned away and wiped at his eyes with a handkerchief.

"I don't know what has gotten into you, Greta," Carl whispered. "Asking this poor man all these questions, and he just lost his brother in a tragedy."

"Not to worry." Robin turned back and gave a sharp laugh. "Everybody's interested in everybody else's business in Glamis. Your wife is already acting like a local. So, what do you do for a living, Carl?"

"I'm retired."

"Oh, Carl, the Castle up there!" Greta squeezed Carl's arm as The Glenmore-Pace Mansion perched on the cliff above came into view. "It's glorious. Like a fairy tale. Now, Robin, tell us every little thing you know about it."

"Ernest G. Glenmore, my great-great grandfather, built Glenhurst Castle, as he named it. It was completed before the Opera House, in about 1870. That was an era before income and estate taxes in the US. If you had money, you could *really* build yourself a showplace. Ernest made his fortune with the Glenmore Stationary Manufacturing Company, which supplied traveling inkwells to the Union Army during the Civil War. When it was first built it had river vistas spanning close to a mile. A journalist back in that day described Glenhurst as 'a castle phantasia with a view worthy of the gods'.

"Even immense family fortunes dwindle over time," Robin continued. "The Castle fell out of Glenmore hands during The Great Depression when Oswald Pace, the Broadway musical composer, purchased it for his summer residence. Maybe you haven't heard of Pace. His musicals are out of style today, but he was a big deal once. Movie stars, novelists, and playwrights visited Oswald and his wife Violette in Glamis during their reign.

"After they passed, Oswald's son inherited the property, but he couldn't maintain it. It fell into disrepair and that's when my sister Jade was able to purchase it for a museum with private donations and state grants. We'll see what becomes of it now. It would really be a tragedy to see it close as a museum. I believe it will make it though. My sister would do anything to keep the doors open."

CHAPTER TWENTY-SIX

Monday, April 3rd - 10:00 p.m.

Satisfied Greta's gentle snores were genuine, Carl crept downstairs to his office and locked the door behind him. He checked his phone. Two text messages. One from Sarah asking if she could join him on his run tomorrow morning before work, to which he replied enthusiastically yes, and the other from Sal Marotta, which gave him a different feeling in the pit of his stomach. The text from Sal read:

> *EXTREMELY DISAPPOINTED YOU DIDN'T MAKE IT TO SUNDAY BRUNCH. This is your ONE get-out-of-jail-free card. I CAN'T have the kids thinking attendance is optional for them too. FAMILY IS THE CORNERSTONE OF LIFE. Want to get lunch together tomorrow or a drink at Thane's to make it up to me LOL? Your Bestie, SAL*

"This man," Carl turned the phone face down.

He opened the package he had picked up that evening at the police station, while he was out supposedly running errands. He began to read the photocopied pages.

Glamis Police Dept. Status Report

Re: Evidence Relating to The Death of Merlin Glenmore

Description: Photocopy of documents found in file labeled "Arielle" inside desk at 7 Main Street, Apt. B, Glamis, residence of Merlin and Arielle Glenmore.

Note on Evidentiary Document A: The following is NOT an historic document. Arielle Glenmore informed us it is a letter, handwritten by Merlin Glenmore as if he were Ernest Glenmore. She initially found this note on her desk at The Glenmore-Pace Castle last September. -OFC Andrew Keane

5 July 1870

My Dearest Catherine,

You ask me to describe to you the spiritual work which has taken me a decade of intense study to master. That I cannot do for you in a single letter.
Come to me at Glenhurst. Stay for a week or more and see if I cannot grant your every wish.
I leave you with the gentlest of kisses on your blushing cheeks. A teasing brush of my lips on your sweet throat and atop each of your round shoulders.
And I will let you imagine how I progress from there.

Your ever devoted,

Uncle EGG

> Notes on Evidentiary Document B: The following is also NOT an historic document. It is a fictional reply handwritten by Arielle Glenmore as Catherine Rogers. According to Mrs. Glenmore, she gave this note to Merlin Glenmore in person in September.
> -OFC Andrew Keane

6th of July 1870

Dearest EGG,

Since your last letter I haven't stopped imagining the progress of which you spoke.
I will arrive at Glenhurst Castle by nightfall tomorrow and anxiously await the hour when I can put myself and all my greedy wishes into your hands.

Yours Now, Tomorrow, Eternally,

Catherine

Carl picked up the last document from the package. It contained information of a different sort. These records related to Merlin Glenmore's finances. Carl winced as he looked over the numbers. Before his inheritance came through, Merlin was deeply in debt. In the fall, his bank account dwindled further under the weight of home mortgage payments beyond his means, combined with monthly payments for two luxury vehicles, eight hundred dollar a month Pilates instruction for Maeve, a membership to the Glamis Hills Country Club, and twice weekly equestrian lessons at the Glamis Riding Academy.

In December, after Maeve's death, Merlin sold the house he once shared with his first wife and moved into Arielle's apartment on Main Street. He resigned from the country club. That month, he used credit cards to buy a thirty-two-thousand-dollar engagement ring for Arielle. In January, he spent twenty thousand on a wedding and a honeymoon in Spain. As he embarked on his second marriage, he had over a hundred thousand dollars in debt. But relief was in sight.

On March 29th, his father's estate wired a deposit of nearly forty million dollars into Merlin's account. He purchased a new sports car the next day for cash from the account. The report revealed Merlin was in talks with a real estate agent in Palm Beach about making an offer on a luxury condo unit listed for approximately ten million dollars.

Carl could not find any unexplained one-time expenses or large withdrawals from August of last year onwards. There was no evidence to indicate Merlin got the money to pay for a hit man by selling valuable possessions either. The police had shown photos of Merlin to pawn shop owners in the area, but this had so far been a dead end.

Was Maeve's death in October an accident after all? Something to think on.

Back to Merlin's deadly birthday celebration. The statements from the witnesses sounded very similar, recounting the party's events. All the witnesses commented on the challenge of seeing in the dimly lit castle. No security camera footage available during the party. Only two of the guests at Merlin's party did not have alibis. One was Justin, without motive, and the other Doctor Boyd. Lewis Waterhouse wasn't in the clear. His alibi depended on his nephew's sighting of a face in the cabinet window right before the discovery of Merlin's body.

Carl examined the enclosed photographs of the body taken at the crime scene. The designer loafers on the man's pale, exposed legs. Carl pressed a finger to the center of his forehead, willing himself to understand. Why put the body in the cabinet? Why take the risk to come back and remove the dead man's pants? To make the corpse appear more pathetic? Could it be symbolic, a message or warning? *Or is there some mundane, logistical reason which motivated the killer to do this? Probably*, thought Carl, *unless we are dealing with someone who is compulsive, theatrical even, who did not feel the work looked right and returned to fix it up.*

No, this killer is clever, more careful than that. There is something critical here I am missing.

Carl slid the evidence back into the envelope, locked it inside a drawer, and shut off the desk lamp for the night.

CHAPTER TWENTY-SEVEN

Tuesday, April 4th - 6:00 a.m.

"Look, Carl," said Sarah. "Right over there!"

"I don't see. What are you pointing at? The weeds?" Carl asked.

Sarah jogged in place on the asphalt next to a tuft of yellow flowers in bloom along the wooded roadside. The snow had melted completely, and the temperatures had risen rapidly into the low 50s, warm enough to run in a tee-shirt and shorts.

"These daffodils survived the snowfall. You'll see how much fun it is to have the different seasons," Sarah went on.

Winter was one season up here Carl could do without. He was starting to wonder if Spring was too.

"Do you think you will like living here in Glamis?" Sarah asked, as they jogged down the slope of the hilly street.

"I will be honest with you, not yet," said Carl. "It has been only three days. What I enjoy most is seeing you and Rosie and Justin more. What I don't like about it...Sal Marotta hounding me non-stop. He is texting me all the time."

"You have to be direct with him," said Sarah. "Establish boundaries, as you remind *me* all the time."

"I have no problem being direct with most people. I didn't move up here to start problems with your father-in-law. Sal is so sensitive. Like a child."

"I know," Sarah said. "Maybe that's why he has such a kind heart though. Not unlike someone I know."

Carl's eyebrows shot up. "Me? I am nothing like him."

"You have to admit you both love your families and spending time with them."

"That's true, but he is not my family, not really. He annoys the you-know-what out of me. I am also annoyed with *you* right now."

"Me? Oh no! Why, Carl, tell me."

"You've led me to a taco desert! They don't have queso fresco, or the right kind of tortillas, or even habaneros at the grocery store in Glamis. You could have warned me."

She laughed elbowing Carl, "I was scared you wouldn't move up here, if you knew the truth."

"Hmm. I haven't given up. I will keep looking. You know me."

"I know you alright. Has it been three miles yet?" she asked.

Carl checked his watch, "Not quite."

"My sides hurt."

"After only two miles?" Carl asked. He used to struggle to keep up with Sarah when they ran together years ago.

"You realize I haven't run in years. Not since college. If we make this a regular thing I am going to need new shoes. I don't think these ones are designed for running."

"We can walk for a bit?"

"No. Let's keep going," Sarah said. "I'll run until I touch the ferry gates at the bottom of this hill. The way back up, I'm slowing to an easy trot."

"How are you doing?" Carl asked.

"There's a stabbing pain in my left side every time I take a breath. Or do you mean how am I doing in general?"

"With work, with being a mom, with all of it. Let's slow down the pace," said Carl.

"Sounds good to me. Rosie's a handful, but I love being her mom. It's my job that is just a lot. I know I don't work on Wall Street or anything, but the stakes are so high for our clients. Brides and grooms and their parents all have these intense emotions and dreams for their one big day. I don't want to get cynical about it, but some people look for anything to complain about to vent their anxieties. I'm working with this mother-of-the-bride who treats me like I'm her personal assistant. She texts and calls me in the evening, as late as midnight. If I don't respond within a few minutes she complains to Catia that I am being 'unresponsive'."

"Would you consider talking about it with Catia? Tell her it's important for you to unplug in the evening after a certain time to be with your family."

"I don't think she would respond well to that. You should see the way that woman works! She doesn't take a single day off, unless she's deathly ill. I don't think she'd go for me saying anything that indicates I'm not all in to making The Lavender Inn a success. Catia brags to our brides and their families we are there for them day and night. It's part of her pitch when they tour the venue. Of course, I'm the one who gets bombarded. Catia doesn't have to give out *her* personal cell phone to clients."

"I think you need to say something," said Carl. "Your mother and I can see the stress you are under. We're worried about you."

"Don't worry about me. Justin thinks I'm being overdramatic. I've stopped talking to him about it. Nobody likes a whiner. Besides, there's a lot I like about my job. My coworkers are great. I like how close The Inn is to our house. I can take Rosie there to use the pool in the summertime. The pay is decent. I don't want to disappoint anyone or stress you guys or Justin. I'll just keep plugging along."

Carl didn't think Sarah was whining, considering the way she was being treated by her clients. He didn't like that Sarah was tiptoeing around her husband and that he was being dismissive of her feelings. He decided to keep all of that to himself for now. One problem at a time.

"It is worth it to tell your boss what you are feeling about these after-hours calls. She will not want to lose you. I don't see how she could not take your feelings about this issue seriously and work with you. In the long term, you will wish you had spoken up for yourself."

"Before I burn out?"

"That is correct," said Carl.

They reached the road's end at the ferry landing. Sarah touched the gates. "Made it. Three miles?"

"We are over three miles now." Carl gave Sarah a high five.

"Just a quick rest," she said. "See The Glenmore-Pace Castle up there across the river?"

"I do. It must have an excellent view," said Carl.

"Hard to believe a murder happened there a few days ago," said Sarah.

They began to retrace their steps, walking this time, up the road's sharp incline.

"At least the police investigators have backed off Justin," Sarah continued. "We haven't heard from them since Sunday. Oh, Carl, I might have found out something significant to the case, pertaining to my boss. You know Catia and her husband, Doctor Boyd, were at Merlin's party that night. Well, the other day at the Inn, I learned from one of my co-workers that Catia's mother was the housekeeper for the Glenmore family, until she was accused of a theft by Merlin, who was a teenager at the time. Mrs. Glenmore went around town smearing her former employee's reputation. Catia's mother couldn't find a new job in Glamis. I'm sure the whole thing must have upset Catia—and it's surprising she agreed to go to the party, considering what Merlin and his mother did to her mom. But Catia couldn't have killed Merlin. She was apparently with the others the whole time Saturday night. Her husband Owen Boyd could have done it. At Catia's request? Justin doesn't think he did. He said the doctor wouldn't have left the room to commit the crime, without knowing how long he could be absent undetected. But who knows? Doctor Boyd could have taken the risk. What do you think?"

Carl found himself blinking. That was a lot of information. "Sarah, I think the solving of this case is best left in the hands of the authorities," said Carl.

"Don't be like that, Carl. Come on you must have some theory," Sarah said.

"I will tell you, the number one reason people kill is not revenge. It is for financial gain, making Doctor Boyd unlikely, in my opinion. What happened to Catia's mother happened a long time ago, so it seems doubly unlikely Catia would have asked her husband to kill Merlin now to avenge her mother."

"I get that," said Sarah. "But everyone who might benefit financially from Merlin's death couldn't have done it, at least as far as I can see. I heard the will is being read to the family today. Sal is having dinner with Jade tonight. He'll get the scoop for us. This murder is all anyone can talk about in town. My hairdresser Liza told me the local news stories have been good publicity for her, all those pictures of Arielle with her fabulous hair. The women in town are finding out she gets her blonde highlights from Liza at The Taming of the Do. I might give Arielle Blonde a try myself," Sarah flipped her ponytail.

"Careful. A truck is coming," Carl jogged onto the scrubby, roadside grass, as a gray pickup rumbled downhill towards them. Carl waved at the truck, its lights temporarily blinding him, giving them such little space Carl swung his arm in front of Sarah. The vehicle sped up and passed them heading down towards the ferry gates at the bottom of the hill.

"Stupid driver," said Carl.

"Seriously," said Sarah. "In a hurry to get to the ferry that isn't even open yet."

They resumed their walk uphill.

"Back to the important matter we were discussing: my hair," said Sarah. "I would only do it one time just to try it. Three hundred dollars a pop Liza is charging for it. Imagine Arielle has been going to her every three weeks to freshen up the color. That adds up."

Carl glanced over his shoulder. Bright headlights blazed, advancing uphill, on the wrong side of the road, now rolling up the shoulder, flying straight toward them. *Holy hell!* Carl seized Sarah's hand and yanked her across the road. The truck veered left, following them. With seconds to spare, Carl wrenched Sarah off the pavement into the brush.

"Run!" Carl shouted. They stumbled into the woods, picking their way downhill between bare saplings. There was no way the truck could follow them through the woods, but their adrenaline was coursing. Whoever this was could choose to follow them on foot. They splashed across a shallow icy stream and scrambled up a slope slick with muddy leaves, stopping only when they reached the asphalt of the empty parking lot above.

Carl prodded his smart watch, "Why is there no service in this town?"

"Was it a drunk driver, do you think?" Sarah gasped for breath.

"The driver of the truck intentionally meant to run us off the road— *twice*. I can say that with certainty. We aren't safe yet. Keep moving," said Carl.

They bolted across the lot behind a commercial building and climbed over a low wall. Their wet sneakers squished as they landed in the garden behind Doctor Boyd's office. They climbed the wall on the opposite side, using the uneven bricks for footholds, and dropped down to the parking lot of The Black Sheep bakery on the other side.

Abby Upham flung open her van door. "Are you two alright?"

"No," Sarah panted. "Someone in a truck tried to run us down on Ferry Road."

"Dear God, let's get you both safe inside," said Abby.

"We need to use your phone please," said Carl. "We need to call the police."

CHAPTER TWENTY-EIGHT

Tuesday, April 4th - 6:00 p.m.

"Enough's enough, Jade. I waited all through dinner for you to bring a certain topic up, and now dessert is on the way. Are you going to tell me what happened or not...?" Sal leaned toward Jade in the carved wooden booth inside Measure Pho Measure, Glamis' Vietnamese restaurant. Oversized woven pendant lights gave a warm glow to the space made moody by dark purple walls hung with gold framed mirrors. Sal picked the place because it was the second most romantic restaurant in town. Dolce Far Niente of course being number one.

"The attorney adopted a new cockatoo from the animal rescue," said Jade. "She was flapping around his office all through the reading of the will. He kept trying to get the bird to perch on his shoulder, but she kept biting his ear. By the look on your face, you're impatient to know the contents of Merlin's will. Is that it?"

"By the look on *your* face, you have some good news?" Sal asked.

"My brother executed a new will in March. Robin and I will inherit three million each. Much more than I expected. The rest, about thirty-two million, goes to Arielle, after Merlin's debts are paid."

"Okay for me to say congratulations?" asked Sal.

"I could live comfortably on what I will inherit, but my priority is funding for The Castle. This will get the museum on steadier ground, especially if Arielle also contributes."

"It doesn't surprise me you would put The Castle before yourself. How about Robin? Is he pleased?"

"None of us are 'pleased', per se," said Jade. "We're in shock; we're frightened; we're grieving in our different ways."

"Understandable," said Sal.

"In answer to your question, the money does come at the perfect time for Robin and Paul, and for me. I have to tell you this! Merlin left Hotspur to Paul."

"Ha! Well, good for him. I won't mind having that beautiful sports car parked in front of Dolce on a regular basis either. I'm curious, how did Arielle react when she found out she was getting the bulk of the fortune?" Sal asked.

"She just looked melancholy," said Jade. "She made a point to say Robin, Paul, and I are her family in her eyes. You absolutely cannot repeat this, Sal. She feels a portion of her share ought to go to The Castle to preserve The Glenmore family legacy. She begged us not to say a word about it to anyone yet. The lawyer did too. Please keep it to yourself. I pray she won't change her mind. Lewis will have the last laugh. His enemy vanquished and Merlin's greatest fear coming true—a chunk of his unenjoyed inheritance going to The Pile," she knocked on the table. "Lewis is seeing someone."

"Oh?" Sal perked up. "Not you, I hope!"

"Don't be silly. Not me, no. On Sunday, I popped over to his house just after you left. I went to thank him for helping me. There was an attractive woman about my age there with him. You know everything that goes on in Glamis. Is Lewis dating someone?"

"I haven't the faintest idea," said Sal. "Sounds like he could be."

"God, Sal, I hope it wasn't him," said Jade.

"You mean who...?"

"His alibi isn't airtight. Not to my mind. He could have, right before the séance...And there's one more thing."

"Tell me."

"Remember when I led the police into the Armory to show them where the plug bayonet is usually displayed, and we noticed wet splotches on the carpet? It was water, Detective Bell said. Thankfully, it wasn't from a leak in the ceiling. I've been thinking. It could have been melted snow from someone's shoes."

"Meaning whoever stole the weapon had just come in from outside?" asked Sal.

"And that leads me to Lewis," said Jade. "He has a stronger motive than Owen Boyd. I don't want to believe it but…"

"Jade, you and I have known him our whole lives," said Sal. "I really don't think so. And this comes from someone who regards Lewis as his chief rival." He reached out to touch her hand resting on the table.

Why had she accepted this invitation? Clearly Sal thought they were on a date. She couldn't tell him without giving a major blow to his ego that there was no rival for Lewis. It had always been Lewis and only Lewis. But he had told her once, twenty years ago it had to be now, that he would never date her. He hadn't explained why. Jade assumed it was because he saw her only as a friend. He might have broken her heart, but she didn't think he was the killing kind.

"It's out of the question. Not Lewis. You're right," Jade withdrew her hand into her lap and straightened her posture. "And besides he has Scott to think of."

Sal gave a loud sigh. "Are you going back to work at the museum soon, or taking the week off?"

"I am going there tomorrow actually."

"Want a friend to come along with you? It might be hard going back for the first time?"

had been four missed calls—all from the same person. Someone Arielle didn't want to talk to.

Dominic drove up High Dunsinane Road and took a left onto Main Street. Arielle lived a block past Dolce Far Niente. He parked in front of the wooden staircase leading to her apartment. He got out and opened the door for her. He stood tense, not looking at her. She desperately wanted to get inside and be alone.

"Thank you for watching out for me," she said.

"I'll be here all night. Officer Timmons takes over after my shift. You have my number if you need anything."

"Are they any closer to finding who did it? Can you say?" Arielle asked.

"Our team is working to find answers. That's all I can tell you for now, Mrs. Glenmore."

"You can't tell me anything really," she said. "That's okay, Dom. You don't know how comforting it is for me just to know you are here."

She said goodnight and climbed the stairs to her second-floor apartment. Letting herself in, she flipped on the light switch, illuminating the kitchen. She deadbolted the front door and set her vibrating purse on the countertop of the granite island. When Merlin shared it with her, the apartment felt like home, despite its lack of personality. But now it felt like she didn't belong here. She couldn't stand the lost sensation of being somewhere that felt as though it was already in her past, though she hadn't moved on from it yet. She felt like a ghost walking through it.

When she accepted the job at The Castle last April, this was the only one bedroom in the town of Glamis she could afford to rent. Right before she moved in, the owner updated the space in the most impersonal way Arielle could imagine: beige walls and white trim, faux wood floors in the kitchen and living room, cheap office carpet in the bedroom, bathroom, and walk-in closet. Inoffensive, she supposed, by being to no one's taste specifically.

She had done her best to charm up the four bland rooms and make them more inviting. Without going to much expense, she filled the apartment with vibrant green plants and hung bold museum prints she purchased from a Salvation Army nearby. Merlin surprised her when he wanted to move into her apartment instead of getting a new place. He explained it was temporary. They would move somewhere much grander with ample bedrooms for their future children soon.

He insisted on installing the modern furniture he kept from the house he once shared with Maeve: a coal gray womb chair Arielle despised and a clear acrylic dining table and chairs which cluttered the living room. She might offer the pieces to Robin and Paul. They wouldn't do for Jade's cottage.

Arielle opened the coat closet across from the kitchen. Merlin's shirts hung there, every piece bespoke and costly. She touched the starched cuff of a white oxford. She remembered the feeling of his possessive arms around her.

She slipped off her heels, and walked into the sparse bedroom. She went to the dresser and picked up the glass bottle of Merlin's cologne. She sprayed her wrist and closed her eyes. She found him in the sandalwood scent, for what seemed like the hundredth time since she came home that awful night, dazed and bewildered by her sorrow. Still in her dress, she climbed in on Merlin's side of the unmade bed, pulling the white duvet over her head. There was no comfort to be found in Merlin's memory. Not when she could hear the buzz of the phone in the kitchen. She could only hide for so long. *If he wants to see me now, nothing will stop him, not a cop parked downstairs. He'll find a way.*

A rap to her left shocked her upright. He must be at the bedroom's sliding door. He must have climbed the fire escape and onto her balcony which faced the back of the building, the side Dom couldn't see from his patrol car on Main Street.

Arielle held her breath to better listen, hoping she had imagined the sound. Then, he called her name.

She pushed the curtains aside and found him standing there. "Open up," came the voice muffled by the glass. More afraid to defy him than not, she unlocked the door, slid it open, letting the cold air inside.

He gripped Arielle by her shoulders. "Did you think I wouldn't find a way to see you tonight?"

CHAPTER THIRTY

Wednesday, April 5th - 1:00 p.m.

In the park, Catia Boyd lingered on the ornamental bridge over the pond, feeding bits of croissant to a pair of ducks.

"Good afternoon," said Carl.

Catia looked up in surprise. "Good afternoon."

"Catia Boyd?"

"That's me," she said. "And you are?"

"I'm Sarah Marotta's stepfather, Carl Sarabia. My wife and I moved here from Houston last Saturday."

"Oh, what a pleasure," Catia smiled. "I heard from Sarah you were moving here, and that you are a retired homicide detective? Though I am skeptical about the retired bit." Catia tossed another corner of pastry to the circling ducks. "You look like a blood hound tracking a scent! I hope your nose didn't lead you to me. You were in the police force in Houston, is that right?"

"I served for thirty-two years in the Houston Police Department, ten years of which I headed up the Homicide Division," said Carl. "Most people who haven't been in law enforcement can't imagine what it demands of you—everything, in every arena of your life, at all hours of the day and night. I am grateful to be entering this quieter chapter of my life. Sarah tells me you are a hardworking person yourself. You hardly ever take a day off. Are you giving yourself a break?"

"Just for lunch. I'm meeting someone. When I can nab a moment for myself, I like to come here and feed the ducks. Think about nothing for a minute. I'm bringing a sandwich to Arielle Glenmore at 1:30. She is the one whose husband was horribly killed this past weekend."

Dominic had mentioned to Carl he had heard through the Glamis grapevine—no doubt from Sal—that Catia's husband Owen had eyes for Arielle Glenmore at Merlin's party. Carl decided to make his conversation with Catia slightly unpleasant to see if there was any truth in it.

"Oh? The same woman your husband, the doctor, is so infatuated with?"

Catia's brows drew together in shock. "That's so stupid. A complete lie. You must have misunderstood whoever... English isn't your first language, is it? Whatever you heard, I think you got confused."

"No, my English is just fine, Mrs. Boyd. I heard your mother worked as a housekeeper for the Glenmores. It did not end well."

"Who is the outrageous gossip you've been speaking to? It better not be Sarah. You're bringing up ancient history. I've moved past all that."

Carl relaxed his forearms on the stone railing, leaning out over the rippling water where he could see his own reflection. He didn't like that Sarah had involved herself in this murder investigation by sharing details about Catia's mother, but now that he knew the information, he couldn't disregard it, especially considering someone had tried to kill them. He needed to find this killer and quickly. He had meant it when he told Sarah that it seemed unlikely Catia would murder Merlin for revenge, especially decades after his lie hurt her mother. But unlikely didn't mean impossible.

"My father was a police inspector in Mexico City," said Carl. "The best man on the force. His colleagues admired him. One day a man younger than my father came in to head the department. This new boss accused him, ironically, of taking bribes, and fired him. My father was never the same. Many years later, I left my own work in the crime lab in Mexico City and moved to Houston. It became my new home. I became a police officer and eventually was hired by the HPD. I find myself a bit homesick. I miss my friends, the food, running at my favorite park, and especially my two sisters. Perhaps it was a mistake to leave."

Catia raised her chin, looking up at the white cloud strewn sky through the budding trees. "Mrs. Glenmore believing her son Merlin's word over my mother's was wrong. It hurt for a long time what happened to us. Your theory would be that Owen helped me do it? Helped me kill him?" Catia glanced over at Carl. "Laughable. Do you think a man who doesn't hold the door for his wife anymore, would commit murder for her?"

"You can take care of things for yourself," said Carl.

"I didn't kill him. What I did was move on and heal myself. You must know as well I the best form of revenge is success. The Inn is becoming profitable. I've created something beautiful. I have humbled the community that once turned its back on me and my mother, and earned its respect and even its admiration. That's all the revenge I need.

"No," she continued. "It is not shocking someone disliked Merlin more than I did and acted on it. This may surprise you: I would rather he hadn't been killed. I would have savored witnessing his downfall."

"I don't follow," said Carl. "He just inherited a fortune. He was happily remarried."

"Merlin wanted loads of children—his idea of living forever. I was having drinks with Arielle about two weeks ago. We've been friends since last summer. She told me she was scared to tell Merlin how she really felt. She pretended she wanted children too. Let's just say she had something in place to prevent it from happening. Merlin started pushing her to see a doctor last month. He didn't want to waste another second. She wriggled her way out of the appointment with some last-minute excuse. Merlin died believing he was on the cusp of a better life, when he was really on the cusp of marital catastrophe. Arielle knew she would be forced to tell him the truth soon. You can imagine the calamity from there. He wasn't the type to handle disappointment well. It would have been a scene to behold. I hope my disappointment at this tragic outcome becomes clearer to you. I wish you luck, Lieutenant...I mean for your continued retirement."

***

Back at his desk later that afternoon, Carl scrolled through The Glenmore-Pace Castle Archives of the museum's website. He clicked on a file titled 1870-71 diary entries of Celestin Mabille. Carl read in the introductory description Mabille was the personal valet to Ernest Glenmore. Arielle Glenmore translated his writing from the original French last year. A note prefacing the diary explained the entries from the valet described events at The Castle following the arrival of Mr. Glenmore's widowed niece, Catherine Rogers of Boston. Arielle noted: M. was an abbreviation for "Monsieur", which Celestin Mabille used to refer to his employer Ernest Glenmore. Carl soon got lost in the diary's tale.

7 July 1870

M. in a merry mood all day. His newly widowed niece Mme. Rogers arrived at Glenhurst accompanied by her maid before nightfall. M. lifted Mme. into the air and kissed her cheeks.

"I'm so happy," I heard Mme. say. "Everyone is dead now. We can do as we please."

M. Glenmore and Mme. Rogers took themselves away to M.'s private study upstairs. They had much to discuss, for they did not come down for hours and dined late.

8 July 1870

Rain showers could not dampen M.'s spirits this morning. M. and Mme. Rogers breakfasted at nine and spent the rest of the day in M.'s study. He ordered us not to disturb them.

At dinner, Mme. Rogers surprised in a pale blue gown with silver ribbons. Unusual attire for a lady in mourning. No other guests were present besides

M. and Mme. They sat side by side, eating from each other's plates, drinking from each other's cups.

9 July 1870
Mme. Rogers intended to leave tomorrow, until a fervent scene unfolded tonight between her and M. "Why should I care what anyone thinks?" I heard M. shout. She will extend her visit with us at M.'s insistence. He is most devoted to Mme.

15 July 1870
This afternoon, I found M. and Mme. Rogers asleep in The Conservatory, their arms about one another. I shut the door and kept watch outside the room for a full two hours to make sure no one saw the sight I had come upon. Is M. unafraid of scandal?

Fortunately, our housekeeper Glancy is a complete naïf. She told me the maid has found Mme. Rogers's bed unslept in every morning this week. It took all my strength not to laugh outright when Glancy asked if I thought Mme. Rogers might be suffering from the heat abed and sleeping instead on the divan without a blanket. Mme. Rogers works so late into the night in M.'s study too, Mme. Glancy remarked with concern.

Does she not know the secret of M.'s study cabinet? I will not be the one to tell her, tempted as I am!

3 August 1870

M. told me today in the strictest confidence he asked Mme. Rogers to marry him, and she accepted. They will have to receive special permission to wed. M. is friendly with Bishop Crawford, who will help arrange it. The ceremony will take place soon and privately.

I receive this news with great personal relief.

15 August 1870

M. and Mme. Rogers are wed. Father Lambert married them in The Oratory this evening with myself, Mme. Glancy, and Mme. Rogers's maid Mlle. Barton, as witnesses to the ceremony.

While we cannot yet know how the village will receive the news, the burden of their secret has been lifted from the household staff.

28 September 1870

M. told me today Mme. Glenmore will have a child. M. is most determined for every comfort to be Mme.'s as they await the arrival of their firstborn.

The chamber in the southwest tower will be remade into a nursery and preparations begin immediately under Mme.'s close direction. I am told the chamber must be completed in January as the infant will be born this winter and could arrive as soon as February! How Mme. Glancy's illusions must be shattered.

19 February 1871

Born today a son to M. and Mme. named Ernest Joseph Glenmore. The infant is in good health. The doctor expects Mme. to regain her strength in time. M. asked me in the strictest confidence to secret away a jar of blood of Mme.'s—I know not how he obtained it. Sickened, but trying not to think of what the vessel contained, I removed it to the vaults, where M. and Mme. hide their other objects. We three are the only ones who know the place. I could not deny M. in his frantic state. He is desperate to see Mme. improve. I fear he will return to demon magic if he believes it can restore her.

21 February 1871

Three days have passed since the child's birth, and Mme. has weakened pitiably. M. does not leave her. The doctor instructed me to send for Father Lambert.

23 February 1871

We are grief stricken by Mme.'s death. M. locked himself inside his chamber with her and refuses to answer anyone. The doctor tells me it is best to leave M. undisturbed until tomorrow morning, when we shall break down the door if necessary.

26 February 1871

M. rang for me in the early hours. He asked me to bring from the vaults the jar I hid there. He believes it will allow him to communicate with Mme. when used with his sorcerer's mirror.

It is as I feared. Forgotten is his promise of a year ago.

I do not wish to leave him in his hour of sorrow, but I am frightened by that which he invites into this place in his desperation.

M. told me Mme. will be entombed inside a mausoleum to be constructed west of The Prior's Garden. M. Black, the architect from New York, arrives tomorrow.

I visited the infant Ernest in the nursery today. He is in robust health, and in the hands of a skilled nurse found by Mme. Glancy. God protect the child's soul. The father's, I fear, is past saving.

1 March 1871

M. showed me a black obsidian disc in his study. He tells me it is an ancient mirror, a devil's looking glass, with which he communicates with Mme. Glenmore any time he wishes. "The price is terrible, Mabille," he said, "Yet for her I will continue to pay, even as they demand greater portions of my soul."

I reminded him of his promise.

He insists it is only with the aid of the mirror and its spirit magic that he may reach Mme. Glenmore through the veil. She visits him and sleeps by M.'s side whenever he wishes it. He hopes he might one day begin to feel her touch.

I hope Mme. does not try to touch or come anywhere near me!

I am in constant fear. Every sound startles me and sets my heart racing.

M.'s monstrous rites violate the laws of God. He calls them 'spirits' but I know he seeks the aid of a host of demons to keep contact with Mme.

He summons them at night by name.

10 March 1871

Enough! M. has invited a court of demons upon this place. We hear running feet in empty passages, the clock in the hall groaned and fell, windows unlatch themselves and fly open. Ghastly faces peer out from shrouded mirrors.

I write this at the gates of Glenhurst as I await the carriage. I pray for M.'s soul, but I will never again step foot inside his accursed dwelling. Mme. Glancy returning from a trip to town came across me in my waiting place and bid me a hearty goodbye. All blushes she asked, on impulse I believe, if she might put a delicate question to me. She thought I might be the only one who could answer. How, she wondered, did M. and Mme. conduct their liaison in such secrecy last July when, she surmised, the child was conceived. I laughed at her audacity to ask such a question upon my departure.

"Madame Glancy," I replied, "Have you worked all this while at Glenhurst and never known the cabinet in Monsieur's study has a false back which connects to Monsieur's bedchamber?"

Carl grabbed his phone and dialed Detective Bell.

"Bell, can you get me inside the Castle tomorrow morning? I have reason to believe the cabinet in the upstairs study opens on to the bedroom next door. This changes everything."

CHAPTER THIRTY-ONE

Thursday, April 6th - 10:00 a.m.

"Welcome to the Glenmore-Pace Castle," Scott stood in front of the steps leading to the entrance. He led Carl back a few paces away from the Castle to get a better view of the façade. "The exterior is stucco in wedding cake white. Note the quatrefoil windows, crenelations, battlements. We have two round towers, walled gardens, and a family mausoleum on site. To the north is The Prior's Garden, with a coiled stone labyrinth and a fountain of frolicking gargoyles, which will not be turned on until May. To the south, is St. Catherine's Garden, which I am told bursts with roses in June and dahlias in all shapes and colors in September. Carved screens inspired by those found in medieval abbeys bookend both gardens."

Arielle would be proud of how smooth his tours had gotten. Scott shoved the thought away. He was sick of obsessing over her all the time. The thought of her used to give him a rush, but not anymore. He felt totally unloved at this point. She couldn't be into him. He hadn't heard a word from her since the murder. If she cared, now that she was free from Merlin, she would have called, texted back, something. No, she didn't care. He wouldn't think about the pain of that.

"Any questions so far?" Scott asked.

"I'll have some for you," said Carl. "I'm most eager to see the room where the body was found."

"Of course," said Scott, leading him inside.

"You must be Lieutenant Sarabia," Jade greeted them inside the entry hall. She reached out for a handshake. "I'm happy to walk you through the museum and answer any questions you might have."

"I am so sorry for the loss of your brother, Ms. Glenmore," said Carl. "Thank you for accommodating me in your schedule today."

"Rest assured, no one wants to see my brother's killer apprehended sooner than I."

"The guests entered through these doors the night of the birthday party, correct?" Carl asked.

"That's right."

"The front doors remained unlocked all night?"

"They did," said Jade. "Unlocked doors, no power, security cameras off. Stupidity all round. It's my fault."

"You couldn't have known what would happen," Scott said. "Unless *you* are the murderer. She's not the murderer."

"Aren't you supposed to be drafting the email blast about the reopening?" said Jade.

"Not when there is a famous detective here who might need my help," Scott winked at Carl.

Carl hoped the kid was joking. He worried the more people who knew he was here at the Castle, working with the police, the more likely it was Greta would find out. He had to take the risk. He had to see where Merlin died. Photos, descriptions, and videos weren't enough. He had to walk the crime scene in person whatever his concerns about getting busted by his wife.

"I'd like to start upstairs in the room in which the body was found," said Carl.

"Right this way," said Jade.

Carl followed her and Scott to the grand staircase.

"The Glenmore-Pace Castle is all about contrasts," Scott launched back into the tour thinking it might be helpful to fill the silence with some information. "Rooms of light and rooms of shadow. All for dramatic effect, to make you feel differently depending on which room you are in. For example, this hall is the brightest in The Castle, but notice—"

"The Lieutenant is not here for an architectural tour, Scott." Jade put her foot on the first step and paused, holding tight to the banister. "I'm sorry. I haven't been to the second floor since the night of the tragedy. I'm freezing up."

"I can show him, Boss," Scott touched her shoulder.

"If that's alright?" Jade asked Carl.

"Perfectly fine," he said. "We can visit more after I have taken a look upstairs."

"Thank you," said Jade. "I'll be in the staff room. I don't know what's come over me."

"Considering the recent trauma you experienced, your reaction is perfectly understandable," Carl assured her.

"Lieutenant, I do have a question for *you*," Jade said. "Is there a date we could settle on to have the museum reopen to the public?"

"I'm afraid that is not something I can answer. It would be for Detective Bell to advise."

"I'll try him now from the office."

Scott led Carl upstairs past the knight's armor to the second-floor landing. "I would like to start in Ernest Glenmore's bedroom," said Carl. That must have been how Merlin entered the cabinet that night. They stepped inside the opulent bedroom. Carl's eyes fell on the spot in front of the fireplace where a piece of the wooden floor had been cut away.

He was stabbed here, Carl thought. *In this fireplace, investigators found remnants of burnt cloth fibers and metal buttons, no not buttons, snaps. Someone at-*

tempted to burn a pair of gloves, likely the killer, after the murder.

"Maybe you've pieced together how it happened. I sure haven't been able to," said Scott. "Merlin's in the bedroom standing here, let's say. Someone comes in. Stabs him. When does the killer place his body inside the cabinet? How without being seen?"

"The sequence of events remains unclear to me," said Carl. "What we know is Merlin leaves Justin Marotta and Doctor Boyd downstairs in the Conservatory. He tells them he is going upstairs to pull an April Fool's prank on the others. He gives none of the prank details away to either man. He goes upstairs and stands here in this bedroom. Is he waiting? For what? For whom?" Carl wondered if this opening might prompt Scott to reveal something he shouldn't.

"Is he looking for a signal from someone in the Study?" asked Scott. "I remember we heard a knocking sound a couple minutes before we found his body."

"You're suggesting this might have been a cue for Merlin that it was time for the prank? That would indicate a collaborator sitting at the table next door."

"Right," said Scott. "I couldn't say which one of us was doing the knocking though."

"Returning to the victim," said Carl. "We know Merlin is stabbed near the fireplace in this position. He doesn't drag himself inside the cabinet." Carl felt certain of that, considering there was no blood trail between here and the cabinet. He decided to see what Scott might say on the subject. "At least I can't see why he would do that, unless...You, Scott, saw the face in the cabinet window. Think back to what you saw. Could it have been Merlin looking for help?"

"I couldn't say who it was. It was dark. I only saw a moving head shape for a second."

"Let us assume Merlin's body is placed inside the cabinet by the killer. Why the killer does this, no, we cannot say why yet." Carl continued. "You call out that you see a face. Zip goes over to the cabinet, opens the doors to discover Merlin stabbed inside. Why did the killer take the trouble to put the victim inside the cabinet? Here, the corpse will be quickly found, giving the killer less time to escape."

"So why?" Scott asked.

"I don't have the answer yet."

Scott pointed to the words engraved over the fireplace. "*Nil Admirari*. The Glenmore family motto. It translates to 'Let Nothing Astonish You'."

Carl approached the bookcase. "I will never stop being astonished by the ingenious variety of ways Evil expresses itself." Carl reached under a shelf holding a set of black leatherbound books on the occult. He found a lever and pulled. The bookshelf eased into the bedroom, opening like a door.

"A secret passage between the study and the bedroom!" Scott exclaimed.

"It would allow Ernest Glenmore to move between his study and his bedroom unobserved by servants or guests."

"But why?" Scott asked.

"I think it was designed with amorous purposes in mind. You had no idea about this false back to the cabinet? Would Jade know about this?"

"I don't think so. I mean you'd have to ask her. I'm sure she would have told the police if she knew."

Carl stepped inside the cabinet, examining the walls, ceiling, and floor with his flashlight. He looked through the leaded glass window on the left-hand door. A chill crept up the back of his neck at the sight of the dark octagonal room with a mirrored table surrounded by oddly shaped black chairs.

He imagined Merlin peering out about to play his prank on everyone, seeing Scott, drunk and flirting with his wife all night. He imagined the annoyance, no, the hatred he would feel for the young man aglow with hope and excitement. A man suspected of killing his first wife could easily also be a man who would hate his nephew, especially one he was related to by marriage only and who had designs on his current wife.

Merlin wanted to continue the name of Glenmore in his own way and make it better in the next generation, only to be frustrated there as well, despite the beautiful wife he married the second time around. A woman who felt kinship with The Castle, who tried to bring Merlin under its spell, but could not succeed. He refused to bankroll the enormous, continuous expense to keep this place alive with his newly gained inheritance. Yet, in the letter Merlin wrote to Arielle as Ernest Glenmore, he took his ancestor's voice for his seduction. Here in The Castle, he proposed marriage, in the place he hated.

Merlin must have felt so close to achieving his dreams. Guarded as he was, he believed the fortune could bring him and Arielle happiness. And his new wife? What kind of a heart did she possess?

Let Nothing Astonish You.

A shadow fell across Carl.

"Lieutenant."

Carl tensed. Scott stood over him.

"You need to see this."

Carl grasped the cabinet's sides and backed himself out into the bedroom.

Scott pointed at the gentleman mannequin. "Ernest is missing his gloves!"

"He always wore gloves?" Carl examined the mannequin with intense interest.

"Always," said Scott.

Carl looked the figure up and down and inhaled sharply, "You have seen what everyone has missed."

"I got it! The killer must have taken the gloves," said Scott. "The killer burned Ernest's gloves in the fireplace!"

"No, no, no. The killer desperately needed Ernest's gloves and never would have burned them, no. You pointed out to me what you yourself don't see."

"Lieutenant, tell me! What am I missing?"

"Intentionally or not, you have uncovered a very significant fact."

"Did I help you figure out who did it?"

"No, not yet. But I see how it happened. To prove who will require a careful trap."

The question burst from Scott, "Why was Merlin missing his pants? They were on him when we first found his body. The killer must have come back and taken them off him. But why bother? What did the killer do with them?"

"Nothing at all," said Carl.

He motioned with a patient gesture. Scott's mouth fell open.

CHAPTER THIRTY-TWO

Thursday, April 6th - 5:30 p.m.

Returning home from his walkthrough at The Glenmore-Pace Castle, Carl found the house empty. He went to his office to type up a report on the new findings he gathered from his visit to the crime scene. As he booted up the computer, Greta's tablet pinged at his elbow. He opened the cover and tapped the screen—a message from Sarah:

> Did you find a Carl-proof hiding place?

Carl typed in Greta's passcode and opened the messages. He read Greta's reply:

> Yes. He will never look in back of *little spoons*
> ;)

What on earth were Greta and Sarah up to? Carl spun around in his office chair and made for the kitchen. He pulled open a drawer to the right of the sink, where Greta's collection of tiny spoons sparkled. She loved using them when eating ice cream or yogurt.

He lifted the cutlery holder and looked underneath. Nothing there.

Little spoons? Where had he seen those words before?

He snapped his fingers remembering from yesterday when they had unpacked a box of books. Greta had insisted on piling several on her nightstand, despite Carl urging her she should keep them in the built-in bookshelves where they belonged and reduce clutter. Greta had ignored the suggestion and placed three books beside the bed. Carl climbed the stairs. On Greta's bedside table he found the stack of books, one titled *little spoons,* a gift from Sarah for Mother's Day. He remembered now. Folded in the back, Carl found pages of lined notebook paper covered in his wife's graceful cursive. Notes from her new investigation. It seemed neither of them was that good at being retired.

Greta returned home from her walk thirty minutes later with a baguette, an array of vegetables, and a rotisserie chicken. Carl sat at the kitchen counter, flipping through the pages of a glossy photo book.

"What's that you're reading?" Greta set down the groceries.

"*little spoons* this book is called."

Uh oh. Hoping this was a coincidence while figuring she had been caught, Greta said, "Let me see!" Greta slid the book away from Carl. "So cute. Yes, I remember. This was a gift from Sarah for Mother's Day. You know how I love my tiny spoons."

"Yes, I do. I have to say, honey, in *little spoons*, the most interesting pages," he pulled the book back towards him, "are at the back."

"Oh Lord. How did you find them?"

"I told you a million times, your tablet is connected to your phone—your texts show up on both. When it pinged, I saw a message from Sarah about hiding something from *me*. Are you surprised I became determined to discover what my wife and daughter were hiding from me?"

"On a scale of one to ten how mad are you?"

"I'm not mad," he touched her handwriting on the pages. "I have no right to be."

"You don't?"

"First of all, the work you, Sarah, Justin, and Sal have done together, it is impressive. I wish you had not done it behind my back, but I can guess why you conspired to do it this way. I know you were trying to clear Justin's name while helping me not get pulled out of retirement. But I am going to insist you and your team of sleuths stop now. It is too dangerous."

"I know. I was so scared when I heard someone tried to run you and Sarah off the road on your run yesterday."

"It was not a coincidence. The killer is aware our family is reaching for the truth. It is pretty good investigative research you have done. Now you want me to be the armchair sleuth to solve the case without lifting a finger. That was the plan?"

"Sort of, yes. I'm sorry for keeping this from you," said Greta. "I'm sorry I made you promise not to get involved. You don't feel betrayed?"

"How can I? I have my own secrets. I have been helping Detective Bell and the Glamis PD."

"You have not. *Carl!*"

"Detective Bell and Dominic Marotta called and asked for my help. They said my expertise in homicide would be a crucial asset in solving this case. I insisted my involvement would be confidential and limited. So far, it has amounted to reviewing evidence, making a few phone calls, reaching some conclusions. I have barely left the house. I did go to The Castle today. I had to see the crime scene. Most of what I have done has been from the safety of my desk chair, as you intended."

"Both of us are absolute scoundrels. It's like you say 'ducks with ducks'. Carl, I'm glad we're being honest now."

"I thought *you* would be angrier," said Carl.

"We've been hiding the truth from each other. It isn't right. On my end, we were trying to have it both ways. We were afraid that if you tried to work with the police, they would say you had a conflict of interest like Dom. You're related to Justin."

"I will tell you the police suspect neither Justin nor Sal Marotta. With my background and track record, they are thrilled to have me help them in any way I can. You amateur sleuths didn't do a bad job. You got all this from talking to the suspects casually? Pretty good. Let's review what we know from these notes. Read them aloud to me, please. I will listen and tell you if I disagree with what you observed. Everything you have done will need to be shared with Detective Bell."

"Do we really have to tell him?" Greta cringed.

"No question, absolutely," said Carl.

"I suppose you're right. Here we go:

Timeline of Events on The Evening of Saturday, April 1st

Approx. 4:00 p.m. Arielle Glenmore and Scott Waterhouse arrive at The Castle, after lunch at Dolce Far Niente. Jade arrives a few minutes later to help with the party set up.

Approx. 6:15 p.m. Robin Glenmore and his husband Paul Krebbs arrive at The Castle. Soon after, Merlin arrives.

Approx. 6:30 p.m. Power is shut off by Robin Glenmore.

Approx. 7 p.m. Zip and Rex Davis (uncle and nephew), Catia Boyd and Dr. Owen Boyd (husband and wife) arrive. Party begins. Cocktails in the Library and adjoining Music Room. Merlin catches Scott and Arielle kissing in the kitchen pantry! Scott leaves at Arielle's insistence. Arielle and Merlin seem to make up.

Approx. 7:50 p.m. Justin and Sal arrive to deliver the Dolce Far Niente catering. They are invited by Merlin and Arielle Glenmore to join the party for dinner.

Approx. 8 p.m. Dinner in the Banqueting Hall, attended by Merlin and all party guests including Sal and Justin.

Approx. 8:50 p.m. While guests are finishing dinner in the banquet hall, Lewis Waterhouse enters The Castle through the front door and goes upstairs to hide behind the curtains in Ernest's study.

Approx. 9 p.m. Arielle, Catia, Jade, Zip, Rex, Paul, Robin, and Scott go upstairs to Ernest Glenmore's Study for the séance. Merlin, Dr. Boyd, and Justin opt out of séance and go to the Conservatory.

Approx. 9:13 p.m. The time Merlin is last seen alive by Dr. Boyd and Justin. Merlin leaves the two men saying he is going upstairs to pull a prank on the others during the séance. He doesn't reveal what this prank is. To get to the second floor, we presume he uses the backstairs closest to the Conservatory.

9:15 p.m. Justin goes into the corridor outside the Conservatory to make a call to Greta about Rosie. Dr. Boyd is left alone inside Conservatory during the call; door shut.

Around the same time Lewis Waterhouse emerges from the shadows of the Study curtains, surprising the guests at the séance.

9:28 p.m. Justin's phone call ends. He returns to the Conservatory and finds Dr. Boyd sitting in the same spot as he left him in front of the chess board.

Approx. 9:30 p.m. Working back from when Justin called the police, we deduce this is about the time the guests find the body of Merlin Glenmore in the Study cabinet. Scott claimed he saw someone in the cabinet window, though he could not be sure who it was. This prompted the discovery of the body in the cabinet. Merlin was wearing pants and shoes at the time. Rex runs downstairs to get Dr. Boyd, while the others return to the Library on the first floor. Paul and Robin go down to the vaults to get the power back on.

Approx. 9:32 p.m. Rex comes into the Conservatory to request aid from Dr. Boyd. Boyd and Justin follow Rex upstairs to the Study.

Approx. 9:34 p.m. Dr. Boyd, Justin, and Rex arrive in the Study. Electricity restored. Dr. Boyd examines the body in the cabinet and re-affirms Merlin is dead. However, pants are now missing from Merlin's body!!

9:36 p.m. Justin calls the police for help, then finds the other guests in the library downstairs. Dr. Boyd, Rex, Paul, and Robin join a few minutes later. Everyone waits inside the locked room until the police arrive.

"This is good work," said Carl. "Though the approximate times may not be supported by the evidence. Let's move on to your list of clues."

Greta continued to read aloud:

Clues

Thanks to intel from someone at the Glamis PD (we won't name names...), we know the murder weapon was taken from The Castle's Armory between 6:30 p.m. (when the power and cameras go off) and 9:30 pm (when the body is discovered).

The carpet in The Armory was noticeably wet with splotches of water when the police, Jade, and Sal went in to see if the plug bayonet was missing from the display cabinet.

Scott Waterhouse saw a face in the cabinet right before the body was discovered. Was it Merlin? The Killer? Or...?

Metal snaps were found in the fireplace with charred fabric.

Blood was found near the fireplace but no sign of drag marks, indicating Merlin was stabbed in the bedroom and carried into the cabinet. How did his body get inside the cabinet without the party guests seeing this take place?

How and why did the pants disappear off Merlin between the initial discovery of his body and Dr. Boyd's examination minutes later?

Important Information Learned During Our Conversations with Witnesses:

- Scott and Arielle kissed for the first time the night of the party during the cocktail hour. They were caught together in the pantry by Merlin. Nasty, but non-physical confrontation. Motive for Scott?

- Lewis Waterhouse was Merlin's first wife, Maeve's brother. Lewis believed her death was not accidental, and Merlin was behind it. He is still embittered. Big motive for revenge. Given Scott's infatuation with Arielle, Scott had a motive to help Lewis get revenge, thereby freeing Arielle.

- Despite their sultry dance together that night, Rex said he likes men and is not romantically interested in Arielle. Maybe his Uncle Zip was interested in her at one point? Zip asked her out last August according to Rex. She turned him down. Did an infatuation linger for the lonely

Texan?

- Catia Boyd's mother Inez was a housekeeper for The Glenmore Family when Merlin was a teenager. She was fired for theft, after Merlin lied claiming she stole his father's watch. Motive of revenge for Catia? Dr. Boyd an accomplice?

- Arielle said her great aunt on her mother's side is her only remaining relative, then contradicted herself when she mentioned 'The Cooks' *plural*. What could that mean? Does she have a living relative on her father's side?

"Not bad," said Carl. "Not enough to solve the case, however."

"What are we missing?" asked Greta.

"Let's go through the rest. Good thinking to compile this next list. This is helpful to review, especially now that I have seen—continue."

Party guests and the costumes they wore, according to Justin and Sal's recollections:
- Merlin Glenmore costumed as a Victorian-era gentleman in formal attire, including a black jacket, black pants (location unknown at present), black vest, white gloves, white high col-

lared shirt, black cravat. Merlin wore a pair of designer black suede loafers with gold horse bit hardware.

- Arielle Glenmore dressed as a Victorian woman in dark blue gown and black elbow-length gloves.

- Scott Waterhouse costumed as a knight. Full suit of soft chainmail armor, including a set of gauntlets, breastplate, backplate, greaves, armored shoes ending in points.

- Jade Glenmore dressed as Josephine Bonaparte in empire waist gown, tiara, pearl choker, and long white gloves.

- Robin Glenmore dressed as a Victorian gentleman in a green velvet suit, white gloves, and wingtip shoes.

- Paul Krebbs dressed as a Victorian gentleman in a formal black suit, white gloves, and black patent leather shoes.

- Lewis Waterhouse dressed as his fictional character Lord Talon de Fey in khaki pants tucked into tall black boots, long red velvet coat, white ruffled shirt, white gloves, goggles, and steampunk-style hat with gadgets attached.

- Rex Davis dressed as Count Dracula in cape, tuxedo, black lace-up shoes, white gloves, top hat, and fangs.

- Zip Davis dressed as The Phantom of the Opera in cape, tuxedo, black cowboy boots, and plastic Phantom mask covering half his face.

- Catia Boyd dressed as Elizabeth Taylor in leopard coat, floral turban, purple gown, elbow-length white gloves, heels.

- Dr. Owen Boyd dressed as a famous golfer in American flag-patterned pants, white collared shirt, blonde mullet wig, golf glove worn on right hand, and golf shoes.

- Justin Marotta – no costume.

- Sal Marotta – no costume.

Guests with Alibis (All in Study Together During Séance)
Sal Marotta
Arielle Glenmore
Catia Boyd
Rex Davis
Zip Davis

Robin Glenmore
Paul Krebbs
Jade Glenmore
Scott Waterhouse
Lewis Waterhouse?? (He emerged from behind curtain minutes after the others came into the Study)

No Alibis
Justin Marotta
Dr. Owen Boyd
An Unknown Person who wanted Merlin dead for reasons of revenge or has monetary or other motive?

Concluding Thoughts Based on The Foregoing

Lead Suspect: Our most likely suspect is Dr. Owen Boyd.

Evidence: The damp patches in the Armory carpet could have been from the snow on his golf shoes after he ran outside from the Conservatory exit to the front entrance.

Opportunity: There was time for Dr. Boyd to kill Merlin in the thirteen minutes Justin spent outside the room on the phone. Boyd could have used the Conservatory door leading outside, crept around to the front of the castle, letting himself in through the front doors. Justin would not have seen him. He did not have the line of sight due to the curve of the corridor.

Motive: Boyd helped his wife Catia get her long-awaited revenge on Merlin Glenmore, who ruined her mother's livelihood when he falsely accused her of theft. As Boyd entered the bedroom, Merlin would not have been on his guard against him, allowing the doctor to get close enough to attack, explaining why there was no sign of a struggle.

Initial Hypothesis: Dr. Boyd and his wife Catia, as an accomplice, are the ones most likely behind the death of Merlin Glenmore, in light of motive and opportunity. We have no idea, however, why they or anyone would want to take Merlin's pants after his body was first discovered.

"I can see you put a lot of thought and effort into this," said Carl.

"It's frustrating this piece about the vanishing pants," said Greta. "Would Doctor Boyd have been able to come back and remove them? I don't see how. Or why? Catia, his accomplice, one would imagine, could not have done it either. She was never away from the group. Did someone take the pants off Merlin who was not the killer? What do you think? Is Doctor Boyd a suspect in your mind?"

"I haven't eliminated him, but it's unlikely," said Carl. "He has a medical mind, methodical. He would not take the significant risk of Justin discovering him missing. From all I have heard of Dr. Boyd, this is not a man who would be able to work himself up to killing for revenge on another's behalf and more than three decades after the event to be avenged."

"Would you agree the killer has to be someone Merlin knew well?" Greta asked. "Enough to get close to Merlin without him suspecting he would be violently attacked?"

"I do agree with that," Carl said.

"The rest of the guests have undeniable alibis. We know it wasn't Justin."

"Of course, it was not."

"Does the work we did here shed any light at all?"

"Yes, this is helpful," said Carl. "Especially one or two pieces of information new to me."

"There's possibly more intel coming tonight," said Greta. "Sarah and I met on Monday at The Black Sheep, while you were running errands. We reviewed what I learned from my conversation with Arielle Glenmore on Sunday night at Puck's Tavern. After one too many glasses of wine, I got Arielle talking about her past. There was something that struck me as odd. She said her great aunt was her only remaining relative. Later, she got going about a high school reunion this week. She was vehement about not going. She said, 'The Cooks won't be darkening the high school's doors.' The Cooks *plural*. What could that mean? Maybe we're overthinking this, but Sarah said why not go to the class reunion and see what she can discover about Arielle's family history. Arielle won't be there, after what she told me, so that shouldn't be a problem. Sarah looked it up online, and it's tonight in a town called Woolsey."

"Sarah is going? It's not safe. You encouraged her to go?"

"It's just a class reunion. And on a weeknight, no less, which means attendance should be light. She won't know anyone there. No one knows she'll be there. I don't *think* anyone does. There were a few locals at The Black Sheep, but I'm sure they weren't listening to us. Anyway, she's already at Woolsey High School by now I would think."

Carl searched his phone. "It's about a twenty-five-minute drive. I'm going there now."

"I'll go with you—"

"No, mi amor," said Carl. "It could be dangerous. I will call you as soon as I know Sarah is safe."

CHAPTER THIRTY-THREE

Thursday, April 6th - 7:00 p.m.

The man with blue-framed glasses behind the check-in table at the Woolsey High School Class Reunion turned the page on his list and ran a sharpened yellow pencil down the names alphabetically listed. "C, Cook. There you are. We didn't get your RSVP."

"I am so sorry about that. I got the courage to come to the reunion at the last minute."

"These should help. Drink tickets." The man handed her two red rectangles. "That will be seventy-five dollars please."

Sarah began to pull out her credit card. "Oops, I can't use this one at the moment." She shoved it back down into the sleeve. "Do you take cash?"

"Yep, cash works."

"Luckily, I have some." She handed over the bills to him.

"Here's a blank name tag to fill out."

Sarah thanked him and shuffled to the side, slipping the name tag into her purse.

The dark gymnasium teamed with strange faces in the unflattering lights tinted blue and yellow, the school colors. What was worse than going to your own class reunion? Going to someone else's. The attendees ensconced themselves back into their old cliques. Sarah searched for an opening.

A man wearing a faux fur coat and a woman in a red leather jacket escaped out a side door. Sarah followed them. The duo turned to look at her as she stepped outside, the door making a loud metal racket as it slammed shut.

"One of these days the roof of this high school is going to cave in," said the woman in red leather. "They still have buckets collecting water from the same old leaky ceiling in the hallways. I don't recognize you." The woman's eyes looked Sarah up and down. "Are you an alum's wife? You don't look old enough to be in our class."

Tension skittered along Sarah's spine. She hadn't considered that she was years younger than everyone here. "Well, aren't you sweet. Guess I have good genes," Sarah said. "I don't recall we were in any classes together. I'm not surprised you don't remember me. I only did my last two years of high school at Woolsey and didn't make many friends. I hung out with Arielle Cook a bit senior year."

"I remember her," the man said. "We were in homeroom together. She missed school a lot."

"I definitely remember her cousin," said the woman. "Jason Cook. He was in our class too. Hot, but crazy. I've never seen either one of the Cooks come to these reunions."

The man exhaled cigarette smoke through his nostrils. "Where are my manners? Did you come out to bum one? Here," he held out his pack to Sarah.

Sarah knew she should take one to keep the conversation flowing, but she had never smoked—the smell bothered her throat. "Oh no, thank you. I only came out for fresh air." As if on cue, Sarah coughed.

"Awkward." The woman turned her back on Sarah, her cigarette poised in the air. "Ian, what were you saying about your restaurant hiring?"

II

As the sun began to set, Carl turned into the parking lot of a former gas station. He hit the grayed-out "Get Directions" button. The wheel on the screen continued to spin. He pulled up his cell phone contacts and tried to call Sarah. The signal was impossible. No ringing, no bars, no service. "Closed For the Season" read the sign on the farmstand across the street. This place gave him the heebie-jeebies.

Bony knuckles rapped at Carl's driver side window. A skeletal man gazed at him, a brown paper bag in hand. "Hey!" the man's hoarse voice whined. He rapped on the window at Carl's eye level, this time harder.

III

Sarah skirted past the line of alums eager to redeem their drink tickets at the bar. A table in one of the gym's corners held a stack of Woolsey High School yearbooks. Sarah nabbed the one dated 2007 and searched the class photos. Each senior got a whole dedicated page. She found Arielle's, a photo of her at eighteen in a white cotton dress, a headband in her waist-length auburn hair, and a black ribbon tied around her throat. The poem beneath her photo read:

THE DANCE
"This is a dance."
I ask what kind.
A Motown prance,
or waltz divine?
A dip too deep
We both fall down.
Your words I keep,
a private crown.
Will you, dark prince, delight, inspire?
Will we set our lives on fire?
How much more do I dare?
You chide "Arielle", intense and rare.

Enticement real,
your pull is strong.
Let myself feel.
Is it so wrong?

Sarah raised her eyebrows and snapped a photo. She flipped to the next page, Jason Cook's, and took another picture. There was no photograph of him, lots of blank space, and one short quotation:

"Dance for a minute, and I'll tell you who you are."
    - Mikhail Baryshnikov

Sarah froze as two fleshy hands clamped over her eyes.

"Guess who?"

"Get your hands off me!" Sarah spun around to face a bearded man, suited up as if he had come straight from the office to the Woolsey reunion.

"My bad," he said. "You're not her."

"No," Sarah said. "You startled me."

"I apologize. It's a mix up. I'm Gunner Lacy," he said, as if she ought to know him. "Gun, student body president, captain of the debate team. I played Judd Fry senior year in *Oklahoma*."

"Yes of course! You were made for that role."

"Well I wouldn't say—"

"Yes, yes, hi, Gun," said Sarah. "Maybe you don't recognize me either. I'm Lindsey..." Sarah's eyes landed on the glowing red sign across the gym, "Exit...er. Lindsey Exeter."

Gun readjusted his tie, "Jerod at the check-in table let me look at the list of attendees. I saw Arielle Cook's name checked off. He pointed me to you."

"Arielle is here?" Sarah asked. "I was friends with her. I would love to see her if she's around."

"Well, she must be somewhere," Gun scanned the line for the bar.

"I hope she's doing okay," Sarah said.

"I do too. She was not in a good situation our senior year. I wouldn't be surprised if that cousin of hers, Jason Cook, ended up behind bars."

"He was a little crazy, huh," said Sarah.

"You're telling me. I asked Arielle to prom our senior year. She'd been flirting with me all semester in French class, but, whatever, she turned me down. Jason cornered me the next day in the locker room and asked me if I'd asked Arielle to the prom. I told him I had, and the psycho gave me a black eye. The principal suspended him."

"Wow." Sarah's amazement was real. "I'm surprised I never heard about that."

"Me too." He tilted his head at Sarah in a way that made her nervous.

Shoot. As Arielle's "friend", Sarah probably would have heard that story. "Maybe I just forgot."

Gun nodded, and Sarah had to fight not to let out a sigh of relief.

"Arielle," he said. "I couldn't figure her out. I guess you can tell I had a bit of a hopeless crush. I've been partial to redheads ever since. Do you know if she ever married?"

IV

The part of Carl that grew up wanting to help people collided with the part of him that investigated murders for decades. In the end, Carl cracked his window, "Good evening. You need help with something?"

The man cradled the brown sack and squinted, "I thought *you* might be the one wanting something from *me*."

Carl wagged his finger 'no'. The man slumped back towards the gas station's former shop.

"One moment! Excuse me, sir. I do have a question, please," said Carl.

"Yeah?" the man limped back.

"How can I get to the nearest police station? My GPS is not working."

"You passed it about a mile back." The man's brows drew together as he scowled. "What do you want the police for?"

V

Gunner Lacy, dabbing his forehead with his pocket square, made his way back to Jared to sort out the whereabouts of Arielle Cook. *Time to go.* Sarah fled the gym through an open door away from the check-in table and jogged down a deserted hallway hung with painted signs on butcher paper. Drips of liquid from the ceiling plunked into orange plastic buckets. Reaching the door at the end of the hall, Sarah prayed the bar beneath her hands would yield. It did. The chilly air stung her cheeks as she ran into the parking lot. Flag ropes rattled against a metal pole. She sprinted to her car parked next to a line of trees where the woods began.

As she grasped the door handle, a loud voice behind her barked, "Hands in the air! Drop the weapon now."

Lamp light flashed along the blade as a knife clattered to the pavement beside Sarah's feet. Her hands shot up into the air.

"Turn around slowly."

Wild eyes peered at her behind a black ski mask, gloved hands in the air mirroring her own. The masked figure charged at Sarah, knocking her against the car door, before disappearing into the woods.

VI

After Sarah finished giving the police her statement, Carl escorted her to his Jeep Cherokee. "We can come back for your car tomorrow morning. I am not letting you out of my sight until you are safe at home."

"I'll drive us, Carl. I'm fine. I know the way. Do you think they'll catch him?"

Carl said nothing in response.

Sarah turned out of the parking lot. "You're awfully quiet, Carl. I'm guessing I must be in the doghouse?"

"You and your mother."

"Didn't I almost help trap the killer?" asked Sarah.

"You almost got yourself killed. If Greta had not told me... Then the GPS would not work. I couldn't reach you. A drunk man at a gas station helped me find my way to the Woolsey Police Station. Thank God we arrived just in time. You didn't know what you were doing coming here, drawing the killer to you."

"I didn't think I would be followed from Glamis."

"You don't know if you were followed from Glamis or not, Sarah. The killer could have been at the reunion and recognized you. Either way, what you did was reckless."

"I know. Thank you, Carl. You saved my life." Sarah stopped at a red light and glanced over at him. "I don't get any kudos at all?"

"None! You and your mother and these in-laws sneaking around behind my back. None of you comprehend the danger you put yourselves in. Unbelievable!"

"You found out about everything?"

"Of course."

"Everything everything?"

"I read your mother's notes on the case from the research your cabal did. Is there something else you are holding back?" Carl asked.

"No that should cover it," said Sarah.

"One thing is for certain," said Carl. "The killer did not want you at the school snooping around tonight. He thought you discovered something incriminating. You're lucky he didn't kill you too."

"How do you think he knew what I was doing?"

"Your mother told me you two talked in The Black Sheep about your plan for tonight. I believe you were overheard. Did you recognize anyone around you while you and your mother were talking there?"

"Glamis is a small town. I would have recognized a few people if I had been paying attention," said Sarah. "I was so into going over the clues with Mom, I didn't notice if there was anyone around us. Not the smartest move talking in public about our plans."

"Not the smartest, no. Now tell me please what you learned tonight at the high school? This could be important," Carl said.

Sarah described her conversations with Arielle's former classmates. She handed her phone to Carl.

"Open up my photos. The two most recent ones are of Arielle and her cousin Jason's yearbook pages. They had the senior class yearbook on a table in the gym. Arielle wrote this mysterious poem about a 'dark prince' she wasn't supposed to be in love with. Unfortunately, Jason didn't bother to give a senior photo. He did provide a favorite quote and a surprising one. The classmates I spoke with described Jason as violent. They thought he might be in jail now. Is any of this helpful?"

Carl zoomed in on Jason's quote. He sat back in his seat. "I was mistaken. Totally mistaken."

"Tell me!"

Carl's eyes turned guarded and owlish beneath his salt and pepper eyebrows. "Soon we will have everything out in the open."

"Carl, you can be so *annoying*."

CHAPTER THIRTY-FOUR

Thursday, April 6th - 8:45 p.m.

"Permission to come aboard, Captain Davis?" Scott asked.

"I'm the first mate," said Rex. "Uncle Zip is the captain, make no mistake. Come on and take a seat."

Scott climbed onto the boat and seated himself on a wooden bench in the cockpit. He pulled out his newly arrived packet of Gauloises. Faustine had the goodness to mail them express but the cruel vixen hadn't had the decency to include a note. One word from her would have made Scott's week. He hunched over to light the cigarette, protecting the flame from the chilly wind blowing across the river. He wasn't warm enough in his suede jacket. Rex didn't appear cold in his denim jacket.

"How you holding up, kid?" Rex asked.

"In case this murder investigation hasn't been stressful enough, my mother got a scathing review today."

"On Yelp or something?"

"In the *London Times*. She's a stage actor. You know in a theater?"

"I know what a stage actor is, thank you," said Rex.

"The critic's problem with her performance is that she is too old to play the role of a young courtesan. To the reviewer, it ruined the believability of the play."

"That's harsh," said Rex.

"She'll be inconsolable," Scott said. "I don't know what to say to her. There is no one more loving or more charming than my mother when she is getting rave reviews and standing ovations, and there is no one snippier when she isn't. She emailed me the review a few hours ago. I want to say something comforting. Everything I can come up with will set her off."

"Ah, just don't leave her hanging. Say something nice, even if it isn't perfect, your mama will understand."

"She will not understand," said Scott. "I'll figure out just the right thing to say. Maybe something about the controversial review boosting ticket sales! No, she'll hate that. She'll accuse me of agreeing with the bad review. I wish I could just sail away from all this, float into the night. Do you like living on a boat?"

"I like being flexible and mobile. I'm going to sail around the world one day. First, head down to the Caribbean, float from harbor to harbor, me and Zip sippin' painkillers all day in the sun. Don't sound bad, does it?"

"I can't imagine living with Uncle Lewis in such close quarters. His house is cramped enough."

"I'm used to it now. Zip sure has got his quirks, but he's blood."

"Your phone's vibrating."

Rex answered it, an auburn lock falling across one eye. "What's shakin'? Alright, I got you. Yep. Sounds perfect. See you then. Bye now." He hung up and wiggled his eyebrows at Scott in a self-satisfied manner.

"Who was that?" Scott asked.

"Listen, kid, I'm meeting someone for a date tonight down in Fairfield. I don't think this one goes for the disheveled sailor look either. I gotta get cleaned up quick. Time to get back to Rex the clean-shaven cowboy gentleman. Gotta live up to my profile picture. If you don't mind."

"Sounds like it's time for me to make my exit," Scott stood. "Permission to disembark?"

"Yeah, goofball. Go on. Catch you later."

Scott hopped onto the dock. "Later!"

Rex had already disappeared below and shut the door behind him.

Scott walked back to the boat house whistling an old Marty Robbins western ballad from the '50s in the chilly night air. Arielle would know it too, he bet.

"Dang," he whispered. A golden moon loomed above. He wondered if Arielle had seen it too tonight. What was she doing right now? Getting torched at Puck's, he'd heard. He hadn't tried to contact her since Sunday. He wasn't going to corner her at a bar where he couldn't even drink legally. He refused to surrender any more of his dignity. Why was he still obsessing over her?

After sitting on the dock and smoking one more Gauloise, he decided to avail himself of some free hot chocolate in the boathouse. He found Robin leaning into the glow of his computer in his office.

"Hey Boss," said Scott. Robin made a quick motion with his mouse, minimizing his screen. "What are you up to?"

"Fine. You busted me. Want to see something?" Robin asked.

"Is it dirty? X-rated?"

"Well, some would call it nauti," Robin motioned to a 46-foot Nautitech catamaran on his screen.

"That's stunning," Scott gaped.

"My new boat, assuming I get Paul's blessing. Not a word to anyone about it for now. You're sworn to secrecy. You smell like cigarettes, yuck."

"Mea culpa," Scott shrugged.

Rex Davis strutted past the window, touching the brim of his cowboy hat in salute to Scott and Robin.

"Ah! See the pink moon up there tonight?" asked Robin.

"You mean the gold moon?" Scott asked.

"It looks gold, but it's called The Pink Moon."

"Are you sure?" asked Scott.

"You have a lot to learn about this world, my young friend. It's a good thing you came to work for me."

"Yeah, yeah. The Pink Moon. Are you pulling my leg? I'm gonna look that up when I get home."

"Do!"

CHAPTER THIRTY-FIVE

Friday, April 7th - 4:00 p.m.

"There are a few suspects whose whereabouts last night remain unproven," Detective Bell said to Carl, as they exited the highway in Bell's Explorer. "Paul Krebbs says he went home early from the restaurant and conked out at 6:30. He didn't wake until the morning he says. Robin Glenmore returned from The Marina around ten last night and said he found Paul asleep at that time. Zip Davis was at the Animal Rescue until about 9:30 he says, but no one else was working there to confirm. Lewis Waterhouse claims he remained home all evening brainstorming plot ideas for his book, using pen and paper. There are no witnesses or digital timestamps to back him up. Scott Waterhouse returned from The Marina around nine forty-five, dropped off by Robin, and said when he got inside the house his uncle's bedroom door was shut, and he'd presumably gone to bed. We're still getting information on the others, but that's what we know for now."

Detective Bell parked along the curbside in front of a ranch-style house.

"There was something the killer didn't want Sarah to discover last night," said Carl. "What could you find out about the cousin, Jason Cook?"

"No criminal record. A 2019 license showed a man with a shaved head and stubbly beard. Hair listed as red, height six foot three. Arielle Glenmore said she and Jason haven't spoken in over a decade."

"Hmm," said Carl. "Let's hope we learn something important here about him from the aunt."

Bell removed his aviator sunglasses, a birthday gift to himself. He wiped them with a small cloth and nestled them into their case. He gave a grim look at the house. "Well, Lieutenant," he said. "Let's hope we don't have to bust up a cat orphanage."

"Indeed," Carl said, his eyes fixed on the bars on the windows with blinds shut. He was getting the sinking feeling too that something wasn't right.

A woman in her fifties wearing a blue jean dress and her hair in a braid opened the door before they reached the front porch. "I'm Harriett's daughter, Becca. Becca Fish. She asked me to come over and join for your visit. I hope that's alright, officially speaking?"

"Just fine," said Bell.

"Oh good," she blushed. "Please come in. I'll show you to the living room. Mother is just finishing her hair."

"I hope she's not going to the trouble on our account," Detective Bell breathed through his mouth to avoid the odor of death.

"You know the weather is nice today. It's warming up. We could sit outside," Carl suggested.

"I love that idea," said Bell.

"Oh no, no," said Becca. "My mother said the living room was where I should bring you. I don't want to upset her. She can't wait to see you. She didn't want me to miss whatever it is you're going to tell us either. I tried to tidy up in here before you arrived."

Carl and Bell followed her into the living room. A cabinet of curiosities displayed an army of taxidermized squirrels in Victorian garb enjoying a tea party.

Becca gestured to a fainting sofa covered in stained peach silk. "Please have a seat there. I see you noticed Mother's collection. She did all of that herself."

"My." Bell looked away from the squirrel installation, blinking rapidly at Carl. He let out a high-pitched wheeze.

"Are you alright, Detective?" Becca asked.

Bell nodded furiously but didn't say a word. His nose made a whining sound this time, a hint of a smile creeping up one side of his mouth. Carl felt a tickle in his own throat as he realized Bell was holding back desperate laughter.

"Here's the artist now!" Becca announced.

A woman of eighty with deep wrinkles and bright coral lips, wearing a black caftan and orange bead necklace flipflopped in. She smelled of ammonia and overapplied lily of the valley perfume. "Lieutenant Sarabia and Detective Bell, be welcome in my home. I am Harriett Fish."

"The officers were admiring your artwork, Mother," said Becca.

Bell didn't risk uttering a word.

"Yes!" Carl managed.

"Oh I'm flattered," said Harriett. "I've got other installations in the bedrooms if you'd like to see more."

"No," said Bell. "Thank you. I'm Detective Bell. This is Lieutenant Sarabia."

"Sticking to business, I see," said Harriett approvingly. "You're very professional, as I would expect you to be."

"I've never seen eyes greener than Detective Bell's in all my life," added Becca.

"A little less enthusiasm, perhaps?" Harriett admonished her daughter. "But you're quite right, my dear. Before we get down to it, may I offer you gentlemen light refreshment? May I tempt you to try my famous deviled eggs?"

"Oh, no thank you, we're stuffed," Carl winked at Bell who was turning purple at Carl's choice of word.

"If you get peckish, you must let me know," said Harriett. "You called saying you have questions about my great niece Arielle. Rest assured, I am willing to cooperate."

A mouse chittered as it neared Carl and Bell. Bell's feet fled the floor as Carl trapped the creature beneath an empty popcorn bowl before it reached him.

"Rodent problem?" Bell asked.

Harriett gave her daughter a rueful look. "I can't have cats anymore."

"Let's jump into a few questions," said Carl. "We don't want to interrupt too much of your day."

"I don't mind at all," said Harriett. "I know what you're up against. The politicians don't let you come down with the needed force on criminals. I expect Arielle has joined their disgusting ranks? No amount of fancy words or books could fix what was bred into her blood on the father's side. The Cooks from England," she chuckled. "My niece, Arielle's mother, was so proud when she married that Thomas Cook. His grandfather was the third son of Lord Something or Other. Doubt if any of it was true. Thomas 'the great architect'. More like a lazy drunk who was so picky about the jobs he took he never had any. When he died, Arielle moved in with us. The airs that teenage girl put on! She didn't know how to do her own laundry or wash a dish when she moved in with us, did she, Becca?"

"No, Mother. She was terribly spoiled," said Becca. "But she was sweet and amusing in a way."

"Why defend her?" Harriett scowled. "She didn't care a fig about you. I am only glad her stay in our home was brief."

"How long did she live with you?" asked Carl.

"One summer. She preferred to live with her father's brother, the con man, and his son Jason. She rode her bicycle there to visit them a few times a week, eventually she chose to move in with them. 'Go,' I told her. 'You belong with the Cooks. We're proud, moral Fish women here.' I washed my hands of her."

"Do you recall the uncle's first name?" Detective Bell pulled himself together despite the squeaks coming from the overturned bowl at his feet.

"A moment," said Harriett, "His first name will come to me. I saved the papers with the stories when his robbery made the news. The MacDougall-Walker Prison is where they had him. Look for the articles in my office, Becca. I think they're in the filing cabinet. The paper did more than one on him."

"You said it was a robbery the uncle was convicted of?" Carl asked.

"Larceny in the first degree. They only gave him a ten-year sentence," said Harriett. "He used the children, Arielle and his own son, as his cover. He had them train in dance classes together. He signed them up for a competition at a hotel in upstate New York. He broke into the room of a woman known for flaunting expensive jewelry at the banquets of these dance events. Wilbur Cook! That was his name. He had the schedule of the dances in advance and knew exactly when his target's room would be unoccupied, when she would be watching her daughter compete. Timing it so, he entered the room disguised as a hotel worker, broke into the safe, took a diamond necklace and bracelet worth something like a hundred thousand dollars combined, and returned to the ballroom, thinking he'd carried off the scheme undetected. A hotel housekeeper picked out Wilbur as the man she witnessed getting off the elevator at around the time the robbery was committed. They put him behind bars and should have kept him there. I am none too surprised to hear Arielle is in trouble. Becca, any luck?" she shouted.

"That's alright, Ms. Fish," Carl stood. Detective Bell shot to his feet as well. "I've written down the name, Wilbur Cook. That's sufficient. Thank you for being generous with your time. We'll go now."

"You just got here. I was hoping you would stay for supper with me and Becca. She's single you know." Harriett gave Detective Bell a significant look.

"You're too kind, Ms. Fish. Thank you, thank you both!" Bell fled the room.

As soon as he and Carl were back inside the SUV, Bell amply availed himself of hand sanitizer. He tossed the mini bottle to Carl who was just as desperate for some. "I've been inside a lot of unpleasant homes," said Bell, "but I can't say I've ever seen taxidermized squirrels having a tea party before. Lieutenant, did you hear what I just said?"

Carl hummed to himself as he rubbed the gel into his hands.

Detective Bell peered at him. "You've got it all figured out, don't you, Lieutenant?"

"Bell, it is clear to me who did the murder, why it was done, and how it was committed."

"Will you be sharing any of these insights?"

"Of course," Carl said. "However, I have no evidence beyond what I have pieced together logically in my mind. There is further research to be done to confirm much of what I believe happened. I expect we will be able to make an arrest tomorrow."

"Oh?" Bell asked.

"But here is the tricky part," said Carl. "I believe we will need a confession to trap our killer. Fortunately, I have a plan. Let's go back to the station in Glamis. I will explain on the way. I want to know if you think my plan is too dangerous."

CHAPTER THIRTY-SIX

Saturday, April 8th - 5:00 p.m.

"Go ahead into the restaurant. I need a second," Scott said as he and Lewis arrived in front of Dolce Far Niente.

"You're not going to have a...?" Lewis pantomimed smoking a cigarette. "You promised you gave it up for good."

"I did. That's not why I'm lingering. There is something important I have to do."

"Ah." Lewis spotted Arielle Glenmore walking up Main Street. "Can I hope you are going to give her up as well?"

Scott said nothing in reply. He didn't know what he would do yet, only that he had to speak to her before they went inside.

Lewis patted his nephew's shoulder and disappeared inside Dolce Far Niente.

Scott leaned on the restaurant's entry ramp railing as Arielle approached. Her eyes met his with no trace of the usual sparkle. "How are you?" asked Scott. "I'm not trying to ambush you. I've been worried."

"I don't want you to be dragged into this anymore than you already have been," said Arielle.

"I want to be there for you," said Scott. "But you've got me wondering what this... friendship ever was for you. Are you still my friend?" God, the words sounded pathetic as soon as he uttered them. He felt ashamed and heartbroken as he spoke them.

"I'm too old for you, Scott," she said. "And even if I wasn't, you're just...too good for me."

"No. I don't buy that," he said. How could she when all along they had been perfectly matched in wit and temperament and humor?

"Give it time," said Arielle. "You'll know I was right. Let's get this over with. I would like another drink before they start."

"Wait," said Scott. "I have to ask, was it a *true* kiss?"

"True *'in my fashion'*," she replied.

For some reason unknown to Scott, it took him courage to look her in the eyes in this moment, but he did now. "I want to be serious with you for once."

She looked away. "Serious? The last refuge of the desperate man. That's not you. Never you. Let's go inside."

***

They assembled in The Vault. Sarah and Greta sat across from Justin at the green marble bar. Rex came in swirling a toothpick in his mouth. Catia and Owen found a seat at the dining table at the center of the room. Robin and Paul entered next and took their seats. Carl, Detective Bell, and Officer Marotta spoke in hushed voices nearby. Officer Keane stood guard by the spoke-handled door, original to the Glamis Savings Bank. Sal bustled in with an overloaded cheese and charcuterie board, just in case. No one would go hungry at Dolce Far Niente on his watch.

"I recognize you," Jade said to Greta as she approached the bar.

"We met briefly the other day when I was visiting Lewis," Greta said.

Jade's eyes widened as she placed Greta as the mysterious woman who had been visiting Lewis in his writer's shed the other day.

"Please forgive my rudeness that day. I was surprised not to find the hermit alone. Are you two…?"

"Heavens no!" said Greta. "I was only asking him for advice on a literary agent. I am happily married to Lieutenant Sarabia over there."

"Oh, I see," said Jade, surprised at the intensity of her relief. "I certainly had it all wrong."

"Uncle Lewis remains single," Scott chimed in over Jade's shoulder. "I could have told you that."

Jade felt her face warm, realizing what Scott thought. *Did everyone think it?* "Beast," said Jade. Thank God Lewis was in the men's room.

Justin poured a martini for Arielle at the bar. No one else felt inspired to order alcohol. Arielle found a seat at the table between Jade and Paul.

Once everyone was seated, Bell cleared his throat, "As most of you know, my name is Detective Nemo Bell. I am a homicide investigator from the Connecticut State Police's Eastern District Major Crime Squad. Thank you all for being here this evening. Today, Zip Davis was taken into custody. He was charged with assault and attempted murder of Sarah Marotta and Lieutenant Sarabia. He is being held without bond."

"You've made a mistake!" Rex leapt to his feet. "My uncle is innocent."

"Sit down, Mr. Davis. Let me finish. As Sarah Marotta was almost a victim," Bell continued, "We invited her and her mother, Greta Klein, to this meeting. I will introduce now Retired Lieutenant Carl Sarabia, who consulted with the State Police and the Glamis Police Department, on this homicide investigation. His involvement has been in strict coordination with us. With Lieutenant Sarabia's over thirty years of experience in the Homicide Division of the Houston Police Department, we were grateful he agreed to our request for his consultation. You will have the opportunity to hear how the criminal events occurred before I give an official statement to the media. This community and the State of Connecticut owe a debt of gratitude to you, Lieutenant, for solving the murder of Merlin Glenmore and also the murder of Maeve Glenmore." A murmur went through the room. Lewis leaned forward over clasped hands, eyes shining with an urgent need to hear the truth about his sister.

Carl stepped forward, "Working in the homicide division of the fourth largest city in the United States for over thirty years ingrained in me the importance of a collaborative endeavor. The information, evidence, and analysis supplied by the police investigative group has been vital to our combined efforts. We were faced with solving a murder case, which, at first, seemed impossible to decipher. Based on the initial investigation of the facts, we did not have a viable suspect. It was not until I discovered the secret of the cabinet connecting the study with the bedroom of Ernest Glenmore that I began to see the elaborate deception played out to create an alibi for the actual killer. Then Scott Waterhouse helpfully pointed out a mannequin missing its gloves.

"When I moved to this town less than a week ago, I learned of a Glamis resident named Merlin Glenmore, who recently inherited a tremendous fortune. His first wife, Maeve Glenmore, had died in a fatal car accident this past Fall. The suspicious timing of her death— that is, right after her husband fell in love with another woman—left many wondering, myself included. Was Maeve's death a lucky stroke for Merlin, who no longer loved her and did not want to share his fortune with her? Or, was he behind the death of his first wife? Later that night, this same man, the subject of town disapproval and gossip, was found stabbed to death at his own birthday party. A maddening detail emerged. The witnesses reported seeing Merlin with pants on when the body was discovered, but moments later when Doctor Boyd comes to examine the body, the pants are missing. Who took them? Why? How? I knew understanding what happened to the missing pants would lead me to the answers needed to identify and capture the killer. For the longest time, I could not fathom the solution. Could it have been someone other than the killer who took the pants from Merlin's body? And how and when had Merlin's body gotten inside the cabinet without witnesses in the room seeing this?

"My thoughts turned to Maeve's brother."

Everyone's eyes locked on Lewis, who crossed his arms and leaned back in his chair looking amused that he was about to be accused of murder.

Carl continued, "Lewis Waterhouse has the creative mind to devise a perplexing scheme of murder. Physically he can move a body weighing one hundred and sixty pounds from the bedroom into the cabinet. He had an obvious motive. He was a grief-stricken brother who believed his sister had been killed by a hit man hired by her husband."

Jade put her hand on Lewis' shoulder. He allowed it to rest there.

"But Lewis did not have the opportunity to commit the murder of Merlin Glenmore," said Carl, "unless Scott lied to give his uncle an alibi, when he claimed to see a face in the cabinet, right before the body was discovered."

"Me?" said Scott. "A suspected murder accomplice? For the second time in a single year, and it's not even May. Volume one of my autobiography will be scintillating."

Carl ignored Scott's cheeky remark. "If Scott had not seen the face in the cabinet," he continued, "It was possible Lewis Waterhouse committed the crime prior to the time he surprised everyone during the séance. The lie would mean Scott assisted his uncle in helping to avenge his Aunt Maeve's death. Unexplained, however, was the problem of the missing pants, which neither Scott nor his uncle could have taken unobserved. After the body was discovered, both remained with the others from the time they left the upstairs study, until the police arrived.

"The younger Waterhouse once looked suspicious, this time in a new light, when we learned he had been involved with another woman whose husband was murdered, stabbed in fact. This did not distract me. There was no way around Scott's alibi the evening of the party. I did wonder if this similarity between the two killings could be by design, an attempt to frame the young man. I presumed the killer must have known about Scott's past. I knew Scott was not protecting the killer, when during my visit to the crime scene he pointed out the mannequin missing its gloves. This clue gave me an epiphany. If Scott were trying to conceal his uncle's or anyone else's crime, he would never have pointed this out to me.

"Most of you who were there the night of Merlin's murder were in the company of others the entire time leading up to the discovery of the body. I asked the basic question how could the crime have been committed by those who will gain the most financially from Merlin's death? How could these people provide themselves with the perfect alibi? My thoughts turned to Robin Glenmore. Perhaps he knew he would come into money if his brother died? Robin and Paul were dressed in white gloves like those worn by the mannequin. I could imagine the killer's gloves soiled with blood, the urgent need to get rid of them, and the fortunate replacements provided by the mannequin."

"I didn't kill my brother," Robin objected. "There were others besides Paul and me who wore white gloves that night."

"I happen to agree with you on both points, Mr. Glenmore. Both you and your husband are innocent of any wrongdoing. I wondered about Doctor Owen Boyd. Merlin wronged Catia Boyd's mother when he was a boy. She was a housekeeper for the Glenmore family, fired after Merlin accused her of stealing his father's watch. For the record, we found among Mr. Glenmore's personal effects the watch described in the police report filed at the time the theft was reported."

"Did the doctor commit the crime to help his wife Catia achieve her revenge on Merlin, or possibly did he kill him for another reason, all his own?" Carl turned to Doctor Boyd, who made a silent appeal for mercy with his eyes. "He had the opportunity when Justin was on the phone in the corridor outside the room. The Conservatory opens to the lawn outside. He could have left that way, gotten back into The Castle through the front door, and taken the murder weapon from the Armory. The snow sticking to his shoes would explain the damp patches found on the carpet in the Armory. He could have gone upstairs undetected, committed the murder, rushed back down the way he had come. He appeared calmly waiting at the chess table when Justin re-entered the room. Why would he take the mannequin's white gloves, when he had no use for them with his golfer's attire? No, that piece did not fit. Boyd was an unlikely suspect anyway. This murder required strength, speed, and agility."

"He makes that sound like an insult, doesn't he?" said Catia.

"He's never seen me swing a golf club," said Owen.

"I did not mean to insult, only to say I did not think you fit the killer's profile. My English maybe." Carl stared at Catia pointedly.

Carl fixed his gaze on Arielle, "You, Mrs. Glenmore, would have the most obvious motive: an inheritance which you could expect to receive as Merlin's wife. What use would you have for the mannequin's white gloves, I wondered? You wore long black ones with your costume. There was the problem of when you could have committed the murder. Your alibi is unshakable. You never left the company of the other guests, during the time when the murder could have taken place.

"There were five men at the party who would have use for a replacement pair of short white gloves, based on their costumes: Lewis Waterhouse, Rex Davis, Robin Glenmore, and Paul Krebbs. Note the last four men seemed to have perfect alibis, all being together before and during the séance. Yet they are not all innocent. Zip Davis is in custody as we speak for assaulting Sarah, but he also played a role in Merlin

Glenmore's murder. How did he do it? *When* could he have done it? The answer: he could not—not alone, at least. His fingerprints confirmed what we suspected. Zip refused to give samples of his fingerprints to the police the night of the murder. His prints were collected nonetheless from the cabinet, where he left them when he 'found' Merlin's body during the séance. A detail he had overlooked while planning the crime and choosing his costume. No gloves. Maybe he didn't worry about it because fingerprints are only useful if you have something to compare them to, such as if the murder weapon had prints on it. That was not the case here. When we realized Zip likely was using another name—a specific name—we ran a computer search comparing the prints we collected with those of the person we suspected he was. They matched those of a convicted felon, who served a ten-year prison sentence for felony larceny. Once we confronted Zip with his identity, I led him through the exact steps of how the crime had been committed. He admitted to being an accessory to Merlin Glenmore's murder."

Carl's eyes fixed on Rex Davis, "'Dance for a minute, and I'll tell you who you are.' Mikhail Baryshnikov. You made the mistake of dancing. Now I will tell everyone who you really are. You are agile, powerful, bold, and quick. You are a man who could approach Merlin at the fatal moment without him becoming defensive towards you, his close friend. I saw you as capable of carrying out a plan with flawless execution. *When* could you have done it? Everyone vouches for you leading up to the discovery of the body. *Why* would you do it? You're not an heir named in Merlin's will.

"This brings me to the story of Arielle. She told her friends she went to live with a great aunt after her father's death. She left out a key piece of information. There was another home she moved into, when she and the aunt proved incompatible. She moved in with her Uncle Wilbur and his son Jason. Jason Cook is your real name, isn't it, Mr. Davis?"

Rex folded his hands together in front of him and gave Carl a stoic stare.

"I imagine," continued Carl, "for you and Arielle it couldn't have been easy, living under the rule of your father, a man with a forceful personality who was both a thief and a con artist. Though perhaps, Mrs. Glenmore," Carl turned to Arielle. Her body was visibly trembling. "Perhaps to you it was a romantic adventure? *'Will you dark prince, delight, inspire? Will we set our lives on fire?'*

"You and Rex Davis danced remarkably well together," said Carl. "Why, I wondered. Two people having a secret affair do not go to dance class together. The truth? The two of you trained together as teenagers to supply Wilbur Cook with an alibi during the robbery he committed at a hotel hosting a dance competition. Wilbur Cook, or Zip Davis, as he was known, was arrested for the theft of a diamond necklace and bracelet. After his release from prison, he stayed out of trouble, until he stopped in Glamis one day and overheard a local talking about Merlin Glenmore's impending inheritance."

Sal thought about the day Zip helped him pick out the kittens for Jade. Was Zip—an admitted killer—an actual animal lover or had he only been volunteering at the shelter so he would look like a nice guy? There was no way to know, which bothered Sal immensely, given how he loved to know everything. Maybe, he thought, he could visit Zip in prison to find out.

Carl turned to Rex, "I suspected you were a liar from the first time we spoke at Thane's. Your orange vest gave the lie to your claim that you are a Texas A&M graduate. It would be unlikely for a proud Aggie to wear the famous color of A&M's longtime rival. When I noticed the requisite Aggie Ring missing from your hand, this all but confirmed my suspicions. And though English is not my first language, having lived in Texas for most of my life, I knew you and your supposed uncle's accents were fake."

"You don't have proof I killed Merlin Glenmore," said Jason. "As you said yourself, I was in the room with the others the whole time leading up to the discovery of the body."

"I told you we never should have come here," Arielle whispered, eyes downcast in defeat. "There's no use pretending anymore, Jason."

Jade gasped, her hands pressing to her heart in shock. Merlin wasn't the greatest brother, but she had loved him. And, she had adored Arielle, leaned on her in so many ways for a year. Yet, her 'friend' had conned them all and was part of the conspiracy resulting in her brother's death. It was too much to process.

"*Keep your mouth shut,*" Jason snapped. "Detective Bell, this man has a conspiracy theory, but no actual proof. My father I'm sure has said all kinds of things to make himself look less guilty of this crime. Arielle and I are innocent. We won't be scapegoats for police incompetence. No one has been able to say how this crime was committed. You can't, can you?"

Jason's chair screeched as he stood. Sal could barely believe the scene he was witnessing; he hardly minded he would have to polish out the scuff marks the man had just created on the floor.

"Sit down. I will tell you," said Carl. "Only two people fully viewed the body of Merlin when it was first discovered in the cabinet. Arielle Glenmore and the man you all knew as Zip Davis. But it was an act. There was no dead body present. Not yet."

"But there was," said Jade, "I saw Merlin lying there too."

"You saw the lower half of a body—pants and shoes. It was your brother's clothing, yes," said Carl, "but it was the mannequin of Ernest Glenmore wearing them. Merlin himself put his own pants and shoes on the mannequin and placed the figure inside the cabinet. The face you glimpsed in the window, Scott, was indeed Merlin very much alive. The moment when you all thought you found the corpse, Merlin was hiding in the bedroom next door, enjoying his joke's success. In his mind, it was a prank, one first suggested to him by Rex and Zip, earlier that day at Thane's. Unwittingly, Merlin Glenmore became an accessory to his own murder.

"He waited in the bedroom for Rex to tell him when he could come out into the hall, anticipating giving the party goers yet another jolt when he would suddenly appear behind them alive. It's perfect. Everyone believes Rex rushed from the study downstairs to get Doctor Boyd. But, instead, he enters the bedroom next door and ends Merlin's life with the bayonet plug. You had the opportunity to take the weapon earlier that evening, Mr. Cook, when Arielle conveniently redirected Scott back to the kitchen. You slowed down as you walked behind Paul and were alone long enough to secure the weapon on your person before returning to The Library."

Jason locked eyes with Arielle across the table in silence.

Scott raised his hand. "He was carrying an ice bucket to the Library—that's how the carpet got wet in the Armory when he stole the weapon, isn't it?" asked Scott.

"You are absolutely right," said Carl, impressed.

"Also," Scott raised his hand again, "When Merlin came into the pantry, he said he thought it had been Rex with Arielle, instead of me. It was because Rex hadn't rejoined the party yet."

"Correct again," said Carl. "You, Mr. Cook, must have seen Merlin Glenmore coming down the corridor and waited to leave the Armory, until he walked past you. You kept the weapon concealed in your cape, until you used it on him in the bedroom, when you were supposedly getting Doctor Boyd. Merlin collapsed onto the floor near the fireplace. You removed the Ernest mannequin from the cabinet, returning it to its original place in the bedroom. You removed Merlin's shoes from the mannequin and slid them back onto their original owner's feet. In your haste to get downstairs, you decided you did not have the time to replace the black trousers on Merlin's legs. You left them on the mannequin. You are running out of time like a diver who knows he must come up for air or he will drown. Your alibi will be destroyed if Doctor Boyd and Justin hear a commotion and link up with the others before you reach them.

"You laid Merlin's body inside the cabinet without the pants. Returning to the bedroom, you realize you have a big problem. Fresh blood on your white gloves. The mannequin, so helpful to you all night, helps again with his clean white gloves. You take them for yourself. Where will you put the bloody gloves? You must get rid of them. You pull out the lighter from the pocket of Merlin's pants worn by the mannequin. You set the gloves on fire, tossing them inside the fireplace, returning the lighter to the pant pocket.

"You leave the bedroom, racing down the backstairs to the Conservatory. You breathe a sigh of relief as you reach Doctor Boyd and Justin, still oblivious, involved in a chess game. The others, on The Castle's opposite side, remain ignorant of how long your mission to bring the doctor to Merlin's aid has taken. Arielle and Zip expertly steered the rest of you from Ernest's Study to the Library. It is the furthest possible room from the Conservatory."

"You figured all of this out from the missing gloves?" Paul asked.

"Scott pointing out the missing gloves brought my attention to the mannequin and reminded me of the missing pants," said Carl. "Scott, you remember when I went over to the mannequin and examined it? I found the lighter inside the pant pocket. Scott and Jade verified my suspicions when they confirmed these were indeed the pants worn by Merlin, which had been pulled onto the mannequin on top of his usual pair. Jade had not spotted Merlin's pants on the mannequin before. I am not surprised they went unnoticed. She gave the walk-through to Detective Bell the night of the crime, when she was understandably shaken and exhausted. This detail escaped her notice. Once I saw the pants belonging to Merlin Glenmore on the mannequin, I understood how the killer created a false sequence of events to fabricate an alibi. Rex *did* have the opportunity to murder Merlin. Once we make the connection Rex, Zip, and Arielle are all related, now we can separate the lies from the truth. Arielle would collect the inheritance and share it with her uncle and her cousin in time."

"I never should have gone back to you and Uncle Wilbur. I'm so stupid." Arielle twisted her ring, her hand hovering above her glass. "It's over, Jason."

"It appears so," he agreed bitterly, as two officers approached him from either side.

Scott stared at Arielle. She had tried to set him up as a possible suspect. How stupid he had been. How fortunate he hadn't left the séance at the wrong moment.

"I hate to interrupt you before you are finished, Lieutenant," said Detective Bell. "But it's time. Jason and Arielle Cook, you are under arrest for the murders of Merlin and Maeve Glenmore. You have the right to remain silent..."

"No!" Scott flung himself across the table knocking Arielle's martini glass from her hand. "She's trying to poison herself!"

Arielle, eyes shining with tears, said nothing as Officer Timmons handcuffed her and led her from the room.

Dominic Marotta with Jason Cook in custody followed close behind.

"Good God," said Jade. "That was quick thinking, Scott."

"I was the one who gave her the poison ring," Scott said. "I never thought she would try to kill herself with it."

"Was there poison in the ring when you gave it to her?" Carl asked.

"Of course there was not, Lieutenant," said Scott. "She put that in there herself. Maybe she had a feeling her luck was going to run out."

"You've got quick reflexes," said Lewis. "Lieutenant, I think I speak for everyone here. We need to know the rest before any of us go anywhere. Tell us what really happened to my sister Maeve the night of her death."

"Wilbur and Jason believed Arielle could make Merlin Glenmore fall in love with her," said Carl. "She succeeded. There was one remaining obstacle: Merlin was married. He was against a divorce. Fine, Wilbur would solve this. The cellular data we obtained shows Wilbur Cook was in the vicinity the night of Maeve Glenmore's fatal accident in Vermont, when her car plunged off a stretch of road down a sharp precipice. Mr. Cook has confessed to forcing her off the road with a rented box truck. It was *not* your brother-in-law behind Maeve's death, Mr. Waterhouse."

"What about Merlin asking around for a hit man?" Lewis asked.

"That was a lie created and circulated by Jason Cook. He hoped to implicate Scott and you as suspects. His goal was to distract the authorities, until he and his co-conspirators collected the inheritance and disappeared. After the murder, Wilbur Cook overheard my wife and daughter discussing a plan to go to Arielle's class reunion. He knew they were on to the truth. The following morning, he attempted to hit Sarah and me with a truck during our run. Failing to accomplish that, he went to the reunion Thursday night to silence Sarah once and for all."

"Thank you," Lewis said to Carl. "I hope Zip and Rex, or whoever they are, spend the rest of their days rotting in a cell for what they did to Maeve."

Owen shook his head mystified at Catia.

"I'd like to stay for dinner," Catia took her husband's hand. "A table for two, Sal? We have a lot to discuss, Owen."

Scott stared at Arielle's vacant chair. "*The little flower, white in sun, violet in shadow*. I thought she was my friend. All the work of a skilled con artist. And The Castle. Didn't she really love it?"

"I doubt we'll ever know for sure," said Jade. "It seemed that way to me. She fooled us, spectacularly. A part of me wonders if she started believing what she was acting out." Jade turned to Lewis as the others buzzed with conversation in the aftermath of Carl's revelations. Jade said quietly, "I'm relieved."

"You mean that it wasn't Merlin who killed Maeve?" Lewis asked.

"No, that it wasn't *you* who killed Merlin. The other day in my kitchen you said you had something to confess. Can you blame me for fearing the worst?" Jade laughed.

Lewis didn't. "How grateful you must have been when Sal showed up to rescue you just in time from the dangerous man who helped you bury your cat. I thought you knew me better than anyone. You didn't trust me? For God's sakes, Jade."

"Wait," Jade protested. She wanted to say more, but she didn't want to make a scene in front of everyone.

Lewis stood up from the table. "I've got to get to Grimalkin's before it closes. Thank you, Lieutenant, Detective." He shook hands with Carl and Bell. "Good night, everyone."

Jade blinked desperately. Of course, she trusted him now, and should have always. She couldn't find the words in time. Lewis was gone.

Sal returned to The Vault after seating Catia and Owen at one of the more secluded booths in the main dining room. "I'm bowled over, Carl. Bowled over. We've got to seize the moment. Any day could be our last. We need to really live. Chef Paul, I saw the Ferrari parked out back. How much would you want for it? What do you figure it's worth?"

"It's not for sale," Paul said. "It's something special we have to remember Merlin by." He hugged Robin to him.

"Dad, come on," said Justin. "Leave Chef Paul alone. It's only his first day having the car."

"Hotspur. It has a name," Paul said.

"That's right." Sal pointed at him. "And one day it's last name might be Marotta." Sal caught Jade's eye and sauntered over to her. "How are you holding up, my dear?"

"I am glad to know the truth. Thanks to Lieutenant Sarabia we will be able to lay my brother to rest without worry. Everything has been made clear." Jade gathered her purse and coat and shook hands with Carl and Bell. Sal followed her out of The Vault into the secondary dining room where he stopped her.

"It's a lot to digest," said Sal. "What do you think about dinner together? We can eat here, or take out to my house?"

Jade let out a sigh. "You have been such a good friend to me, Sal. I owe it to you to be direct. I have feelings for someone else. I'm sorry."

"Don't be sorry," Sal's eyes moistened and his voice grew husky as he stumbled trying to take the high road. "Know I admire you, respect you, and think the world of you. Who's the lucky guy?"

"I'd rather not say just yet. Thank you for being such a gentleman. Please excuse me. I have to go."

"You must follow where your heart drives you," Sal said. "Even if I am the one being crushed beneath your wheels."

"I repeat I am not a motor vehicle." Jade forged on into the main dining room towards the exit.

Sal returned to the vault and picked up the untouched charcuterie board from the center of the table. "Justin," he said to his son. "I conclude she is not The One."

"Sorry, Dad," said Justin.

Sarah put a hand on Sal's shoulder. "Just remember, Easter is tomorrow, at your house. That's something to look forward to. You're not short on people who love you."

"That's true. Car!" Sal called across the room. "Tomorrow at my house—you'll be there. It's Easter. A family holiday. It's not optional."

"We will be there," said Carl. "But, remember, for me and Greta, it is optional. We *choose* to go. There is a difference."

"And as long as you keep choosing correctly, we won't have a problem. I am so proud of you. Get in here," Sal embraced Carl, and whispered, "Tomorrow's not optional."

Sarah nudged Greta, "It's nice to see those two getting along. You might say they're in-lawv."

Greta groaned. "You're a dork, Sarah. Ah, but you're my dork. You get the punster gene from your father's side. Keep an eye out. Rosie might be afflicted too."

"A mother can dream," said Sarah.

CHAPTER THIRTY-SEVEN

Saturday, April 8th - 7:30 p.m.

The shopkeeper's bell jingled as Jade stepped inside Grimalkin's Wine and Spirits. Lewis stood with his hands on his hips in front of the bourbon section.

He stared at Jade as she approached. He still looked upset, but curiosity shone in his eyes.

"Are you stalking me?" he asked.

She nodded. "I have been wanting to say...to ask...for years..."

"Did the cats get your tongue?" he asked.

"I didn't want those kittens, as adorable as they were. I told Sal no—about ten times and it finally sunk in," said Jade. "Do you have plans tonight?"

"Plans to knock back a glass or two of this, sit on the porch, listen to the frenzied songs of the spring peepers."

"Would you care to do that with me? At my house?" asked Jade.

Lewis tilted his head, with hints of a smile tugging at the corners of his lips. "No felines about, you say? Count me in."

"We can pick out some wine. There must be one we can agree on. Red?"

"This occasion calls for only one kind of wine. Champagne."

"You're right. And I'd like to call tonight a date," Jade added. "If it's not too bold of me."

Lewis' smile broke full out. "Bold? I've been wild about you since high school. My cat allergies getting in the way all the time, and you, so inscrutable. Bold, calling tonight a date? I'm ready for us to *set a date*!"

"Lewis! You wouldn't deprive me of the pleasure of what I am sure will be a most thrilling courtship? We can talk about all the rest... another day. I have a whole folder full of love poems I've been saving to read to you."

"*You* wrote love poems?" Lewis asked, his vision beginning to blur with emotion.

Jade gulped, "Yes."

"For *me*?"

"Yes."

"That's the strangest coincidence," said Lewis, trying to get a grip on himself. "I happen to also possess a folder full of love poems about you. I'll die before letting you read them," he wiped frantically at his eyes, "but I'm okay with you knowing they exist."

"They can't be more embarrassing than mine. Are you crying?"

"It's just...dew."

"No, it's not dew you silly thing."

"I'm so glad you came and...told me. Hang on. Cole," Lewis spun around so quickly he caught the owner gaping at them behind the counter, "a bottle of your finest champagne! I am going to have my first date tonight with the incomparable Jade Glenmore after waiting decades."

"Me and the whole town's been waiting for it as long as you," said Cole. "I have half a mind to call up the *Glamis Times* with this hot tip."

"I wouldn't mind. It's the lady who wants to take it slow," said Lewis.

"And what is so wrong with that?" Jade beamed.

CHAPTER THIRTY-EIGHT

Sunday, April 9th - 4:00 p.m.

Sal stood on the back deck of his house clutching the railing. Nodding daffodils Melissa planted years ago filled the garden. The emerald lawn beyond was right on the cusp of needing to be mowed for the first time this year. A few colorful plastic eggs missed by Rosie dotted the expanse. Sal spread his arms. "68 degrees, flowers abloom. The Hero of Glamis deigning to attend my Easter celebration. You can't beat it. I just wish Melissa were here to enjoy it with us."

"She is Dad," said Justin. "She's here with us in spirit."

A shriek of excitement came from Rosie. She stared up at her father and two grandfathers from the outdoor rug. She wore a ruffled dress and clutched a stuffed bunny with a pink bow. Her great-uncle Dominic sat beside her helping her investigate the contents of the plastic eggs gathered in her basket. "A fun size Twix bar! That's my favorite. Can I have this one?" asked Dom.

Rosie shook her head.

"What if I say 'please'?"

"Okay, Uncle Dominic," she said. "'Please' is the magic word."

"Thanks, Rosie," Dominic gave her a high five. "Sal's right, Lieutenant," he looked up at Carl. "I hope you know how grateful we all are to you. I'm proud it was one of our family who saved this town in its hour of need, when it couldn't be me. This time."

"We all sort of helped, right?" asked Justin.

"Some more than others," said Greta from a lounge chair where she sipped fresh squeezed lemonade. Not that she would say it aloud, but in Greta's opinion she wasn't sure how Carl would have solved this particular case without her.

"I'm so proud to be your daughter, Carl," Sarah gave him a hug.

"Excuse me? Where's my hug?" Greta asked. "I'm the one who picked him for this family. Against your objections too, I might add!"

"A lot of objections," Carl teased.

"I don't know what you're talking about," said Sarah.

"You don't remember collapsing in the front yard for all the neighbors to see when your mother told you we were engaged?"

"Sarah," Sal gasped. "Not you."

"I was only twelve," said Sarah. "I'm glad I didn't drive you away. You are a good, kind, brave man, Carl. I see that now. I love you."

"I love you too. You are the best daughter for me," he said.

"If you hadn't solved this case," said Sal, "who knows what would have happened to The Castle? Without it being a tourist attraction, we don't get all the people coming near and far to shop at our businesses, not to mention the people dining at the best restaurant in the state."

"Are we ready to show him?" Justin asked. Sarah gave the thumbs up. "As a token of our appreciation we have a surprise! If you will follow us, Carl..."

"Trust me you are going to love this," Sal said.

"You definitely will," agreed Sarah.

Carl felt nervous. They seemed to be overselling whatever was to come. Still, he followed them into the kitchen.

"Oh my god," he said. Spread across the breakfast table were habanero peppers, shiny red plum tomatoes, cans of Carl's favorite refried beans, a bag of fresh corn tortillas, packaged towers of both yellow and orange tostadas, ripe avocados, a head of lettuce, and two gleaming wheels of queso fresco.

"We did okay, Car?" Sal asked.

"Not okay. You did *excellent*. Where did you buy all this?"

"There is a supermarket in New Haven," said Sal. "It carries everything you've been looking for. We went there yesterday. About a thirty-five-minute drive away. Not too far."

"Chef Paul told us about it," said Justin.

"I wrote down a note in my phone when you told me the list of foods you hadn't been able to find at the grocery store here," said Sarah.

"We found every single item," Justin said. "Including chicharrones and your favorite brand of crema."

"Muy bien, Justin," said Carl. "I have a good son-in-law! And a good whatever-in-law!" he said to Sal. "And definitely the best daughter!"

"Food is a passion we all share," said Justin. "I hope now that we've found a store with the ingredients you need, you will feel more at home."

"I really appreciate this," Carl said. "It is more than just food to me, yes. Thank you."

"With Sal's blessing, we thought for our Easter Sunday dinner tonight, we could make tostadas," said Sarah.

"With meatballs and pasta available for whoever wants," Sal leapt in. "But I will happily try a tostada."

"This is a great idea," said Carl. "Italian food as an option and *also* delicious Mexican food for those who want it. Now, *that* I can get on board with."

"Every Sunday together for the rest of our lives," said Sal.

It was the same words Sal had been saying all along, but now Carl found himself more amused than annoyed. "Correction. Sundays when my wife and I are *available*."

Sal wiggled his head in response. "Good thing I've got tough skin dealing with the likes of you. Let's get moving on cooking. We've only got an hour before everyone arrives!"

"Who is coming?" asked Carl.

"Twenty or so relatives. Oh, they are so excited to meet you and Greta."

"Before the others get here, I have another surprise everyone needs to hear," said Sarah.

"Do you know about this?" Carl asked Greta.

"No," she said.

"I have an announcement," Sarah said. "My dad and Lyda just told me they are going to be renting in Glamis for the summer. They are moving up here, possibly forever, if they enjoy their test run. They want to be closer to us and to Rosie too."

"Alright! That's fantastic!" Sal cheered.

"Oh, they're moving right here? To Glamis?" Greta gulped.

"Yep," said Sarah. "They found a cute apartment right around the corner from you, on Main Street. Carl, you look ill."

"Just processing this new information," he said.

"The more the merrier!" said Sal. "Cheers to the Future of one Big Happy Marotta-Sarabia-Woods Blended Familia!"

Carl raised his glass along with the others. He had major misgivings about this development. Justin's wide-eyed expression indicated he did too. Carl and Greta had coexisted before in a city of five million inhabitants with Whip and Lyda. Glamis possessed a population of only three thousand.

Greta rubbed Carl's shoulder reassuringly, though inwardly she cringed at the thought of her ex-husband and his wife being anywhere near them, even if only for a few months. Odds were good they would not take to life in Glamis. Greta doubted if Lyda would be able to survive a week without immediate access to Nieman Marcus, SoulCycle, and Drybar. Greta knew Lyda's favorite haunts because Sarah would send her screenshots from Lyda's Instagram. Lyda reported every step of her daily itinerary to her adoring eight hundred followers. And how would Whip be able to stand not being within driving distance from his ranch? Greta's divorce was ancient history she would prefer not to remember. There had been some overlap between her era and Lyda's on Whip's romantic timeline. She didn't feel angry anymore. She was grateful not to be married to the man and to have found her true soulmate in Carl. That didn't mean she wanted to live in the same vicinity as Lucifer and Jezebel.

Rosie grinned at the commotion. *In this little girl's eyes,* Carl thought, *everyone here is one family. Perhaps it is possible to peacefully add two more—extremely potent—ingredients into this small melting pot.*

"Sal, maybe you will want Whip to be your new bestie," said Carl.

"I don't need a new bestie," said Sal. "I already have my bestie. Will we be including Whip in our revelries? Of course! We'll call ourselves the three musketeers!"

"Now you go too far," said Carl.

"It'll all work out."

"We'll see. We will see."

To: Arielle Glenmore
   York Correctional Institution
   Niantic, Connecticut

Arielle,
This is not an invitation to correspond with me. If you write a letter back, I will burn it unopened.
This is just to say I have plucked from my heart the love I once bore you like a burr from my foot.
You taught me an important lesson.
I would be wise to let nothing astonish me.
Scott

ACKNOWLEDGEMENTS

My dad Ron read through countless iterations of this book, catching errors big and small, making suggestions that improved this story tremendously. Thank you for your unwavering love, enthusiasm, and support for this project.

My mom Elaine has been a believer that I am and always will be a writer even during times when I had doubts if I would write again. Thank you for the excitement you have shown for this book.

My stepfather Miguel was the inspiration for Detective Carl Sarabia. I appreciate you letting me borrow some of your many wonderful qualities (and a few quirks too) in constructing my hero. I love you and look up to you so much. Thank you for always being there for me when I've needed you the most.

Barb Goffman, my editor, brought my work to a higher level of polish and improved the book so much. I have been lucky to work with you, Barb. I admire your own writing so much.

Heartfelt gratitude to powerhouse authors of the genre Meg Gardiner and Kris Lackey for your kind endorsements. I am honored by your generous support as I embark on publishing my first book.

I wish to thank my three amazing brothers. Blake, for your guidance and patient help making the audiobook everything I envisioned it would be. Brandon, thank you for being one of my early readers. Chris, I'm grateful for our bond forged in Iron! I look up to you and have so much to thank you for. A special thank you as well to my family members Michelle, Audry, Phoebe, Ben, and Luke for the love and encouragement.

Thank you to my friend and colleague from my publishing days Jeff Yamaguchi, a talented writer and one of the savviest minds in publishing. I was very fortunate to have your input and guidance.

Thank you to my cousin Quique, who gave me the push to publish I needed at just the right time.

Thank you to my Connecticut and Texas friends. Many of you were some of my first readers or listeners and showed me so much kindness over the years. Nancy Anderson, Alicia Prete, Diane McQueeney, Susie Sutfin, Maureen McGowen-Schwartz, Kathy and Mike Conroy, Terri and James Neill, Tara Mills, Haley Grill, The LoRicco Family, Nina and Danny Courville, Davida and Steve Pepe, Karen and Charlie Smith, Lauren and Sam Mencoff, Bobby and Andrea Frye, Galvin Kennedy, and my coach Fernando Lopez all cheered me on at various stages of the book's development. Diane McQueeney connected me with her nephew Chris Whibey who worked in Connecticut law enforcement. Thank you to Chris who gave me insights into police work in the state.

I am grateful to the faculty forensics experts at Henry C. Lee College of Criminal Justice and Forensic Sciences at the University of New Haven who explained so much about criminal investigations in Connecticut.

Finally, thank you to my love, Josh Robinson. Since we met, we've been writing the best chapter I could imagine. Crazy about you.

ABOUT THE AUTHOR

LAUREN OPPER is the author of *Let Nothing Astonish You*. She worked for many years in publishing in New York and Connecticut. She now lives in her hometown of Houston. Lauren is an Ironman and in her spare time can be found coming up with story ideas while swimming, biking, and running. Visit her at www.laurenopper.com.

www.ingramcontent.com/pod-product-compliance
Lightning Source LLC
LaVergne TN
LVHW091702070526
838199LV00050B/2250